RAVEN'S RUNES

RAVEN AND HUMMINGBIRD

BOOK FOUR

NIKKI BROADWELL

AIRMID PUBLISHING
TUCSON, ARIZONA

Raven's Runes

Copyright © 2020

ISBN: 978-1-7326173-6-0

Formatting by: Polgarus Studio
Cover Design by: Daniella Colleo—www.stunningbookcovers.com

OTHER BOOKS BY NIKKI:

A Witch in Time Saves Nine
The moon in Her Eyes

The Last Keeper of the Light

Rosemary for Remembrance

Burning Night

Siobhan's Secret—book 1 of
Raven and Hummingbird series
Dagda's Daughter—book 2 of
Raven and Hummingbird series
Kat's Conundrum—book 3 of
Raven and Hummingbird series

FOREWORD

The Norse and Celtic mythology in this book may differ slightly from other versions you may have read. There could be a crossing over of time lines and cultures, variations in lineage. Ambiguous characters may have traits never before mentioned. Fiction and mythology are open to interpretation, and I hope the one I chose does not offend anyone. Please know that these characters seem to come unbidden, surprising me as they fill the pages with their words and deeds. I am merely the typist.

PROLOGUE

Myrddin gazed at the rolling snow-covered hills and the turreted castle he remembered from the distant past.

"Why have you come?"

He turned to his mother, noticing her narrowed eyes. "You expect me to stay away when the continuation of life hangs in the balance?"

She scoffed. "It doesn't hang in the balance—it is already destroyed."

"Not from where I'm standing," the wizard said.

"Be careful," a deep voice intoned.

"Who is speaking?" Myrddin asked, looking around.

Carmun let out a cackle, her black dress swirling around her as she addressed the invisible voice. "You think you can control me? You have no idea what I've become. I will stay or go according to my whims. And if I decide to destroy you and this castle you love so much, there is nothing you or our son can do about it."

A wind came up, sudden darkness spreading across the exposed hillside where they stood, menacing clouds swirling. Myrddin had a vision of the beloved castle in ruins, a shiver running down his spine. He saw a shadow towering over his mother. A man or a giant with wild hair that blew in the wind. "Heed my warning, my son," the shadow intoned before it seemed to dissolve, tattered pieces scattering into the wind.

"He called me son. Who is he?" Myrddin asked.

But Carmun was watching the place where he'd been, and didn't answer.

LAST CHAPTER OF KAT'S CONUNDRUM
(TO REFRESH YOUR MEMORY)

K at returned from the woods feeling strange and not herself. But when she tried to relay what had happened, Bran wasn't interested, his concerns making themselves known as he grabbed her arm and dragged her away from the others.

"Your father just made it clear that he will never approve of us."

"I don't care what he thinks, Bran. Do you?"

"Yes, I do. He used to be the all-father god, Kat. Do you realize how powerful he was? I can't ignore his wishes and act like he has no authority."

Kat stared at him in surprise. "He is no longer a god, and the two of us can do whatever we want. It's not like you have to ask him for permission. I'm not a medieval maiden."

Bran didn't get the humor, his frowning face turning even darker. "Giving up my powers was the wrong move," he muttered. "If I hadn't done that your father would

3

respect me. As it is, I can't live with him."

"Do you want to find another home for the two of us?"

"What about your brother, your Mom and now your baby sister?"

Kat shook her head, and stared into the distance. "Did you see what Mior and I did up there?" she asked, pointing. "We can repopulate the earth with plants and trees and maybe even animals."

Bran glanced where she pointed and turned back to her. "What I'm talking about is the continuation of *us*, and you're going off about plants?"

"This is my home and what I'm doing here is of paramount importance! Do you want to live in a wasteland?"

His eyes narrowed dangerously. "I don't want to live where I'm not wanted," he muttered.

She grabbed his arm. "Bran, what has gotten into you? Of course, you're wanted here!"

He pulled out of her grip and shook his head. A second later he was Raven. Kat watched him fly up and away, a black dot disappearing into the distance.

Kat and Mior worked together for the next few months, bringing life back. Kat had no idea how other places on earth were faring, but she was ecstatic about what they'd managed in such a short time. Now there were deer grazing along the edges of the forests, more rabbits than they could eat, and berry bushes where they collected gooseberries, blueberries, raspberries and blackberries. Deer grazed in the meadows, foxes roamed, skunks could be seen—black and white shapes waddling across the hills.

When she wasn't doing magic, Kat agonized over Bran's continuing absence. Her father had been too occupied with Siobhan's recovery to question, but as her mother improved, she finally confronted him. "Dad, were you responsible for Bran leaving?"

Dagda frowned and stared into the distance. "I only told him he wasn't worthy of you."

"But I love him!"

"What has he accomplished, Kate? While you and Mior have been restoring the world, he's been sitting on his ass twiddling his thumbs."

"That isn't fair! You haven't helped restore the world either."

"I didn't willingly give up my abilities. They were torn from me. To be a god one must behave like a god—I know that now. He could have helped down here, but instead he spends his days either flying around in raven form, or bringing back what the coyote catches and maybe skinning and cooking it. Powers are not to be taken lightly, and to act like you never had them is shameful. He doesn't deserve you, especially after what we all witnessed during Tus Nua's birth. You are much more than I could ever have imagined. He left because he knows this."

"He left because you shamed him, Dad."

Dagda shook his head and turned away. "You'll thank me one day."

But Kat couldn't accept what her father had said to Bran, or how Dagda felt. Giving up his powers for *her*, was what Bran had done. Had he done it willingly? She didn't really know. All she knew was that he loved her enough to sacrifice what he'd always been. But now he was gone and she had no idea if he'd come back.

She thought back to the months they'd been here, how there was no privacy. They were both pent up, frustrated about not being able to express their affection. She'd suggested building a place for the two of them—why hadn't he gone with that plan? He seemed to be behaving as though he'd asked Dagda for her hand in marriage and her father had refused him. Old-fashioned in the extreme, and very out of character for him.

The baby was one month old when they had the naming ceremony up in the woods by the spring-fed pond. Kat presided as her druidic persona, saying the words that came to her to protect the baby. The name Dagda and Siobhan decided on was Tus Nua, Gaelic for new beginnings. Siobhan had regained her health, her eyes sparkling as she shed her clothes and carried the baby into the pond. Mior was next and Kat followed, the festive feelings sending their happy laughter cascading across the landscape. When Dagda finally took off his clothes and joined them, they shouted it to the treetops. His grumpiness made them all laugh as he complained about the cold water and pretended he wasn't having the time of his life.

They had fresh caught rabbit for dinner, along with blackberries and greens they found growing along the newly established streams. Dagda skinned the animal and cooked it in a firepit with the downed wood they'd gathered. The only thing missing was Bran, an emptiness that continued to plague Kat. She'd expected him back, but there'd been no sign of him.

It was barely a week later that they came upon the survivalists, a clan of around twenty-five people who had built a house into the side of a hill. They'd been there before it all started, with food enough to last them at least a year. There were men, women and children in the group, all of them wearing crosses around their necks. They looked at Kat's family with suspicion and distrust.

"Do you worship the devil?" one of the men asked, staring at her waist length braided hair, the tattered Fae dress she wore and her bare feet.

"No," Kat told him. "We worship the goddess and the trees."

"That's the same as devil worship," he informed her. "Stay away from us and we'll leave you alone."

"I used to be Catholic," Siobhan told them. She was holding the baby in her arms, her long skirt trailing in the mud.

"We fixed the forest!" Mior piped up. "And now we have animals again!"

The man was bald, tattoos on his upper arms. He laughed nastily. "God did that, you little pissant. Who in hell do you think you are?"

Siobhan blanched and glanced at Dagda who was frowning.

"We are living in difficult times and there are not many

of us left," Dagda began. "I suggest you develop a more forgiving attitude, considering the circumstances."

"We'll do whatever the fuck we want, old man. Now, as I said, stay away from us and we won't give you any trouble." He turned on his heel, signaling to the others. "Be warned," he called over his shoulder.

"Well, that didn't go well," Kat muttered. "Hope we don't have any more run-ins with them."

"He's the one who shot the coyote," Mior whispered.

Six months had gone by since Bran's departure, every day that he was gone hurting Kat in a way she couldn't describe. He'd promised her he wouldn't leave and yet he was gone—and it seemed for good. Twice she'd had run-ins with the survivalists, their belief that God had created the woods and the meadows and the flowers, infuriating. She decided not to push it, knowing that with their violent tendencies they could hurt her and Mior. From then on, she instructed Mior to stay away from them and not play with the children. If they got wind of what he could achieve, they could easily do something crazy.

All of her little family had participated in the building of a house along the edge of the woods, the rustic shack reminiscent of the one her father had built on his property. But this one was fashioned out of the curved limbs they gathered and twisted together. It looked like a fairy house from a book, leaves still sprouting as though the limbs were attached to a living tree. Mior and Kat had added a layer of magic to the roof to keep them dry, and Mior had woven a spell around it to keep them safe. They didn't have electricity or even running water, but it kept out the wind and the rain and it was cozy, with thick grass floors that they replaced often, and seats fashioned out of other downed limbs. Their beds were made of pine needles and grass covered with the blankets left from their cave days, deerskins now keeping them warm. Their clothing was torn and ragged, but still functioned. They bathed in the pool in the forest and got their water from the spring. On warm days they went naked.

For some reason the survivalists did not visit the forest, their days seemingly spent hunting and building walls out of the stones they lugged from other places. They were creating a compound to shut out the world, or what was left of it. "They're afraid of us," Mior exclaimed in surprise one day as he and Kat walked through the meadow gathering herbs. "Why?"

Kat straightened from where she was picking chamomile. "Because we're different."

"What's wrong with being different?"

"Nothing, Mior. But there are those who don't want to take the time to understand others. We aren't doing much to bridge the gap between us either."

"But that's because they don't like us."

Kat nodded. "Exactly right."

The fireflies still followed Mior around and helped him locate beehives, instructing him on how to extract the honey. Since then they'd been able to make beeswax candles that lit up their home on dark nights. Kat pondered her earlier feelings of wanting to have a simple life with Bran that didn't include her powers. Lately she'd been grateful for everything she could do, from bringing the forest back, to welcoming her druidic abilities when they appeared. She'd changed since Bran had gone, embracing what had always lived inside her. But it didn't take away the pain of his absence.

She wondered about the dark witch and Danu's warning. She felt Carmun lurking at the edges of her mind. Biding her time. Recently she'd seen a shadow creature that reminded her of the specter. It was a darkness hovering within the branches of the trees and a phantom that followed her across the meadows. When the pooka saw it, he barked and chased it away. It didn't worry her.

She'd felt Danu when she bathed alone in the forest pool or collected hazelnuts, or discovered the mushrooms that grew at the base of the trees. No message had come, but she knew the goddess was watching over them. Mostly she just lived, enjoying Tus Nua and her brother. There was a newfound peace, joy that had been missing for a very long time. Dagda looked younger, a smile replacing the frown he'd worn. Siobhan laughed and sang while she worked. Life was worth living, every day like a precious jewel.

There were dark clouds on the horizon the day it happened. Kat was walking in the meadow with the coyote, collecting herbs for the teas she'd begun to make, her mind on what she was doing. She heard a whisper, a familiar voice that sounded urgent. "If you want to stop the witch, you have to come now." When she looked up there was a door in front of her. It opened, and on the other side she saw a tall smiling boy around twelve years old who looked very much like Val except for the dark wavy hair. Behind him stood the man Kat had nearly forgotten, the father of her child. When she glanced back at the pooka he was staring at her. "Will you watch over them?" she asked. He gazed at her knowingly, his eyes shining with magic. She turned and stepped through.

EPIGRAPH

~Without the darkness there can be no light; without
sorrow there can be no joy~

The house in Alfheim had changed, the understated wood and stone turned into a palace of gleaming glass and turrets that rose so high they were barely visible amongst the clouds. Kat stared uncomprehending, wondering how such a thing was possible.

"It is all due to our son," Val said proudly. "He has a knack with magic that is unsurpassed in recent history." Val put a hand on the twelve-year-old's shoulder. "It is the combination of goddess and Elven blood."

Kat turned to Arwen, afraid for a second. This boy had nearly killed her when he was but a baby. But before she could utter a word, he had moved close and was pulling her into a hug.

"I am so glad to see you," he murmured in a voice nearly as deep as Val's. "I am sorry for how I behaved." He chuckled and pulled back. "A Fae child has no inner restraint unless trained by a member of the Elven race."

Kat was taken into the luminous eyes, not at all sure she trusted him, even now. There was guile behind that innocent look he was giving her. She smiled. "It was a long time ago."

"Yes, too long," Val agreed, moving close to put his arms around her. "Arwen is much changed. There is no need to worry," he whispered in her ear.

In truth it had only been a little over two years, but in that short time her baby had reached his father's height. He looked nearly full grown. Kat glanced at the uninviting monstrosity in the distance, her gaze lingering on the lack of roses, lavender and other blooming plants. This garden was stark, with nothing in it but strange sculptures that echoed the house design. "What happened to the roses?"

Val's expression went dark for a millisecond before he said, "Arwen didn't like them. He felt they were an unnecessary addition to a castle that needed no enhancement."

Kat peered up at the tapered points that resembled skewers. They were sharp like the tips of bayonets or javelins. She suppressed the shudder that went through her body. "It is rather grand, isn't it?"

Val nodded. "Shall we go inside? I have some food prepared and we can talk about why you are here."

Arwen moved to walk beside her, his sidelong glances making her uncomfortable. "I have your hair color," he finally announced. "And your eye shape, I think."

Kat smiled up at him. "Yes. I see it. But your eyes are crystalline blue, like your father's."

"All the Fae have eyes like this," he said smiling. He strode ahead to open the door for them.

Kat watched him, surprised by his need to charm her. Those eyes were where the Fae magic lay, their ability to cast spells with a look, something she'd dealt with in the past. It was why she was mother to Arwen.

The inside of the edifice was just as changed as the outside, with copper tables and gleaming glass everywhere. She missed the wooden benches, the enormous fireplace and the homey feel of the former building.

"Bring in the plate I arranged," Val told his son. "I'll get the drinks." He motioned for Kat to sit at the highly polished metal table.

"Where is Isabel?" Kat asked as she settled into an uncomfortable chair. Isabel had served them the last time she'd been here, and Kat had been looking forward to seeing the diminutive Fae woman who had done her hair and dressed her during the time she was blind from the witch's spell. Val had helped her through it, her sight returning after he worked his own magic. When she glanced at Val, he was watching her, his expression knowing. She was sure he was reading her mind. Hopefully Arwen did not yet have that ability.

"Arwen and Isabel did not get on," Val finally answered, heading to a cabinet set into the wall. He came back to the table carrying a bottle and three glasses which he placed in front of her. "This is some of our best Fae wine," he said, pouring golden liquid into her glass. "It's delicious and I know you will like it."

Kat laughed. "What magic does it hold?"

Val chuckled. "It is merely wine, Kat. It might make you feel slightly more awake, but other than that, it is benign."

Kat examined the room. The ceiling reached up and up to end in a turret, light spilling downward to bounce off the metal and glass below. She squinted in the brightness and shaded her eyes. "I miss your house, Val. The one that burned."

He nodded as he poured himself a glass and sat next to her. "I do as well."

Kat glanced toward the kitchens before she whispered, "Why did you allow Arwen to change the design?"

The question went unanswered as Arwen appeared carrying a platter filled with meats, cheeses, olives and bread. He looked from one to the other. "What did I miss?"

"Just setting the stage for why your mother's here," Val said, reaching for a piece of bread. "But before we get into all of that, how are things on Earth? Is your family safe? How is Bran?"

Kat felt a twinge of apprehension as she glanced at Arwen. The look on his face seemed over-eager, almost greedy. "Everyone's fine at the moment, but the creature is still up in the sky. Bran left six months ago."

Val frowned. "Why?"

"I…I told him I planned on doing this without him."

"Doing this—you mean stopping the dark witch?"

Kat nodded, suddenly feeling guilty about all of it. Bran was the person she trusted most in the world. "I don't know why I told him that. Dagda shamed him too. Possibly the combination of things put him over the edge."

Val nodded slowly, looking down at the drink in his hands. He took a hefty swallow. "As I remember, aside from turning into Raven, Bran is without his god powers."

"Yes, and that's exactly why I worried."

"But yours are back?"

Kat smiled. "I have so much more, Val. Danu…"

Val's eyes widened. "You're in touch with the mother goddess?"

Kat nodded. "And also, a life I lived long ago as a druid priestess."

His gaze met hers. "Possibly that's what's bothering Bran—you've outshined him. Men do not normally enjoy that, not even gods and the Fae. It is a hard thing to accept."

Kat nodded. "I suppose it could be that. He expected us to be a team. But how can we be a team when he's so vulnerable? I would spend all my time worrying about him instead of focusing on the mission." Kat tasted her wine, surprised by the honeyed flavor. It was just as good as Val had said it would be. "So, Val, tell me why I'm here. Is the witch in Alfheim? What have you learned?" She glanced at Arwen who seemed riveted, his eyes wide with interest.

"Arwen? Can you retrieve my notes from the library?" Val asked.

"Where are they?"

"On my desk underneath that stack of missives I'm working on. They are handwritten on yellow paper." Val turned to Kat. "This is a busy time in Alfheim. We've barely begun the process of digging ourselves out from under the terrible damage we suffered. Freyr, Alfheim's ruler, has been in touch with those of us who have land. He wants to commandeer our property for various purposes, some of which sound somewhat dubious."

"He's been threatening," Arwen supplied. "Val has been arguing with him, but so far…"

"Arwen?" Val interrupted. "I need my notes please."

Val waited to continue, watching his son rise and head

off. Once the boy was out of earshot he leaned toward Kat, placing his hand on her forearm. His eyes narrowed and turned gold, his voice lowering to a near whisper. "Remember that favor you owe me?"

Before Kat could answer him, Arwen returned with a stack of papers and put them down in front of Val. "Your notes, your highness," he said, moving to his seat.

Kat was surprised by his sarcasm, but when she glanced at him, he grinned. "Occasionally Father needs to be brought down a peg," he said.

Kat didn't smile back, a shiver running down both her arms. When she looked at Val, his eyes were on his notes, but she could see that the pale skin around his neck had turned red. "What are the notes about?" she asked, rising to look over his shoulder.

Val glanced up. "I have detailed the changes happening here in a diary. The villages have been rebuilt since you were here last, but many of the Fae who were my friends have moved either to other realms or to another section of Alfheim."

"Why?"

"Because this village is a sinkhole of despondency," Arwen muttered. "Old ideas don't work in this day and age, but Father's generation seems to think they can continue in the ancient traditions as though nothing's changed."

"Are you talking about Ragnarok?" Kat asked, tearing her eyes away from the words, *destruction* and *annihilation* on the paper.

"Yes, Ragnarok!" Arwen shouted. "It signaled a new beginning, but…"

"Arwen, calm down," Val said, raising his hand. He

turned to Kat. "Arwen is convinced that the terrible storms were the beginning of Ragnarok and that it's meant to clear out all of our traditions so we can start anew. But these traditions have been in place for millennia and they are here for a reason."

"Stupid things like meetings to discuss our future as a realm and rules on killing and fighting that are so outdated to be laughable? We need to use the magic we have and develop it even further. I say we let the younger generation take over."

"That is not how we do things here, Arwen. We've had this discussion a million times."

"My friends agree with me," he mumbled, looking down at the table with a scowl on his face.

"Your friends are mostly orphans who lost their parents during the latest devastation and are in a state of grief. Grief can make people act irrationally."

Kat let out an exasperated huff and turned to face the arguing men. "The reason I'm here is because you told me if I wanted to stop the witch, I had to come now...what's going on, Val?"

Two pairs of swirling eyes met hers, making her dizzy for a second. "It was true," Val said unconvincingly.

Kat stood suddenly, her chair toppling over and clattering onto the stone floor. "Please do not tell me you made this up to get me here. I have a family about to go through another Ragnarok, a world that needs tending, and a missing man who I love. I don't have time for this."

"The witch is close. She plots your downfall as we speak. We thought it best to let you know what's going on," Arwen said earnestly.

Kat frowned at her son, her cheeks flaming with rage. "Please *do* go on," she said, waving her hand in the air.

Arwen glanced at Val. "Father thinks I'm in league with her."

"What?" Kat's gaze went to Val.

Val shook his head, tapered fingers pushing his straight hair behind his pointed ears. "Arwen, you know that isn't true."

Arwen rose from the table. "It is true!" he shouted. "You think all kinds of horrible things about me!" He glanced at Kat, his eyes troubled, before he turned away from the table.

Val stood and reached out, but Arwen was already striding away. The glass door leading outside let out a clang as he walked through, swinging closed with a bang a second later.

"What is going on?" Kat whispered.

"This is why I wanted you here. I don't trust him, but you're his mother. I need some help sorting things out."

"And this is the favor you mentioned."

Val let out a sigh and returned to his seat, sinking down heavily. "Yes. Arwen has become a problem."

he sun was going down, unrelenting shafts of intense light pouring through the glass into the high-ceilinged room. "I don't like this house," Kat murmured, shielding her eyes.

"Neither do I," Val replied. "But Arwen was adamant."

Kat frowned at her former lover and powerful sorcerer. "What's happened to you?"

When Val looked up his eyes were filled with an undefinable expression. The swirling colors had gone dark, his eyebrows twisted into corkscrews. "If you remember, when you dropped Arwen off things were very bad here. Alfheim had just been devastated and I was not myself. I'm sorry to say I didn't take proper precautions with him, telling myself that getting things up and running was the first priority."

"In other words, you let him run wild."

Val nodded, his sad eyes meeting hers. "I'm afraid he's taken a dark turn. The friends he runs with are hell bent on destruction rather than working with the rest of us to bring back order. Arwen is impressionable and easily manipulated.

If he isn't in touch with the witch, he will be soon."

"So, you expect me to…what, exactly? Bring him back to his senses, discipline him or just determine what he's doing?"

"I've been watching you from afar, Kat. You're not the same woman who shared my bed. I'm limited when it comes to my own kind, and he's devious and can hide himself from me."

Kat nodded slowly, thinking about how she'd felt in Arwen's presence. "He seems false. I felt that right away. As to whether he's truly in touch with dark magic, I can't say."

"I want you to spend time with him, study him. Let your clairvoyance open so that you can see who he is inside."

Kat exhaled her annoyance. "I don't like this, Val. You brought me here on false pretenses."

"I wasn't lying. I do think the witch is nigh. It's why I'm so concerned about our son. She's very clever and can enter others and use them to do her dirty work."

Kat thought about Airmid. "Yes. I've seen it. Do you think she's physically in Alfheim?"

"As far as I know she lives in the Underworld. But there's a clear pathway from there into the Norse realms. What she did here before couldn't have been handled from a distance."

"And she's poised to come back to Earth as well. If I'm not there when she does, it will be the end of what Mior and I have accomplished, not to mention my family."

"I will keep an eye on them while you're here."

"The serpent is still there. I haven't seen it, but Mior has. He thinks he can tame it."

Val laughed. "No one can tame Jormungand."

Kat didn't smile. "You'd be surprised. But why is Jormungand there? Does the witch control him too?"

"As I said, she can inhabit any creature she chooses to inhabit, and that includes Jormungand."

"Stopping Carmun is far more important than bringing our son to heel."

Val turned from where he'd been staring at the floor. "Is it?"

"Yes, Val, it is. Once she's gone Arwen will have no reason to take a dark path."

Val stood and began to pace. "There are many dark paths, Kat. Carmun is only one of them. Our son seems to be drawn to the darkness."

"But Carmun is the most powerful. Danu said my destiny is entwined with hers."

Val nodded. "That is what I've seen as well. It was what I attempted to warn you about when you were here the first time."

"As I remember you refused to tell me what you saw in my future."

Val smiled a sheepish smile. "True enough. But I did try and shield you." He came close, his hands on the back of her chair. When she turned to look at him his eyes had changed color again, an all too familiar expression in them. "I am having difficulty staying focused on the matter at hand," he muttered huskily.

Kat shook her head. "I can't, Val. Bran…"

Val looked away, his pale cheeks reddening. "I understand." He moved to his chair and sat, a brooding look taking over his features.

"Bran took off without explaining why," Kat said, watching him. "I don't understand what he's feeling or why he left, other than my father's boorishness."

"As I said earlier, it's his pride. He will return."

"I'm not at all sure that he will."

Val's eyes narrowed. "If he doesn't, he's a damned fool."

By now the sun was a sinking orange ball on the horizon. Kat was tired, her thoughts beginning to tangle. "Where am I sleeping in this glass house?"

Val rose and took her hand, tugging her up the wide steps into another section that had a normal roof height and several shuttered rooms. "I had my way with this area," he laughed, showing her into a small darkened room.

"This is more like it," she said, sinking down on the bed.

Val sat beside her. "To tell you the truth I spend more time up here than I do in the main rooms. It suits me better."

Kat lay back on the bed and closed her eyes. "Me too." She heard Val settle next to her, his breath close to her ear. She felt the waves of his energy, tendrils of his essence entering her and making her tingle all over. "Stop it," she muttered.

"Stop what?" he asked innocently.

When Kat opened her eyes and turned her head, his face was inches from hers. Before she knew it, he was kissing her. And she couldn't seem to stop him.

Kat woke naked in the bed. Val was gone and the room was dark aside from a candle on the table next to the bed. All her resolve had gone out the window in just the first few hours of being with him. She was furious with herself and furious with him for taking advantage of her. But when she thought back to what they'd done together, his tenderness and the way he made love to her as though she was a precious jewel, she had to smile. It had been very pleasurable, especially after the celibate months she'd been through. And if Bran had abandoned her why shouldn't she enjoy Val's attentions? But the guilt nagged at her, nonetheless.

"Kat? Are you awake?"

She turned to see Val enter the room carrying a plate of food. Light surrounded his body, allowing her to see him clearly. She pushed herself up and leaned back against the soft pillows, watching him approach. He hadn't bothered to dress or even pull on a robe.

"Thought you might be hungry after all the exercise," he said, sitting next to her and placing the plate between them.

"I take it Arwen isn't back?"

"No. When he leaves in a huff as he did, I don't normally see him for a day or two. Thought it might be different this time with you here, but..." he shrugged.

Kat reached for one of the tiny sandwiches, surprised by the sudden hunger that rose up in her. "Yum. Do you have any help here now?"

Val shook his head. "Arwen won't allow it."

"My god, Val! You have to stop letting him dictate your life!"

"I know, but when we argue and he takes off it makes matters worse. I have to rein him in somehow."

"Giving in to him isn't reining him in. It's capitulating.

Use some of that magic you just used on me."

Val frowned. "I didn't use magic on you."

"Are you saying that what we did together wasn't generated by your sorcery?"

"I did nothing but kiss you, Kat. You have feelings for me. They may have been buried, but they're there."

Kat stopped in mid chew, staring off into the shadows. If it wasn't magic, then…she had no excuse for her behavior. "I thought I loved Bran," she whispered.

"You do love Bran, but I think you might love me a little bit too. We have a child together and our chemistry is impossible to ignore."

Kat didn't answer as she finished the last of the sandwiches.

Val picked up the plate. "Shall I sleep in here or would you rather be alone?"

"I think I'd rather be alone."

He nodded and headed toward the door, pausing to turn to her. "Why can't you admit that you're in love with two men?"

"It isn't right," she muttered.

"There is no right or wrong when it comes to affairs of the heart." He opened the door and shut it quietly behind him.

Kat stared into the darkness. Without Val's glowing body to dispel them, shadows had raced in. She pondered what he'd said before she slipped under the covers and curled into a tight ball. All she could see was Bran's face staring at her in shock and bewilderment. And no amount of telling herself he deserved it for leaving her, changed the guilt that washed over her.

Bran woke with a gasp, the dream images making him shudder. Kat had been in Val's arms, the expression on her face making him feel sick inside. Why hadn't he returned to her? He didn't know the answer, only that something kept him away. He was heartsick with missing her but at the same time he was ashamed of who he was. Dagda was right. He was unfit to be a god. He lurched to his feet, determined to seek answers to his questions.

Airmid waited until he'd finished his diatribe before peering at him with her eyes narrowed. The look of him worried her, his face gaunt, his eyes red as though with sickness or possibly despair. "You must seek out the wizard. Myrddin is adept at magic. He can help you with your confusion. I wish I could say that I could, but whatever is going on with you is beyond my abilities."

Bran watched Airmid to make sure she hadn't been taken over by something dark. After what had happened in the past, he'd stayed away from her spring, afraid of what he might find. But she seemed herself, her hazel eyes full of sympathy. "This Myrddin is here in Otherworld?"

She nodded. "He's ageless and immortal, as are we, at least those of us who haven't given up our powers," she added, giving him a sharp look.

"You don't think I'm immortal anymore?"

"Do you?"

Bran let out a frustrated sigh. "I've royally fucked up my life, Airmid. Not only did I give up what makes me who I am, but I also gave up the woman I love."

"Seek out Myrddin."

"Where will I find him?"

Airmid shook her head. "He likes to dwell in caves. Maybe start up in the mountains to the north?"

"That could take the rest of my mortal life!"

Airmid scoffed and shook her head. "Call to him to help you, Bran. You've certainly turned into an idiot these past few years. It's as though losing your god powers made you forget everything you once knew."

"Oddly, that's exactly right. I don't remember half of what I could do, or even who I was back then."

Airmid made a sound in the back of her throat. "Being mortal is no way to go through life, especially if you've been immortal for a thousand years or more. Use the raven to search. Apparently that bird knows a lot more than you do."

Bran gazed into her clear eyes. The misty spring beckoned behind her, luring him with its shimmering warm waters. "You're right about that. Raven is all that's left of who I once was. Can I take a dip before I go?"

Airmid smiled for the first time. "Of course. The spring

will help you regenerate. As to Kat, what she feels for you will never go away, even if she finds another. And once you're a god again, Dagda will no longer have the power to humiliate you."

"Did I say I wanted to reclaim my god status?"

Airmid peered at him, frowning. "Do you want to remain mortal? Because I wasn't kidding earlier. Your hair is going gray, and you've developed lines across your forehead and along your cheeks. You look like crap."

Bran reached for a strand of his hair, attempting to pull it around to look at it. "Gray?"

Airmid nodded. "Gray. Your beard too. If you wait too long, you'll be a grizzled old man."

Once Airmid was gone, Bran stripped off his clothes and climbed into the spring. He ducked beneath the water, remembering the last time he'd been here—with Kat. It was a bittersweet memory, reminding him of why he was here now. He had to figure things out or he would lose her forever, not to mention die of old age. He hoped this aging wouldn't keep going until he looked a thousand years old. He shook his head, laughing to himself—he'd be long dead before that happened.

Raven flew high, his sharp eyes taking in the landscape below. The forest where Cernunnos ruled spread beneath him, the trees a sea of green. He was intent on his mission until the moment he spied the other raven. She was female and his mating instincts took over, whatever he'd been doing lost in the moment. He chased her, the two of them diving and rolling before landing together in the top branches of a cedar tree. When he mounted her, everything disappeared into a haze of unknowing. Nothing mattered but making a nest and raising their young. The two of them flew side by side to find the twigs and to search out the perfect spot to build their nest.

"Where in hell is Kat?" Dagda roared, staring at his son. Hours had gone by since he'd seen his daughter, worry taking up residence in his stomach. Beside him Siobhan clutched their baby girl tight, her eyes wide with worry.

"I don't know," Mior answered, glancing at the coyote who in reality was a magical spirit sent to keep him safe. "Coyote says she went through a door."

Dagda shook his head. "That Fae bastard, Val, lured her into his realm, Siobhan. He's devious and has powers that I can only dream about."

"And they have a child together," Siobhan murmured, gazing down at the baby in her arms. "It's a strong connection, Dag."

He let out a roar, his hands turning into fists. "God damn it! I'm sick of feeling so fucking weak!" Dagda yelled, staring at his wife and the mother of his three children. His god powers were long gone, and he was aging—he could not get used to it, no matter how much time went by. This latest one, Tus Nua, had no powers at all, merely the progeny of two human beings. It was amazing the baby had survived after the deprivation Siobhan had gone through. It was Kat who had delivered her, some ancient druidic priestess taking over to give her the ability to save Siobhan from certain death. The girl was beautiful like her mother, but that was all she was. A tiny useless human in a world so dangerous that every day was a challenge.

Being mortal enraged him in ways he couldn't seem to control. He'd frightened Siobhan with his tirades and scared Mior on more than one occasion. Being hurled out of Otherworld to live out the rest of his mortal life on Earth, was a punishment nearly worse than death. At least they had Mior, whose powers seemed to grow with each passing day. The boy was able to communicate with the coyote, and had also done amazing things to re-animate the barren world they lived in. But Jormungand was still there, the son of Loki curled up in the sky and waiting for the right moment to strike. Was he part of the witch's plan too, or was he merely a feature of Ragnarok that didn't include Carmun's sorcery?

"Dag!"

Dagda turned to see his wife pointing up the hill where a small band of men approached. And they were carrying weapons. "Mior!" he shouted, hoping the boy could stop them. He felt like an inept fool and yet this was how it was now.

Coyote and Mior were already on their way to greet them when Dagda took hold of Siobhan and pushed her behind him. They watched their son send a blanket of fog toward the group. A second later chaos ensued and men were running every which way, weapons discarded in their haste to escape the noxious cloud. Mior gathered the guns and returned, a wide smile on his face. "Now we have guns!" he said proudly.

33

Siobhan frowned. "That is nothing to crow about, Mior. Do we want to become thugs like they are? Nothing good can come of that."

"And yet if we can't defend ourselves, we'll be killed," Dagda intoned morosely.

She shook her head glancing at their son. "We have Mior. And Kat will be back soon."

"And now I have my own gun!" the six year-old yelled, waving the gun around.

"Mior, be careful!" Dagda shouted. But it was too late. The gun exploded in his hands and the boy dropped like a stone.

Kat woke with a pounding headache, her dreams still fresh in her mind. Bran was gone, lost in a haze that made no sense. Kat had searched but it was as though he no longer existed. She rolled over and groaned, realizing where she was.

A second later there was a soft knock before Val entered the room, his swirling eyes searching hers. "Are you all right?"

Kat pushed herself up and reached for her clothes. "Not really. I had a bad dream."

Val nodded as though he already knew. "I figured as much after what happened between us. You don't do well with uncertainty."

Kat pulled on the dress he'd laid out to replace the tattered muddy mess she'd been wearing. "Is that what you call what I'm feeling?"

Val hesitated for a moment before he came close to sit on the bed. "You're feeling guilt mixed up with desire, Kat. That combination always wreaks havoc with your mind. Try and remember that you're here to help me deal with our son. If you choose to act on your feelings for me while you're here, please don't be so hard on yourself. I love you and I'm not planning to hide it. Since you've been gone, I've thought of you every day, wishing you were here. I've been with no other woman, Fae or otherwise."

Kat smoothed the dress over her body and ran her fingers through her tangle. "Thank you for the clothes. I was afraid I'd be wearing those rags until they fell apart."

Val chuckled. "You did look a mess. If you wish to bathe there's a hot spring behind the house as well as the elaborate bath our son erected." He gazed at her for a second before he added, "And I promise not to force myself on you."

Kat let out a light laugh, despite how she felt. His presence was having an effect on her that she didn't want to acknowledge. "Is Arwen back?"

Val shook his head as he rose to his feet. "I've made breakfast." He waited until she'd walked through the door before following her out of the room and down the stairs into the brightness of the glass room.

The table was filled with platters, a carafe of some coffee like substance sending enticing vapors into the air. She grabbed a mug and poured herself a cup of the dark liquid. "I understand what you expect of me, but what about Ragnarok and why I thought I was here? Does that have any importance to you? Boys Arwen's age are trying out their wings, finding what fits. Perhaps this is just a phase."

Val motioned for her to sit, his forehead furrowing. "The Fae grow up fast, as you've seen. What Arwen's into right now will impact the rest of his life. The gang he runs with is not exactly what I'd call evil, but they are far from virtuous. If this continues, I fear for the elders in our community. The young want us gone and they have the means to do it."

Kat's mouth dropped open. "You're saying they would attack you?"

"That's exactly what I'm trying to tell you. Arwen is dangerous."

Kat shook her head and looked down at the array of food on the plate Val had served her. She'd suddenly lost her appetite.

It was midday when Arwen appeared, his face leached of color, his eyes dulled by lack of sleep and perhaps drugs. Kat and Val were in the garden when they saw him stumbling down the hill.

"Arwen looks terrible!" Kat whispered.

Val nodded, his mouth a thin line. "They pick berries that grow in the forests and ingest them. Arwen insists that they give him answers to his questions."

Kat smiled sadly. "Hallucinating sounds more like it."

"The Fae have used these substances forever. We have rituals around them. But what these young boys are doing has nothing to do with ritual—they have no respect for the magical essences or for the process."

"Hello parents!" Arwen called out just before he reached where they were standing. "Have you been having fun in my absence?" His sneering face spoke volumes.

"With your mother here, I expected you to stick around," Val answered.

Arwen gave a humorless laugh. "Don't you appreciate the time you had to rut?"

Val grabbed him by the arm and jerked him close, his neck turning magenta. "You will show some respect, Arwen!"

Arwen laughed and pulled away. "I need my beauty rest," he mumbled, glancing at Kat before he headed for the house. "Looks like you two haven't been sleeping much either," he added over his shoulder. His laughter floated toward them as he strode away.

"That little bastard," Val muttered under his breath.

"Don't rise to the bait."

Val's eyes were narrowed when he glanced at her. "Aren't you the calm one," he said, surprised.

Kat shrugged. "I know kids and he's no different from others I've been around. He wants to shame us because he's ashamed of what he's doing."

Val shook his head. "I doubt he's ashamed, but I hope you're right."

The day was warm and bright, birds singing behind them in the forest. Kat breathed in the clean-smelling air, sighing in pleasure. The branches in the distance swayed in the gentle breeze. Oddly, she was relaxing. At home on Earth she'd been plagued with responsibilities, worried about keeping her family safe and watching for the witch or the dragon's arrival with her heart in her throat. With Bran's disappearance she'd felt even more bereft, his absence eating away at her like a wasting disease. Yes, they had a house now, and yes, they'd managed to eke out a pretty good life, but she knew deep down that it was only a respite and wouldn't last. There were too many variables.

When she glanced at Val, he was watching her, a smile hovering around his mouth. "You like it here," he said quietly.

"Yes, but I don't like the house."

"You like being with me."

Kat smiled and shook her head. "I can breathe here, Val. I don't have the duties I have on Earth. That's all."

"And yet I've placed an enormous assignment on your shoulders."

"Can we replant the garden?" she asked, ignoring him.

"Only outside the gates."

Kat frowned. "Why do you tolerate this behavior from your son?"

"*Our* son, and in order to get along with him I have to."

"And yet you asked me here to rein him in—you think I'm stronger than you are?"

"With Arwen at this point in time? Yes, I do."

Kat's good mood faded. "I'll have a talk with him, but I doubt I'll get very far."

"You'll have to do more than talk," Val said, taking her hand to tug her toward the house. "Use that druid priestess persona you told me about to persuade him."

When they came inside, Arwen was sitting at the table with his head in his hands. "Are you all right?" Kat asked, placing a hand on his back.

He shook her off and glared at her, his eyes narrowing into slits. "I'm fine. Mind your own fucking business."

"Arwen!" Val shouted, but the boy had already risen and was disappearing up the wide staircase. "Do it, Kat. Make him hear you," he hissed, pointing after Arwen.

"Now?"

"Yes."

Kat thought of that part of her that had delivered her mother's baby—the persona who knew things and commanded respect. Would Arwen listen to a priestess? And more importantly, could she summon her at will? She walked toward the stairs, conjuring the strength she felt when that wise woman took over. When she turned to glance back at Val he smiled. "Yes, that will do nicely," he said. Was it that obvious?

By the time she reached Arwen's room she felt fully in the grip of the druidess, calm strength coming over her as she knocked.

"Go away!"

Kat took a deep breath and opened the door.

5

Siobhan was on her knees cradling Mior. Dagda held Tus Nua, his face gray with worry. "Where did the bullet hit him?"

"Straight through the heart, Dag—he won't live more than a few minutes." Tears flowed down her ashen face as she held Mior's small body close.

Dagda kneeled next to her. "Isn't there something we can do?"

Siobhan looked up at him, her eyes red and filled with tears. "No."

A second later Mior's eyes popped open. "Mama. What happened?"

"The gun, Mior. The bullet hit you." She laid him across her lap and smoothed the hair back from his wide forehead, watching blood gush from the wound in his chest. It flowed across her skirt, staining it red.

When Mior tried to sit up he grimaced and fell back. "The fireflies…" he murmured. "They can help me. But I…" his head lolled back and his eyes closed.

"Dag? Can you call the fireflies?" she sobbed.

Dagda shook his head. "Mior is the only one they listen to."

Siobhan shook Mior's shoulder, trying to wake him. When his eyes opened again, she said, "Call to them, Mior."

Mior raised his hands into the air, his fingers moving in symbols. A second later his arms dropped, and went limp. Siobhan placed her fingers on his neck, feeling for a pulse. "He's gone!" she wailed. A second later the air was thick with bugs. They hovered around until she placed Mior on his back and let them come closer.

Dagda handed her the baby as he watched the fireflies settle on Mior's chest. There were so many of them he all but disappeared, his body covered from his head to his feet.

The coyote arrived a few seconds later, his liquid eyes on Mior. A spark came from him, a golden speck that radiated in tandem with the lightning bugs.

"He's magic," Siobhan murmured in surprise, looking up at Dag.

"You didn't know? The coyote's a pooka."

Siobhan didn't answer, her eyes wide as she watched the bugs lift her son and cradle him within their light. When they placed him on the ground fifteen minutes later, Mior's eyes were open. A second later they swarmed and flew away.

"Mama, Papa? What happened?"

Siobhan cried tears of relief as she watched her son sit up. Before she could put an arm around him, Dagda had lifted him in the air, letting out a cry of joy that scattered the birds perched in the trees. The coyote let out a bark and rose on his hind legs to lick Mior's feet.

A second later Mior was running circles around them.

"The fireflies saved me!" he crowed.

"As did the coyote here," Siobhan told him, her hand resting on the wide gray- brown head.

"The pooka," Mior corrected, hugging the creature around the neck. "I was dead, Mama. I went somewhere and…" his eyes darkened, "and there was a bad man there and a woman whose eyes were like black holes."

Dagda frowned, staring at his son. "You saw Carmun. Where was she?"

"She…I don't know. It was too dark to see much of anything." He looked around. "Where are Bran and Kat?"

Dagda and Siobhan exchanged a look. "Bran flew away several months ago in the form of a raven, Mior. And your sister—you told us she went through a door. Don't you remember?"

Mior looked puzzled, his dark brows pulling together. He shook his head slowly.

"You don't remember?" Dagda asked, grabbing his arm.

"I remember being in the meadow with Kat and…" he shrugged. "Bran was still here too. Why can't I remember?"

"I don't know," Siobhan murmured, reaching to kiss his cheek. "All I care about is that you're alive."

The sun was sinking, a shimmering glow against the darkness of the forest, when Dagda led the way back to their fairy house of twisting limbs. Leaves had sprouted even though the tree trunks were no longer anchored in the ground. Kat's sleeping spot was empty now, her things together in a small pile. Siobhan stood next to Dagda, her eyes filling as she looked down. "When will she come back?"

Dagda shook his head. "I assume she's with the father

43

of her child now. Would you want to leave me?"

"Never—I would never leave you, Dag. But what about Bran?"

"Bran left her, Siobhan. He let her down badly."

"I hope she's all right. You weren't okay with this the last time we talked."

Dagda frowned. "I'm not okay with it now, but I understand what happened. If she's happy with Val then I'm happy for her."

"If it really was Val who took her."

"It was Val—who else could lure her through a door?"

Siobhan stood in the doorway watching the last rays of the sun sink behind the trees. Dusk sent fog creeping through the understory, birds flying to find their roosts for the night. "But now Mior doesn't remember her leaving." Her eyes met his. "What could that mean?"

When the baby let out a mewling cry Siobhan hurried inside to sit on one of the stools fashioned from twisted tree limbs to feed her.

Dagda watched her, his thoughts spiraling away in confusion. Mior had died and seen the witch and some unidentified man, and had no memory of either his sister or Bran leaving Earth. Something magic was at work here, and whatever it was did not bode well.

Bran shivered. He pushed himself up, trying to free himself from the rotting odors and the gray slime. "Where have I been?" he muttered as he registered the cold wind. Memories of the past months came back slowly, his thoughts hazy as he remembered his time as Raven. Raven had mated and raised three chicks. Why was he here on this flat plain filled with nothing but rocks and puddles of ice?

Once he was on his feet, Bran had a moment of *deja-vu*, his thoughts coming together. He was on Earth and close to the place where he and Kat's family had discovered the injured coyote. He hurried away, his arms tight around his slime-covered body.

K at stared hard at Arwen, her eyes narrowing when he turned away from her glare. "Arwen, look at me," she ordered in a voice that didn't sound like her own.

Arwen's head swiveled toward her. "Who *are* you?"

"I'm Katel, your mother. Whatever else I may be does not concern you. Now tell me what you've been up to and why. I want to hear every detail about your supposed friends, your drug use and what you have planned for the future."

"I…" He struggled not to speak, his stuttering voice echoing in the glass room. In the end he could not control himself, confusion on his face as he began to talk, the words pouring from him like a faucet that had just been turned on. "I run with a gang—I guess my father already told you that. We have a plan to take out most of the old ones who refuse to listen to reason. We want a new world order that does not include all these fucking rules." He paused to take a breath, gulping in air, his face scarlet with resisting. But there was nothing he could do. "We've been talking about contacting the witch to help us. One of us knows where she is. But so far that person has been too nervous to do it. He says she's so powerful that it scares him. She could take over the entire plan and destroy all of us. But we want what she wants!"

"And who is this person? What is his name?"

Arwen kept his lips tightly shut but he was unable to keep the information back. "His name is Elrie." He clamped his hand over his mouth, tears coming into his eyes. "How are you doing this?" he asked querulously.

Kat smiled. "In truth I don't know how this is happening. I've never had this kind of power. Perhaps it's because of the extra magic in the Elven world?"

"Please stop. I can't reveal all the secrets without getting into a lot of trouble."

Kat cocked her head to one side. "How will they know unless you tell them?"

"We don't keep secrets from each other. It's part of our pact."

"And the drugs you use? What are those?"

"Berries," he blurted. "Magic red berries. They help us see things and know things."

"Like this witch?"

He nodded. "I've met her in the dreamworld."

Kat gazed at his face lit up by the afternoon sun's rays; his vivid eyes looked translucent; the pupils were enormous. "And do you think this meeting was real, Arwen?"

"I don't know—maybe it was…don't ask me any more questions!" He was openly crying now, his hands over his face. He pushed back against the wall trying to escape her.

Kat took pity on him, realizing how terrified he was, but she had to know. "You will tell me the next time this happens. I want to know every detail of where this witch is and what she says to you or your little gang. Do you understand?"

Arwen nodded, his eyes wide.

"And what is the plan if you don't meet up with her?"

"We have to meet with her—she's the only one strong enough to take out the elders," he muttered through his tears.

"The elders? Will you knife them, shoot them, fill them full of arrows or use sorcery to kill them?"

"Stop!" he cried out. "I'm going to be sick." A second later he was running for the open window. He leaned out and retched, his body sagging against the sill.

Kat moved behind him, her hand on his back. "I'm sorry for this, Arwen, but I cannot have you destroy your father or the ones he loves. How can you even think about doing something so heinous?"

"It isn't just me," he mumbled, wiping a sleeve across his face. "Elrie...he's our leader."

"And what would happen if you quit?" Kat asked softly, rubbing soothing circles on his back.

Arwen let out a groan and retched again, his body convulsing against the window ledge. "They would kill me," he muttered, crumpling to the floor.

Kat found a rag to clean him up before she helped him to bed. "Sleep now. We will talk again later."

Arwen's eyes closed, his chest heaving as he drew in ragged breaths. "If I tell them what you did, you'll be in danger," he muttered.

Kat sat next to him. "So, don't tell them."

"I have to," he murmured just before he fell asleep.

It was dusk when Kat returned downstairs. Val was drinking from a tankard, his eyes clouded when he glanced up at her. "You've been up there for over an hour."

"Our son is in danger, Val. The boys he associates with are in touch with dark magic. They've contacted the witch."

Val was on his feet in an instant. "Carmun is a lot more than she seems. The boys are foolish to mess with her."

"Arwen's sleeping right now—I exhausted him with my questions."

"And he answered willingly?"

Kat smiled. "I wouldn't call it willingly, but he did answer."

Val frowned. "You have power over him."

"I guess I do, or at least the druid priestess does. I think the magic in the atmosphere here helped. We need to keep him here for his own safety. Those boys will hurt him if they find out what he told me. This witch—I've seen what she can do. I'm really worried for them and for all of us."

Val ran agitated fingers through his long hair. "If they've already contacted her it's only a matter of time before she's here and inhabiting someone who we least expect. I need to talk with the elders and come up with a feasible plan. Can you stay here and watch over him if I head out?"

"Now?"

"I think now would be better than waiting until tomorrow. From what he told you, time is of the essence."

"True. What if he tries to leave?"

Val smirked. "I'm sure you can manage to keep him

here, Kat." Val grabbed his cloak off a peg and gave the dark material a theatric swish before wrapping it around his shoulders. A second later he opened the glass door and let it fall shut behind him, his shadowy form disappearing into the night. She took in a breath and went to the kitchen to get herself some food and a tankard of some alcoholic beverage. She felt oddly drained by her conversation with her son and the anticipation of what was to come. Val's reason for her coming had been right all along.

Kat was still sitting at the table when she heard Arwen's door open. She looked up to see him slinking down the stairs. "Where are you off to?"

He stopped, his gaze traveling to where she sat in the dark. "What's it to you?"

Kat rose from the chair and moved closer to where he paused halfway down the stairs. "You should know the answer to that question. I suggest you stay here."

"Where's my father?"

"He went to meet with the elders."

Arwen let out a moan. "They'll kill me," he muttered, his eyes flicking from left to right.

"Not if you stay put they won't. What do you hope to accomplish by talking with them?"

"I...I have to tell them that you know. It's part of our..."

"Pact...yes, so you said. But what happens if you decide not to participate in their plans?"

Arwen looked confused, his eyes bulging. "I...I don't

have a choice anymore. We did a ritual and my blood was part of it."

"You cut yourselves and pledged yourselves to darkness?"

He held his hand over his mouth but the words came anyway. "We have one more blood oath to go to summon the witch. We have to kill an animal. It's supposed to happen tonight."

Kat glared at him as she straightened her spine, rising up to her full height. "You will not be attending."

Arwen looked around frantically, his eyes wild. "If I don't go, they…they'll come here to get me. I'm a necessary part of it now."

Kat heard Val opening the door, her attention drifting from Arwen. In that instant Arwen streaked by her and ran by his father as he was coming in, nearly knocking Val down.

"Stop him!" Kat cried out.

When Val reached out for Arwen, he stumbled, his knees hitting the glass floor with a crack. He let out a sharp cry before pushing himself up to gaze at the disappearing figure of his son running as fast as he could up the hill. Val rubbed his knees, turning to Kat. "Where is he going?"

"His gang is holding the summoning ritual tonight," Kat told him, her blood running cold in her veins. "It's a blood ritual, Val."

"Summoning…the witch?"

Kat nodded, hurrying to where he teetered on legs turned rubbery. She grabbed hold of his arm to steady him and led him to chair where he dropped heavily, his face leached of all color. "This is it, then," he muttered gazing up at Kat hovering over him. "This is the beginning of the end."

"Not if I can help it," Kat murmured. "Now tell me what you learned from the elders?" she asked, staring at him intently.

Val frowned. "Do not try and use your magic on me, Katel."

"In order to stop this ritual, I have to know what was said. If Carmun responds to the summoning it will be over for all of us."

"The elders are doing a summoning of their own tonight. Freyr should be here by midnight. He is our king and leader. He's had dealings with sorcery and he knows this witch from centuries ago. With him here we'll know what to do."

"Know what to do? I know what to do and I'm not your leader! Midnight will be too late!"

The Fae man's eyes widened. "And you think you can go up against her by yourself? She is full goddess, Kat, and a witch on top of it."

"I didn't say that—but maybe, if I have some help. Danu said my destiny is entangled with hers. We are fated to find each other."

Val smiled. "You are not the little bird I knew from before."

Kat ignored his comment, continuing, "If we stop our son and his friends tonight, we won't need Freyr."

Val glanced away, reaching for his tankard which still contained a small amount of ale. He downed it in one gulp. "And just how do you propose to do that?" he asked.

7

Bran struggled through the cold night trying to keep his teeth from chattering. Last he remembered it was warm, sunlight glinting off his feathers as he flew to find carrion and other delicacies to feed the nestlings. Earth seemed an unlikely place for Raven to take him—unless—unless there was some reason for it that he had yet to discover. Perhaps Kat had called for him? He didn't know how he felt about her now, his anger having solidified into a shield wall he couldn't begin to penetrate. Her new powers had addled her, any love she'd had for Bran disappearing into a haze of selfishness—or at least that's how he'd seen it at the time. Now he wasn't sure what to think, only that being Raven had given him a respite from the constant pain of missing her.

But then he remembered what he'd been doing when Raven took over his psyche. He'd been on his way to find Myrddin when the female raven tempted him. With the wizard's help he'd hoped to find answers to his questions, the ones that had plagued him since he'd left Kat and her family. His heart beat erratically, reminding him of what it had cost him to leave her behind. A moment later he was Raven again, his awareness on his surroundings and finding his way back to Otherworld. But first he would take one turn around.

The sun was peeking above the eastern horizon when Raven circled the small camp below. Even in his Raven form he knew the boy who spied him before calling to the others. A man and a woman appeared from within the odd house that reminded him of a raven's nest; a baby was held tight within the woman's arms.

"Bran!" the boy cried out, his hands held around his mouth.

Raven circled again, waiting for another, but no one else appeared from within the structure.

"Kat is gone!" Mior shouted, his voice hoarse. "She went through a door!"

Raven tried to puzzle out the words, but his bird mind didn't understand. The only thing he knew was that someone was missing. And the missing someone had at one time been very important to him. He let out a caw and circled upward until he was amongst the clouds. It was hard to fly with the heaviness that weighed him down, a sensation he did not understand.

"Why didn't he stay and turn into Bran?" Mior asked, his tear-filled eyes on Dagda.

"Perhaps he knew that Kat wasn't here, Mior. No reason for him to be here without her."

"But I thought he loved us," Mior murmured, his head down.

"He does love us," Siobhan told him, pulling him against her. "But he loves Kat in a different way. I think he will attempt to find her now that he knows she isn't here."

Mior looked up at his mother. "I hope he finds her and brings her home."

"So do I," Siobhan answered, turning to gaze at Dagda.

"I hope Katel realizes how close we are to a showdown with that monster in the sky," Dagda muttered, frowning. "We need her here to fend off what I fear he's about to do."

"What makes you think it's imminent?" Siobhan asked, handing him the baby.

"He's unfurled, Siobhan. He lies across the entire length of the heavens now." Tus Nua, let out a happy chortle, blue-green eyes focused on the man who held her, but Dagda didn't notice, his narrowed gaze on the sky where the enormous winged serpent was just barely visible amongst the clouds.

"What could Kat possibly be doing?" Siobhan asked her son. "What did she say before she left?"

Mior shrugged. "I didn't see her leave, Mama. Coyote said there was an opening in the sky. And a man lit up on the other side."

"Yes, the father of her child," Dagda grumbled, frowning. "As your mother said, she has every right to be with him. I only hope she remembers what's happening down here in our realm. Without her we're helpless to fight that creature off."

"He won't hurt you!" Mior insisted, but neither Dagda or Siobhan paid him any attention.

Raven shifted, his human eyes on the unfamiliar land around him. He glanced down at his featherless body. Normally shifting left him wearing what he'd had on before the shift. Caves lined the hills above him, caves that could possibly house the wizard. There was nothing to be done but search out Myrddin and hope he had an extra pair of trousers and a tunic, or maybe a wool cloak.

A frisson of fear snaked up his spine as the reality of his situation penetrated. Myrddin was a powerful wizard. He was a recluse, living out here to escape the ones who sought him out. Why had he listened to Airmid? He was better off going to the gods and throwing himself on their mercy.

Two days and nights went by as Bran combed the hills and searched through abandoned caves that led nowhere. He was badly scratched, his legs and feet cut and bleeding from scrambling over the sharp rocks. At night he shifted into the bird to stay warm.

On the third day he discovered a trail that meandered upward, his raw and blistered feet sending rocks skittering as he struggled to find his footing. He scrabbled his way toward a dark opening where bits of bright cloth hung from a tree at its opening. But when a person emerged, scowling down at him, he fell backward, his hands reaching out for branches that weren't there. A second later he was suspended in a place neither here nor there, and before he could think, he was hoisted upward to stand directly in front of a dark-haired man wearing a heavy robe with a hood. Fathomless onyx eyes peered at him.

"Are you…?"

"Who might you be? I do not receive many visitors. I prefer the quiet."

"I…I'm Bran, used to be Bran, the blessed. But I am no longer a god. If you are Myrddin, I've been searching for you."

The man smiled, his eyes lightening into a shade of deep green and crinkling around the edges. "I am who you think I am, but I am not sure why you found it necessary to search me out. What can I possibly do for a god who is no longer a god?"

Bran sighed, glancing down at his unclothed body. "Well, for one thing, do you have a robe I might borrow?"

Myrddin laughed, the sound ringing through the cave behind him and scattering a half dozen birds roosting nearby. "And how did this nakedness come to be? I have the sense there's a story here."

Bran shook his head. "Not that interesting other than I ended up somewhere I didn't expect. I am also Raven, but normally I'm dressed when the shifts happen."

"If you are Raven why have you not shifted in order to stay warm? You could have found me easier as a bird."

Bran sat on a flat stone, wrapping his arms around his shivering body. The sky had turned dark and the wind had come up, raising goosebumps on his arms and legs. He felt embarrassed to be exposed, ashamed of the cuts and bruises all over him and his vulnerability. "Before we talk further, could I borrow some clothes?"

Myrddin waved his hand and a second later Bran was dressed in loose-fitting trousers and a warm wool tunic, his feet encased in boots. "Will that do?"

"Thank you."

"You'd best come inside. Nighttime here is not safe. Even my magic can't stave off the spirits that roam this part of the forest."

Bran frowned, glancing around nervously before ducking his head to follow him thru the narrow opening. A door swung closed behind him, latches clicking into place. "I haven't seen anything bad."

"You are no longer a danger so you are not on their radar. They want me."

"Is the witch Carmun part of it?"

Myrddin turned from lighting candles with the ends of his fingers. "What do you know of her?"

"She...she attacked Earth and my woman has gone after her."

"Your woman...who is this woman who would think she could go up against an ancient witch of this strength?"

Bran looked around as the candles revealed the cave, surprised by the rugs, the wooden furniture and the small bed that occupied a spot under the sloping wall. It was comfortable and cozy with a firepit and grate for cooking, low chairs and hanging utensils that seemed handmade and others that looked to be artifacts from another time. The cave disappeared into darkness and he could hear a stream burbling.

"Have you lost your tongue, boy?"

Bran turned. "I...I'm sorry. Your cave it's just so..."

"Yes, yes. Now answer my question. Your woman?" Myrddin bring the fire to life using the tips of his fingers and his breath.

Bran lowered into a rustic chair made of twigs. "Kat, her

name is Kat. We love each other, or at least we did. She's gone now but the entire thing was my fault," he mumbled.

The god came close, bending over Bran, his gaze intense and disturbing. "This Kat, who is she exactly?"

Bran nearly tipped his chair backward, trying to avoid the eyes that seemed to bore inside him. "She's Dagda's daughter."

Myrddin straightened, his gaze going into the distance. "Ah—the Dagda who is no longer the Dagda. I have heard of this young demigoddess, both in prophecy and also from other sources. She is connected with the witch."

Bran leaned forward, disturbed. "Connected? What do you mean?"

"Connected, you fool! Don't you know what that word means? She and this witch are linked."

"But Kat would never do…"

Myrddin scowled and pulled his long hair away from his angular face. "Linked does not mean they like each other, young fool. Do you not know anything? It means they have a destiny together."

Bran nodded. "She did talk about that. But I assumed she didn't understand."

The god swiveled to stare at him. "You have assumed a lot of things not in existence, haven't you? This is why you are no longer a god. This Kat is wiser than she knows. But Carmun is a worthy adversary."

"You act like Carmun is just a normal person."

Myrddin looked away. "She is a witch—that is all."

"But she caused the beginning of Ragnarok."

Myrddin shook his head. "She is but a part of what has happened and is happening. The true Ragnarok has not begun. Perhaps it will happen when this woman you speak of meets with Carmun."

Bran shivered despite the warm fire and the clothes he was wearing. "Is that foretold?"

Myrddin ignored him and pulled a carafe down, pouring a reddish liquid into two earthenware cups. "Elderberry wine," he said, handing one to Bran. "You have come to get your god powers back," he murmured before taking a sip. "But in order for that to happen you have to take stock of who you are."

"You mean who I've become," Bran grumbled, taking a hefty slug of the bitter- sweet wine.

"Yes. You have allowed your emotions to dictate your every move. Being a god means holding onto a part of yourself that can never be violated, not by love, not by misfortune, not by any circumstances. You have a long way to go, young fool."

Bran snorted. "I wouldn't call myself young."

"Age has nothing to do with state of mind. You allowed this shift to take place without resisting it in any way. You gave yourself over to this woman without once taking into account what it would mean. Why did you do this?"

Bran shook his head, searching for a reason. "I love her…"

Myrddin sneered and shook his head. "When you can answer this question, then and only then can we begin to restore who you are."

8

Val's skeptical expression pissed Kat off. She was sick of everyone doubting her. Having the goddess Danu on her side, as well as an ancient druidic priestess inhabiting her body, was no small thing. "I'm pretty sure I can dissuade them, Val. I just forced our son to tell me everything. If my attention hadn't drifted, he'd still be here. You need to have a little faith in me."

Val shook his head his gaze going to the tankard on the table in front of him. "These are forces from a shadow place, Kat. Have you been to where this goddess lives? No, you have not. I have, and it is beyond your wildest nightmares—a place of no light, no air, only impenetrable darkness."

"I *have* been there," Kat murmured, remembering the sensation of suffocating. It was where Bran had nearly died. "Carmun is my destiny. I know it, you know it—we have to let this play out."

"I will go along with your plan, but only to a point. If you cannot turn these boys, I will contact the elders and call on Freyr."

"Shall we go before they do the deed? Arwen said the ceremony would take place tonight."

"Did Arwen tell you where?"

Kat frowned. "I figured you would know."

Val's lips pursed, his eyes narrowing. "They hold these meetings in secret. I have no idea where they do it."

Kat sniffed in annoyance. "You must have some idea, Val. Kids his age are usually pretty transparent about where they meet. Is there a local wood close to town?"

"Local wood?" Val let out a laugh. "There are acres of forests—the entire realm is covered with trees!"

"And you can't look into his mind like you looked into mine the last time I was here? Have you lost all your magic?"

Val's face turned red. "No, I haven't lost my magic, but he has to be here for me to read his mind."

"Sorry. It just seems that he's holding all the cards right now. Please search your memories for places they might be meeting."

Val ran his fingers through his pale hair. "I do know of one place. It's a short walk from the main town square, a power spot that connects with the rest of the realms. From there you can go through a door into any of the other worlds."

Kat frowned. "You never told me about that when I was trying to find Bran. Instead I nearly died."

"Are we going to argue about the past or try and stop this evil goddess from destroying the world?"

When their eyes met Kat saw the frustration and anger swirling in Val's. She'd been baiting him and she didn't know why. She held out her hand. "Let's go."

When Val's warm fingers slid through hers Kat felt an immediate rush of desire, her cheeks turning pink as she glanced in his direction.

"I feel the same," he murmured. "But we have a job to do first."

A second later she was running behind him through the dark night, her breath coming in gasps.

The village lights twinkled through the tree branches, the sight of the lanterns giving Kat a moment of calm. That is until she glanced at Val's expression. "What's wrong?"

He pointed one long finger in the direction of the town square where a bonfire was sending sparks into the cloudy night sky. "Arwen and his friends are performing the ritual right out in the open," he muttered.

Kat looked closer, shocked to see Arwen and a group of boys standing together in a circle. Beyond the light cast by the fire a dozen robed figures watched. "Is that…?"

"The elders are here and doing nothing to stop them," Val hissed.

"Maybe this isn't the ritual—maybe they're only warming themselves."

Val gripped Kat's upper arm. "Look closer. That's a goat they're holding up."

A tortured scream that sounded almost human split the silence as a silver knife flashed, blood spurting from the animal's throat. Kat watched in shock as the boys dipped their fingers into the blood and covered their naked upper bodies with symbols. A chant went up, growing louder and louder. The elders moved closer, throwing off their cloaks to stand fully naked with the boys. "Val, the elders, they're…participating!"

Val pulled her back into the shadows. "What the fuck," he whispered, his eyes wide with shock.

Kat sagged against him as the scene unfolded like a dark nightmare. There were women among the men, stark-naked beneath their discarded dark cloaks. "It's a sexual ritual to bring forth evil," she muttered, staring in astonishment as the men and women clutched each other and fell to the ground.

Val's body began to shake, his breath ragged. "We have to get out of here," he whispered. "This is…I've seen this sort of thing before."

"But what if Carmun arrives? I can feel the power from here!"

When she turned to Val he looked sick, his face the color of ash. "The elders…how can they be involved in this? I just met with them. This can't be happening." When the ground began to tremble, Val jerked her away, tugging her into the shadows. "We can't be here."

"I'm not leaving our son," Kat hissed. She pulled out of his grip, moving behind a tree where she could view the proceedings. There was a rhythm to the movements, the sexual act ritualized and slowed down as the elders coupled. The chanting continued, the sparks from the fire turning red and illuminating the writhing bodies as the drawn-out moments went by. Arwen was in the midst of it, but it was only the elders who were copulating. The boys danced around them, chanting, caressing the bodies of those on the ground and touching themselves. Some were outright masturbating.

"This is repulsive," Val hissed. "We have to go."

Kat grabbed his arm, her fingers digging into his flesh. "Carmun's coming," she muttered. "I can feel it."

"We can't be here, Kat. She will kill us."

Kat's eyes widened as she glanced from Val to the circle where their son stood transfixed. "You would leave our son here to be subsumed by evil?" A second later Kat took off, running toward the circle, the fire, and her son. She shoved the elders aside as she rushed toward Arwen, nearly falling as the ground shook and rumbled under her feet. An unearthly sound began as a crevasse opened, sucking the flames into the darkness. A few lanterns had been set here and there, revealing the elders as they stopped what they were doing to watch. And from the chasm a dark mist rose, the stench of something foul coming with it. Kat screamed, her gaze riveted on her son who stood watching the thing that was rising from the ground.

Arwen turned when he heard Kat scream, his pale face devoid of emotion—in a trance. But Kat was already upon him, her fingers reaching for his arm. For a second it was as though time stood still, a high-pitched shrieking taking over everything as Carmun rose from the pit. There was a roar of welcome from the elders as they stood waiting with their arms out to greet their queen.

The witch materialized slowly, her dress like shadows that moved and shifted, her eyes holes of darkness. She was hideous, her hair tangled and thin, her skin cragged with age. Through the noise and the sudden chaos, Kat heard Val shouting. And when a shimmering door appeared, standing open, she shoved her son through and stumbled after him.

9

"**S**omething's changed."

Bran turned to see Myrddin frowning moodily into the distance. "What?"

Dark eyes met his. "You can't feel it?"

"All I feel is the wind picking up outside."

Myrddin's eyes narrowed dangerously. "She's arrived. My mother has returned."

"Your mother? Who is your mother?"

"My mother is the witch, Carmun."

Bran shivered, suddenly deeply afraid. "How is *that* possible?"

Myrddin eyed Bran. "How do you think, young fool? My father fucked her and she bore a son."

"Who is your father?"

"I don't know."

Bran willed him to say more, but he simply cocked his head as though listening to something that Bran couldn't hear.

"Your demigoddess…she…" Myrddin muttered.

"She, what?" Bran interrupted, his fear rising even further.

"The daughter of Dagda is involved in this resurrection. She's there."

Panic took Bran into its clutches, his heart beating a staccato rhythm against his ribs as he paced from one side of the cave to the other. "What's happening now?"

Myrddin shook his head. "I only saw the hag rise from the depths of hell and your woman standing there to greet her. After that it all goes dark." Myrddin sighed, rubbing a hand across his face. "My mother sensed me and blocked me out."

Bran shook his head, his pacing taking on a manic speed until Myrddin grabbed his arm and pulled him to a halt. "Sit down, young fool. It is time for you to rest. We have much to discuss, but not until the morrow." When the wizard waved a hand in front of Bran's face, Bran collapsed onto the floor, his eyes closing, his mind going blank.

10

I t was barely light on Earth, very early dawn judging from the streaks of vivid color in the eastern sky. Arwen glared at Kat. "What did you do?"

"I did nothing. I have no control of the doors. It was your father who helped us out of a dangerous situation."

Arwen moved closer, his chin jutting. "It wasn't dangerous for me. I'm supposed to be there."

Kat put her hand up, stopping him. "The witch is dangerous for everyone, Arwen. She plans to bring darkness down on every living thing. Would you like to live in a world devoid of light and life?"

Arwen smirked. "You don't know what you're talking about. She's our future. She will only cull what is no longer of use."

"And who did you hear this from? I've seen where she dwells. I've been there. It is a lightless place filled with the vile creatures who belong there. Now that she'd been resurrected, she wants ultimate power."

"My friends know all about her. They said she has the power to let us begin again."

"Begin again? After she's destroyed the entire cosmos?" Kat gestured to the barren land. "She sucked the life out of this place, sent storms and earthquakes to destroy our world. I was rebuilding when Val summoned me to Alfheim."

"My father is an idiot," Arwen mumbled.

Kat grabbed his arm and twisted. "He is no such thing. Val cares about you, but you're too wrapped up in your own little screwed up world to see it. And after witnessing that scene around the bonfire I can see that Val is one of only a very few who care about the future of Alfheim."

Arwen let out a nasty laugh. "Yes, the elders are on our side. Didn't take much to convince them to join. Only a spell or two. Weaklings, all of them. They'll be killed off soon enough."

Kat frowned, staring hard at her son. "You did this?"

"Me and my friends have learned a few potent spells in the last few years. It seems there is dark knowledge to be had if you know where to look."

Kat frowned and shook her head. "You won't be practicing any dark arts here, Arwen." She lifted her gaze to the rays of sunlight beginning to appear, her spirits rising as she thought about her family.

"You're wrong," Arwen muttered. "I'm stronger than you think."

Kat whirled on him. "Really?" She waved her hands in the air, sending him flying backward to land heavily on the ground.

He rose laughing. "A few parlor tricks," he said, dusting off his pants. "I'm linked with Carmun now, *Mother*." He raised his hand and Kat felt his slap against her face even though he never touched her. A second later she was on the ground and he was standing over her. "I suggest you think again before you do something to annoy me."

Kat stayed where she was, attempting to absorb what had just happened. In the meantime, Arwen strode away, disappearing into the early morning mist rising from the damp ground. When she rose to her feet a few minutes later a familiar stooped figure was approaching from the forested hill in the distance. She hurried to meet him.

Dagda stopped and glared at her. "Where have you *been*, Katel?"

"I was in Alfheim, Dad. Val needed me. Our son, he…"

"We needed you too. Mior was shot and nearly died, your mother…your mother has been beside herself with worry. The gangs are threatening."

"It was about the witch. I had to go."

"And did you stop her?" he asked, watching her. "No, I didn't think so. And what about Bran? Have you seen him lately? He came by as Raven looking for you, but because you weren't here, he didn't stay."

Kat felt a blip in her heart region. "Bran was here? How long have I been gone?"

"We've had two full moons since you walked through that door."

"It seemed like only a couple of days on Alfheim."

"We'd best get back now. Your mother has been up all night with Tus Nua. She's teething or something…I told her I'd gather some herbs to help with the pain."

Kat nodded and followed him toward the hills in the distance. "Who shot my brother?"

"He did it to himself," Dagda muttered. "It was an accident."

Kat wondered how Mior obtained a gun, but the scowl on her father's face told her not to ask more questions. It seemed things had not been going well in her absence. "Arwen's here," she said.

Dagda swiveled to stare at her. "Arwen? Where is he?"

"He took off that way." She pointed into the distance.

"All the gods in Otherworld, Kate! How in hell did this come about?"

Kat groaned, suddenly so tired she could barely keep her eyes opened. "It's a long story. Can it wait until I've rested?"

Dagda scowled, his bushy gray eyebrows drawing together. "No one will be happy to hear this news," he muttered, hurrying toward a field planted in herbs.

Siobhan bustled about, heating water for her herbal concoction and attempting to sooth an irate Tus Nua. "Give her to me," Kat ordered, reaching out. As soon as the baby was in Kat's arms, she stopped crying, too fascinated with Kat's braids to remember why she'd been crying in the first place.

Siobhan let out a sigh. "We've missed you," she whispered, stirring her concoction.

Mior danced around her, a wide smile on his open face. "I want to see my Elven brother!"

"I'm sure you will, Mior. He's only sulking right now."

Dagda glanced at her, his expression one of skepticism.

"Sulking? I have the strong sense we won't see him unless he decides to do something…"

Kat gave him a warning glance, shifting her eyes toward Mior. "He'll show up when he gets hungry," she said, glancing around the small house. "Where's the pooka?"

Mior looked sad. "He's been gone for a while."

"We think he's looking for a mate," Dagda added, shaking his head ever so slightly.

"Breakfast?" Siobhan asked brightly. While they were talking the herbs had cooked down and now Siobhan was spooning cooked grains from the pot into bowls. "It's made from grasses that grow in the lower meadow—it's like a wild rice."

Kat placed the sleeping baby on a pile of blankets and reached for a bowl. Confusion settled in as an image of Bran appeared in her mind. He was with a dark-haired, dark-eyed man who seemed somewhat sinister. Where was he and who was with him? Before she could muse any further, she heard several shots ring out.

Dagda was up and out of the house a half second later, scanning in the direction of the continuing reports. When Kat joined him, he turned, a deep frown furrowing his forehead. "This has to be because of Arwen. We've had no incidents with these people in many months."

"Arwen doesn't have a weapon, Dad."

"Weapon or not, he's pissed them off somehow."

Fifteen minutes later Arwen appeared, walking up the hill with a sneer on his face. "I took care of your little problem!" he yelled when he saw Dagda and Kat watching him.

Kat and her Dad exchanged a look. "What has he

done?" Dagda asked.

"He's powerful, Dad. He absorbed some of Carmun's energy before I pushed him through the door."

Siobhan grabbed Dagda's arm. "We have children to protect," she hissed. "Will he hurt us?"

Kat frowned. "Not if I can help it." Kat summoned the priestess, closing her eyes and visualizing what she'd felt when the entity was inhabiting her. By the time Arwen reached the house Kat was in the background of her mind. "Stop right there," she ordered, putting a hand up. "What did you do?"

Arwen opened his mouth and the words poured forth, his eyes going wide with his inability to control himself. "I got them to turn on each other. It was easy. There aren't many left now so they won't be bothering you. I thought you'd be happy."

Mior let out a whoop of joy. "The bad ones are gone!" he crowed, running to wrap his arms around Arwen's legs. Arwen tried to back away but was unable to move, a look of horror crossing his features.

"Mior, step away," Dagda ordered.

"But Arwen is my…my…?" He looked at his mother.

"Kat is your sister, Mior, and Arwen is her son, my grandson," Siobhan said. "You are Arwen's uncle."

Mior laughed, staring at the stricken boy standing like a statue. "How old are you?"

"He's younger than you are," Kat told him, trying to keep her mental hold on her son. But the second her attention veered, Arwen took off and disappeared beneath the trees.

It was late in the evening before Kat filled her mother and father in on what had happened in Alfheim. They were both horrified. "Does this mean the witch is in control there?" Siobhan asked in a throaty whisper, trying not to wake Mior.

Kat shrugged. "I have no idea what happened after I left, but I did see Carmun arrive. The elders had all been taken over, but I'm not sure about the townspeople. I'm worried about Val."

Siobhan touched Kat's arm gently, her gaze sympathetic. "Of course, you are, dear. But he's Fae and can walk through a door whenever he wants. I'm surprised he isn't here already."

"I'm sure he's busy doing what he can to save his realm," Dagda muttered, his blue eyes dark in the candlelight. "That's what I would do."

"Makes sense," Kat agreed. "I just hope he's able to evade the witch."

It was deep in the night when Dagda let out a shout, waking them all. "The forest is on fire!"

Kat grabbed her dress and slipped it on, staring out at the red-orange glow in the distance. "It's Arwen."

But Dagda didn't hear her as he took off running, his light tunic flapping around his bare legs in the heated ash-filled air.

"We have no way to stop it," Siobhan said worriedly. "The entire forest could burn down. Do you have the magic to undo this?"

Kat shook her head, watching gray smoke billow upward, red-hot flames moving through the trees.

Mior was now awake, his wide eyes on the trees. "I can help," he said. A second later he was running out the door, Siobhan in hot pursuit.

Kat ran after them, finally catching up with Siobhan. She grabbed her mother's arm. "Go back and take care of the baby. I'll deal with Mior."

Tears ran down Siobhan's white face. "Don't let anything happen to him," she sobbed.

Kat gave her a quick hug and headed up the hill toward the now raging fire. Terrified animals streaked by as the flames encroached, the smoke making her cough the closer she got. In the distance she could see her father standing silhouetted against the brightness, unable to do anything but watch their beloved forest burn. Mior was nowhere to be seen.

11

B ran woke with a gasp. He'd seen Kat surrounded
by flames. "Myrddin!" he shouted, searching the
empty cave for the wizard. No one answered, and
when he ran outside, he was greeted with an ominous
silence. The images were still with him, the terror as well.
He had to help her.

Bran ran, attempting over and over to turn into
Raven—he had to find Myrddin. When he finally came
upon the wizard, Myrddin was standing in a clearing
looking up at the sky, a chant rising like smoke from his
mouth. Bran rushed toward him, panting to find his breath.
"I have to help Kat!"

Myrddin turned, his eyes dark with fury. "I have
important business to take care of and you interrupt me for
this? Do you remember why you came here? You have no
power to help this woman. Not only have you given up
your god powers, but now Raven is gone as well. And you
have done this all willingly!"

"Willingly? Why would I give up Raven? It's the only
way I can get to her now."

Myrddin let out a laugh. "*Was* the only way."

"There was fire. Do you know what's happened?"

The god scoffed. "Of course, I know, young fool. I am aware of all of it, including this Fae boy of hers who started the fire. Trouble is upon her and there is nothing you can do. I suggest you stay here and continue to solve your own problems and leave her to deal with hers."

Bran shook his head, the need to leave making him shake all over. When Myrddin grabbed him by the arm, he followed the wizard back to the cave, his mind suddenly blank. "Now sit and listen to me very carefully," Myrddin said. "What is it you want more than anything else?"

Bran's legs abruptly folded, landing him on the cave floor. He felt weak, diminished and fearful. "I want Kat. I miss her. I don't know why I left in the first place. I guess I was sad because she didn't seem to need me anymore, and…"

"And her father despises you and has no respect for you. You turned your back on all that you were, and gave yourself over to a woman. Is that what you want for yourself?"

"Why not? What's wrong with love? I'm happy to give myself over for love." Bran was taken into the dark eyes, all sense of who he was disappearing in that moment. He struggled against the uncomfortable sensations, but he couldn't escape the feeling that everything he ever was or had been was gone. "What did you do?" he asked in a strangled whisper.

"We have to begin at the beginning," Myrddin said.

Bran sat like a zombie, unable to think or speak. The wizard burned herbs and muttered incantations, the firepit flaming as the dried herbs caught and pungent scents lifted into the air. The chanting seemed to go on and on. When the wizard turned to Bran, his eyes were completely black, no expression on his gaunt face. Bran felt utterly vulnerable, a piece of clay for the wizard to mold in any way he wanted. Did he trust Myrddin? It didn't matter whether he did or didn't. He'd sought him out and now he'd been rendered defenseless, exposed and helpless. He tried to move away from the man who approached him, but he was unable to budge.

"Drink this," Myrddin ordered, handing him a bowl.

Bran didn't want to drink it, the smell was disgusting, but he did as he was told. A second later he was gagging, his eyes watering.

"It is a purge," Myrddin explained. "It will take what you think you know out of your mind so that you can start anew." Myrddin peered at him closely, dark eyes pinning him like a bug. "You did ask me for help, young fool. Remember that I am not your enemy."

Bran tried to answer but his tongue felt thick. He moved his mouth helplessly, staring up at the wizard hovering over him.

"You cannot speak for now, but do not let this disturb you. It is only temporary while I work a few spells. This next few hours will not be pleasant, but in the end, you will thank me."

Bran's insides gurgled and shifted, cramps sending him crawling toward the opening.

Myrddin laughed. "It is a strong potion."

Bran was outside the cave in the bushes, unable to think of anything but what was happening in his bowels. When that part was over, he was heaving, caught in spasms that seemed to go on and on. He lay spent until Myrddin dragged him inside and forced him to drink another cup of disgusting brew.

"This one will only take you back to the beginning, young fool—to when you were born into your god powers. Do you remember?"

Bran was suddenly thrown into a twilight world. His father Llyr, the god of the sea, was standing next to his mother, the goddess, Iwerydd. He felt the warmth and safety of her arms as she held him close, her heartbeat calming him. She sat to nurse him, kind eyes peering down as she slipped off her gown. As a tiny baby he was mostly aware of cold and heat, the feeling of being safe and the hunger in his belly. His fingers kneaded the warm skin of his mother's breast as he suckled.

A second later he was hurled into a future time when where he was playing with his sister, Branwen, their game of catch with an energy ball taking all of his attention. She was pretty, his sister, and sweet. He loved her. He was also aware of his father's second wife, a human woman called Penarddun, who lurked in the background of his mind. She was dark-haired in contrast to his mother's red-brown curls, and there was something he disliked about her. His mother was not happy about this new marriage and her angry scowl was something he dreaded. He was happiest when he and Branwen spent time together, that and his sword lessons with his father.

The scene shifted and he was thrown into a future time,

this one when he was fully grown with all his god powers. He was skilled in poetry, music and prophecy, his strength lauded by the other gods and goddesses. Scenes flew by, scenes in which he was with women, scenes in which he fought for what he knew was right, scenes on ships with his sword hanging by his side, until…the moment when he was mortally wounded by a poisoned spear. After that there was darkness and awareness of something he didn't want to acknowledge. The darkness seemed to last for a very long time, years that he was caught in a lightless place where other spirits dwelled, many of them malevolent. He thought he might be there forever when he was finally resurrected, his god status taking him to the kingdom of Otherworld to live as an immortal.

He was powerful, a god of ravens who were the messengers between the mortal world and the world of the spirits. He reveled in his power, his light, and everything he'd been given. He sat on a throne of gold and silver and wore a crown of bright stones. A woman sat beside him, beautiful, ethereal, her eyes the color of the sky. They had children together who played in front of them. A boy and a girl, both blonde and sweet-faced like his wife. But he didn't love her.

A second later he was careening away again, his love for Kat taking him far from his background and far from who he'd always been. The gods disapproved of this forbidden love, the Dagda, Kat's father, angry and trying to prevent it from happening. Kat was human, mortal. But when he discovered that she was actually half-goddess, his world shifted again. He helped her discover her power, gave her all of his heart and went through hell for her. And somehow during the process he'd lost himself. His powers had been drifting away and he hadn't even known it.

Bran woke naked and curled into the fetal position, his face wet with tears. He sat up, his body exhausted and drained. His mind felt scoured, his heart torn open and exposed. He let out a strangled cry and curled up once again, hugging his knees into his chest. Myrddin watched him from the fire, his expression unreadable. "Come warm yourself," he invited. "And pull on a robe."

"How did I end up like this?"

"Are you speaking about your nakedness, or metaphorically, young fool?"

Bran crawled to the fire and pulled on the robe the wizard handed him. "Both, I guess."

"You shed your robe early on. It seemed that it got in the way of your flailing. You've been raving for nearly two full days. If you hadn't come back to your senses, I would have had to apply powerful magic to bring you out of the past."

"Isn't that what you wanted?"

Myrddin glared at him coldly. "Did you learn nothing from this experience? This was not about what *I* wanted. You came to me with an enigma you needed to solve. Is it solved or not?"

Bran thought about that. He'd been happy as a god, glad to have the respect of his fellow gods and goddesses and the ability to do good works. When he first helped Kat on Earth, he'd only been doing what he'd been asked. But as time went on, he'd fallen in love with her. In order to relieve himself of the guilt, he must have begun to shed his abilities, until he was left without anything but Raven. And now even that was gone. It hadn't been a true choice. "I'm not sure."

"Do you or do you not wish to be a god? Is it your desire to be mortal?"

"I want to be who I was, not who I am now. I don't like who I am...it's why I sought you out."

"I do not begrudge you your love for this woman, but in order to love her you must know yourself. It seems you have lost touch with all that. In order to bring your powers back, you will need to seek out the part of you that you discarded. It will not be easy." Myrddin stared at Bran full a full minute before he said, "My work is complete."

Bran frowned. "But I don't know how to get my powers back."

"When you truly recognize what it is you want, the path will become clear. For now, I suggest you spend time in contemplation."

"Can I stay here?"

"No, young fool. I am not a crutch for you to lean on. You must discover the strength inside yourself."

"And you? Are you going to deal with your mother?"

Myrddin frowned, his dark gaze going into the distance before he turned to Bran. "There is no 'dealing' with my mother. What will happen is not up to me."

"Are you saying it's up to Kat?"

"I may have magic but I do not predict, nor do I know the future. And if I may give a word of warning before you go: do not seek out this demigoddess until you are fully yourself again and know exactly what you want."

Bran nodded, realizing that he was already planning how

to get to her. "Thanks for that."

Myrddin smiled for the first time, his eyes turning pale blue-green, the skin around them crinkling. It changed his entire demeanor. "Trust, young fool. Trust who you are deep inside. The future will take care of itself."

Myrddin watched Bran lurch down the rocky slope, but his thoughts were far away. He was in the past with the woman who birthed him. He saw her as she was then, young, beautiful, with kind eyes. He loved her and counted on her, especially since he'd never known his father. That other half of his existence was still shrouded in mystery. All he knew was what he'd inherited from the man his mother never spoke of. He'd questioned her incessantly about his abilities, abilities that his mother either didn't have when he was young, or had hidden from him. He'd grown up thinking that what he was had come from his mysterious father who she refused to reveal. But now she was all-powerful, an unstoppable force. How had that come to be?

His mother had disappeared hundreds of years ago, and he'd never known where she'd gone. This reemergence called to him in ways he didn't want to contemplate. He felt his part in what was unfolding, but what his role would be was shrouded in darkness. He and Katel's path would cross soon, with or without the young fool's involvement.

The sky darkened and turned black. A low roar could be heard—thunder it seemed. Kat ran toward the hillside, skirting around burning embers and avoiding the fleeing foxes and deer that ran by her with terrified eyes. When she reached Dagda, he turned his worried eyes her way. "Your brother has gone missing."

"I'm going on, Dad."

Dagda shook his head and grabbed her arm. "What good will getting yourself killed do?"

"You forgot who I am now. I'll be fine."

Dagda frowned and then nodded. "Find your brother!" he called out as she took off running toward the burning trees. Kat managed to slip through the flames and smoke as though an invisible shield surrounded her body.

Kat was deep in the forest when she heard a rumbling and looked up to see the creature stir. Through the blazing limbs she saw the dragon's eye open, focusing on the land below. Jormungand was awake. It was then that she heard the tinny, childlike cry. "Please help!"

Was that Mior ahead of her talking to Jormungand? She hurried on, her dress catching fire from time to time, her fingers brushing the ash off a second later. When she finally caught up with Mior he was standing in a clearing looking up, the gigantic dragon uncoiled above him. "Mior!" she shouted, sprinting toward him.

"Stay where you are!" he screamed, never taking his eyes off the creature in the sky. "He doesn't trust you!"

Kat stood still, watching the dragon move closer, sinuous scales shimmering iridescent gold and green in the brightness of the flames. Mior was waving his hands around and muttering.

"He's coming!" Mior finally called, glancing her way. "He's going to put out the fire!"

"How can a fire breathing dragon put out the fire, Mior?"

"You'll see," he said confidently, gesturing for the enormous creature to come closer.

Kat watched in dread as a head the size of a city descended toward her brother, wings tight against his back, the neck and body stretching across the rest of the night sky. Mior was dwarfed by it, his tiny form disappearing as the dragon covered the expanse of forest and hovered over the rest of the visible land. When his gigantic mouth opened it was so enormous it could have swallowed everything in sight, but instead it sucked the flames inside. A few moments later the creature retreated into the dark sky leaving only the hissing of the dying embers. The fire was out.

Kat hurried to her brother and pulled him close. "How did you do that?"

"I told you I could tame him. Jormungand is my friend."

"Are you saying he isn't part of Ragnarok and the witch's plans here?"

Mior smiled. "He's here to protect us. I told Papa but he didn't believe me."

Kat was so surprised she could barely speak. "Will you come with me to find Arwen?" she finally asked.

"Arwen went through a door," her brother announced.

Kat was not aware that Arwen was able to control the doors—he was still very young—younger than this boy standing in front of her. "Did he do it himself?"

Mior shrugged. "All I saw was an open door and then he walked through it. But I do know where he started the fire. Want to see?"

"Yes," Kat said, reaching for his hand.

They walked up the hill and deeper into the smoldering forest, finally arriving at another clearing. A firepit was filled with embers, herbs scattered here and there. A strange odor lingered, but when Kat went to examine the herbs, she was hurled backward. "This is a dangerous place."

"He conjured the witch," her brother muttered, his eyes glazed. "It's how he started the fire and how he got out of here."

Kay gazed at her six-year-old brother. "You are entirely too wise for your years."

"I'm magic like Papa used to be."

Kat laughed and hugged him. "You are much more than any of us could have predicted, Mior. I'm so proud of you."

Mior frowned. "I was made this way."

Kat chuckled, trying to move closer to the pit and the herbs Arwen had left behind. She wanted to know what they were. But as soon as she came within ten feet, the repelling force stopped her. "It won't let us close," she muttered, giving up.

"It's Arwen's magic place. He can come back here whenever he wants."

Kat groaned.

"But we have Jormungand," he reminded her, skipping away.

Kat followed her brother out of the forest, joining Dagda where he waited at the edge of the trees. "You scared me," he muttered, pulling Mior close.

"It's okay Papa. Jormungand is here now."

Dagda glanced toward Kat, his eyes widening. "If I hadn't seen it with my own eyes, I never would have believed it."

Kat shook her head. "Pretty amazing and terrifying."

"Just because he's big doesn't mean he's scary," Mior piped up, taking off down the hill.

The sky was lightening as dawn arrived, a sense of peace drifting like vapor across the land. Dagda and Kat watched Mior. "He's something else, isn't he?" Dagda said proudly. "A god's son for sure."

Kat nodded, smiling. "And he's only six years old. I wonder what else he'll come up with?"

Dagda chuckled. "Your mother is already scared of him."

"Good thing she has a normal child to care for to take her mind off it."

Dagda nodded and led the way along the path down. "Are you planning to stick around for a while?" he asked over his shoulder.

"Not sure, Dad. It depends on what messages I get from the ether and what happens with the witch."

"I'd feel better if you were here when she attacks."

As the path widened Kat caught up to him. "I don't think it will be as direct as that. I wish Bran were here."

"Why? He's completely useless."

"He has good instincts and intuition about things. And he's Raven."

"I was Raven once," Dagda grumbled, tripping over a root. "Now I'm more useless than he is."

"You are not useless! Look what you did with your hands, Dad!" Kat pointed to the house in the distance. Leaves had sprouted across the roof, flowering vines twining amongst the rafters and the poles that held it up. It was alive and a work of art. "And Mom is as happy as I've ever seen her."

"When she's not scared out of her wits," Dagda muttered, watching Siobhan waving from the doorway. The early morning sunlight had turned her wild hair to molten gold. Dagda let out a long sigh, pushing the tangled gray hair away from his face. "She's so beautiful," he muttered.

Kat glanced at her mother holding Tus Nua, Mior close by her side. She was smiling, her loving gaze on Dagda. "Yes, she really is."

Dagda wiped the corners of his eyes and turned his gaze to Kat. "Please alert me to anything you see in our future. I need to keep her safe, Kat. If anything happens to your mother, I won't want to live."

Kat nodded. "What I worry about is Val. He's on his own in Alfheim and the elders are all in league with Carmun."

"There have to be others there who feel the way he does. What about the townspeople?"

Kat shrugged. "I have no idea, but if Arwen's gone back, he's got to be stirring up trouble."

"Maybe Val will come here. It seems that he loves you."

"Maybe." Kat hurried toward the house, wanting to get away from the questions and her confusion about Val and Bran.

Kat was breathless by the time she reached her mother. "Come in and have some breakfast," Siobhan said, taking her hand. "It's been a long and terrifying night for all of us."

It was quite a while later when Kat headed across the hill to the camp to follow up on the shots they'd heard. The entire place had been torn apart, belongings strewn across the ground. Bodies lay where they'd dropped, pools of dark blood drying around them. Kat was bending to examine one of the dead when she spied a woman coming up the hill. As soon as the woman saw her, she turned and ran. "Wait!" Kat called out, but she'd already disappeared. Kat's eyes welled as she counted the bodies. Arwen had managed to massacre nearly an entire village without firing a shot. Her son was a monster.

13

Arwen leapt across the pit, suddenly nervous. The darkness beneath was like the bowels of hell. But when he saw his friends and the elders standing around with smiles on their faces, his anxiety disappeared. "Where is she?"

Elrie turned from where he was talking to a gray-haired man of indeterminant age. "Where were *you*?" he asked, angry.

"I…my mother pushed me through a door."

"Your mother? That human is your mother? Glad to see you've returned. It's time to begin."

"Begin what? She's here, right? What happens now?"

Elrie smirked. "We have to meet with her and make a plan to destroy Earth and all the rest of the worlds."

Arwen felt a shiver. "Alfheim too?"

"We will have a place with *her*, Arwen. No need to worry."

"But my father, and…"

"Your father made his choice, as did the rest of the town. They will be destroyed."

"But…what kind of world will it be?"

"It will be as dark as night and we will be all-powerful. Personally, I can't wait."

Arwen gaped at his friend, wondering how being all-powerful in a dark world was a good thing. "My mother said everything would go dark—I mean really dark—no moon or sun or stars."

"So? I can live in the dark if it means I can do anything I want."

Arwen felt a twinge of uneasiness, but Elrie was the wisest one of their group. It had to be a good thing.

In the distance Val trembled behind a tree, his face wet with tears. His beloved Alfheim was about to be taken over by something grotesque. The powers he'd always enjoyed were nothing in comparison with the evil they'd unleashed. His son and the others were in thrall to her, under spells that he couldn't reverse. There were many he knew who would fight to save Alfheim, but they were not strong enough to go up against the witch. The only one who stood a chance was Kat. But could she manage it alone? He'd seen the force that rose from the pit. The witch had materialized and then disappeared a few minutes later like smoke, leaving the elders and the boys to celebrate her arrival with the thousands of strange birds that had arrived and stationed themselves around the square like evil sentinels.

They had drunk themselves silly, done unspeakable things and then slept on the ground curled up like animals. When dawn arrived, they rose to dance some more, continuing to drink and fornicate with whoever they were next to, be it man or woman. It was like a frenzy of madness that was hard to watch and even harder to fathom, especially when it came to the former staid elders who had always been the beacons of sanity.

Unable to take it in anymore, Val had dozed, waiting for Kat to return. When Arwen arrived without her, his heart dropped. He'd been so sure she would find a way to bind Arwen's abilities and come back to Alfheim to help.

Val moved backward, losing himself under the heavy canopy before turning to run, stumbling over rocks and roots as tears streamed down his face. He'd never felt this powerless, had never wept like this. His hold on life felt like it was slipping, as though his essence was seeping away. When he reached his property and the glass house, he was shaken to see Arwen waiting for him.

"Did you think you could stay here, Dad? I created this house for the witch. *She* will live here."

"Why Arwen? Why would you be involved in this abomination?"

Arwen scowled. "Why wouldn't I be? What have you done for Alfheim or for me? You allowed it to be destroyed and never lifted a finger to stop it."

"It was the witch's minions who came through here and destroyed it, Arwen. You were just a baby then. Do not try and tell me you were already under her spell."

"No, I wasn't. But even then, your weakness made me sick. I saw who you were inside and I didn't want to be like that. I made a vow to myself."

"All I wanted was a safe home where I could raise you

to understand the Elven ways. I hoped your mother would return some day, but in the meantime, I promised myself to do everything I could to…"

"Oh, come on!" Arwen shouted. "What a bunch of shit! All you did was read to me from some fucking boring book and try to teach me to ride! I've always hated you and my life here! It was more fun on Earth where I could perform spells and make my mother crazy."

Val gazed at the frowning red-faced boy. He was like a stranger. "So now you want to destroy the Elven race. Will you also destroy the rest of the Norse realms and Otherworld?"

"Of course. Carmun is the dark goddess who destroys the light. Haven't you read our archives?"

Val stilled. "The dark goddess. Is that who you think she is? That prophecy has nothing to do with Carmun. The dark goddess is not evil, she is the destroyer of evil. It will be the dark goddess who brings back the light. Perhaps she is your mother. I suggest you reread the texts."

"No!!" Arwen screamed. "You're mistaken! The dark goddess is Carmun, not my fucking mother!"

When Val reached for his arm, Arwen jerked away and ran for the hill. "You better be gone when I come back!" he shouted over his shoulder. He sent a bolt of hot white energy surging toward his father, hitting Val in the middle of his forehead. Val fell backward, stunned.

At least I touched a nerve, Val thought to himself as he rose unsteadily a few minutes later. *Where are you, Kat? You need to be here.* The door appeared before he realized that he'd conjured it. He took one last look around and stepped through.

14

Bran wandered for weeks, his thoughts shifting between wanting to search out Kat and heeding Myrddin's strict warnings. Would he ever be able to say definitively what he wanted? He thought of the apartment he'd magicked for himself, the bedroom where he'd first told Kat about her god origins. That was the night he realized how he felt about her. But after that magical night they spent together, her memories were taken by her father, and one day she no longer remembered him at all. He was furious with the Dagda, enraged at what the god was doing both to Kat and to him. The gods were wrong. That must have been the thinking that began it all. He hated the gods and so by association, he hated himself.

"Bran? What are you doing here?"

Bran looked up to see Airmid staring at him with a frown on her face.

Without meaning to, he'd ended up at her spring—the last place he and Kat had been together in any meaningful way. Mist curled upward from the bubbling water and green vines covered in blossoms sent out tendrils around the rim. He could hear birdsong, and could smell the earthy odors of perfume mixed with the sulfur rising from the thermal waters. "I…I've been trying to sort some things out."

Airmid's eyes widened. "That was months and months ago! Are you saying you've been wandering around all this time?"

Bran nodded, realizing how he must look with his filthy tunic and dirty hair. He gazed longingly at the spring.

"Did you find the wizard?"

"I did."

Airmid took hold of his arm, worried. "How long since you've had something to eat?"

Bran shrugged, realizing that his trousers hung on him now, barely kept up by his narrow hips. He tried to remember his last meal but nothing came to him. He'd forgotten how to kill things, his appetite leaving him when he thought of taking a life to feed his hunger. "It's been a while."

"You need food, a bath, and some new clothes, in that order," she said, pulling him along toward her tiny cottage under the trees. "And once that's completed, you can tell me all about the wizard."

Bran devoured the bread and cheese, his belly rumbling. Once he'd rested Airmid made him strip and handed him soap she'd made from wildflowers and her special oils mixed with beeswax. "Wash while I find you something to wear." When he climbed into the water she turned away, her forehead puckering. "One of my lovers must have left clothes behind," he heard her mutter, her voice drifting away as she disappeared toward the cottage.

Bran sunk beneath the surface, rising up to shake the water out of the filthy tangled hair that hung down his back and the long beard he'd grown. He soaped his body and his hair, envisioning Kat's fingers working it into a lather. He heard her laugh in his mind, felt the tingle when she touched him. He let out a heavy sigh. He had a lot to deal with before he could face Kat again.

He heard the rustle of Airmid's tunic, opening his eyes to see her bent at the waist and placing clean trousers and a long tunic next to the spring. She straightened, her gaze meeting his. "I will burn these tonight," she laughed, holding up the rags he'd been wearing.

While his clothes were smoldering over the late-night fire, Bran relayed what had happened with Myrddin, explaining the confusion he felt around his god status. Airmid listened quietly only saying she would do whatever she could to help him. Bran was beginning to relax now that he was with the earth goddess. She'd been his friend forever, and her knowledge of the past and what had gone on with Kat, afforded her a lot of insight. He trusted her and welcomed her advice.

It was a few days later that Airmid questioned him more extensively, her sharp eyes boring into him as she asked where Myrddin lived and how to get there. He answered as best he could, wondering why she was so interested. They'd drunk copious amounts of ale, but he was still shocked when she leaned close and pressed her lips to his. He reared back to look at her, wondering if she'd been taken over by the witch, but her eyes were closed as she pulled her tunic over her head, exposing her small breasts. She touched him then, her fingers working at the string that held up his trousers. Bran groaned when she pushed his trousers down and took hold of that part of him. It had been too since he'd had sex and he simply couldn't stop himself.

Bran spent a week with Airmid, glad of the respite from his over-active thoughts. The sex was nothing but that, an enjoyable interlude that seemed to satisfy both of them. They kept each other warm at night and talked during the day while they foraged for berries and nuts. Airmid now knew everything about where the wizard lived, the paths to take to find his cave, and what was on the wizard's mind. The details about Myrddin's heritage didn't seem to surprise her, as though she knew already.

"You're a good friend," he told her the morning he decided to leave.

"To quote a human saying, a friend with benefits."

Bran laughed. "Thanks for saving me from myself."

Her eyes swirled with an expression Bran couldn't identify. "I suggest you keep this our little secret."

"If I ever get together with Kat, I'm sure this will be the last thing on my mind."

Airmid grinned, giving him a little push. "Go before I decide that your warm body is something I can't do without."

Bran lifted his eyebrows before leaning in to give her a kiss goodbye. He was on his way down the path when he turned to look at her over his shoulder. What he saw was clouded in a foggy haze, Airmid's face barely recognizable within the dark mist that swirled in angry clouds around her. *A storm is coming*, he thought, hurrying down the trail.

It was days later that Bran revisited his time at the spring. His insides twisted with as he remembered the nightly coupling, the depraved things she asked him to do. And what about all her questions regarding Myrddin? If the witch was in possession of Airmid, he'd just revealed everything he knew about her son, including where to find him. Every morning he'd awakened exhausted, as though his body had been drained during the night. As a god it wouldn't have happened to him—he would have recognized the deception.

He was still going over all the clues he should have noticed when he heard a rumble, looking up to see charcoal clouds swirling in odd patterns. Something in the atmosphere had shifted. And that's when he knew for sure. The dark witch was in Otherworld. Rain poured down and gale force winds sent him sprawling. He heard a cackle of laughter as he crawled toward the forest. Once under the trees, he pushed himself up and ran.

Myrddin felt it. The young fool had fallen prey to the witch. It was as clear as the dream he'd had the night before. His mother was searching for him. He'd already vacated the cave where he'd lived for many years, knowing she would find him there. She wanted his help, and he knew that if it came down to it, he would not be able to deny her. Now he had to find a place to hide. And hiding from his mother had never been easy.

15

K at shaded her eyes, trying to make out the hooded figure walking up the hill. When she realized who it was, she ran toward him, throwing her arms around his glowing form. "Arwen is gone," she whispered.

"I know. It's why I'm here." His sad eyes met hers. "I am powerless against him, Kat. I'm useless."

"No, Val. You're in emotional shock." She hooked her arm through his and led him up the hill toward the shelter. "Tell me what's happened."

"Alfheim is under the witch's spell and our son is part of it. He means to house her in the glass house he built. It was his plan all along. I had no choice other than coming here. He would have killed me."

"Oh, Val. I'm so sorry. Try to remember that our son is under a spell. You must not despair."

"Has he always been under a spell?"

Kat smiled. "He was just a Fae child who needed his father."

"I'm not so sure," Val said, his gaze meeting hers. "I so

wanted you to have access to the Fae world. I had no idea what my magic would unleash." He shook his head and wiped at his eyes.

Kat had never seen him like this. Age had claimed him, his haggard face lined, his eyes dulled and hopeless. "Come meet everyone and have something to eat. We can talk more later." Kat tugged him toward the house where her family waited.

Siobhan came forward first. "I've heard so very much about you, Val. It's wonderful to finally put a face to my imaginings."

She held out her hand and Val took it, a look of surprise on his Elven features.

"I was not sure I would be welcomed here," he mumbled, glancing at Kat.

Dagda scowled. "My daughter's happiness and safety has made me hesitant to meet you. I lay all blame on the birth of this monster child directly at your feet."

"Dad, please," Kat said, placing a hand on his arm. "Val had no way to know what would happen. And it's not Arwen or Val's fault—it's the witch, Carmun."

Val straightened before he addressed Dagda. "I understand a father's worry. I would feel the same in your shoes. I am only here because of the witch and what's happening in Alfheim. As a former god you must understand what's at stake."

Dagda's gaze hardened. "Oh, I do, believe me." When Mior hurtled toward Val, Dagda reached to restrain him, but the boy was already flinging his arms around the Fae man's slim waist.

Val looked down, his features registering shock as Mior

said, "I knew you'd come. I saw you in my dream."

Kat laughed. "Well, that settles it. Val is supposed to be here."

"Perhaps I am," Val replied, smiling for the first time.

"Yes!" Mior shouted, flinging his arms in the air.

"Let's go inside," Siobhan invited. "I will make tea and we can talk. I can hear the little one getting restless in there."

"There's another baby?" Val asked, following her inside.

"Dag and I have a baby girl, her name is Tus Nua, and she…" Siobhan's voice drifted away as the door closed behind them.

Dagda's annoyed gaze met Kat's. "Is this a good idea?"

"Why wouldn't it be?"

"The Elven race, Katel. They are not to be trusted. Look what's happened with Arwen."

"Really, Dad? Be reasonable. Val is on our side."

"And what about getting you with child without telling you?"

"His definition of magic is different from mine—that's all."

"He's in love with you."

"What does that have to do with anything?"

"Are you in love with him?"

Kat frowned and turned away. "I don't know," she mumbled.

The door opened and Siobhan stuck her head out. "Are you two coming in for tea?"

When Bran reached Myrddin's cave nothing was there aside from the lingering smell of smoke and herbs and the symbols painted on the walls. When he saw a shimmer in the air he ran for the trees, but he'd already been spotted. "I know why you're here," a female voice rasped. "Do you know where my son has gone?"

Bran crept backward, watching the shimmer morph into a ugly crone wearing a black dress that seemed to be made of flowing mist. Her lined face was in shadow as she moved toward him. "You can't hide from me," she smirked. "Lucky for you I am on a quest to find my son. If you know where he has gone you MUST tell me now!" Her voice rang out and Bran was suddenly unable to move. "I don't know where he went. I was coming to warn him."

The witch cackled. "You are a powerless being with no will of your own. But I did enjoy our little interlude."

Bran gagged, his mind scattering back to the time with Airmid. Hearing it from the hideous witch's lips made it even worse.

When she noticed his discomfort, she let out a cackle. "Yes, that was me, not your precious earth goddess. I need you again. My supply has run dry."

When she waved her hand, Bran was flung backward, his head slamming into the rough trunk of a tree. Dizziness made it hard to focus as he watched her march toward him. A second later her toothless mouth was pressed to his. He fought against her, but in the end, he couldn't stop her. He woke later with scratches all over his arms and legs, his muscles weak from straining to get away. He was naked, drained of all energy. The spell she'd put on him had now worn off, but he remembered the horror of what he'd been forced to do.

Kat woke from a dream, barely managing to stop the scream that rose up in her throat. She'd seen Bran, and witnessed the confusion that had him metaphorically running in circles. The witch had hurt him in some way. Kat sat up, trying not to wake Val sleeping next to her. Bran was clear of the witch now, and on his way…somewhere. To do what, she didn't know.

"What is it?" Val asked sleepily.

"I had a dream about Bran."

Val glanced into the darkness to where Mior slept. "Is Bran on his way here?"

"No, I don't think so, but he seems on a mission of some kind. The witch had hold of him for a while—not sure how."

Val tugged her down and slipped his arm around her. "Rest for a while, Kat. It isn't light yet."

His arm felt good and she wanted to let him hold her, but the dream nagged at her. She'd let Bran go and hadn't searched for him. Why? Her only excuse was the witch and the need to walk through that door into Alfheim. But in retrospect she hadn't accomplished a thing. The time she'd wasted could have been spent in Otherworld seeking out the man who left Earth feeling unappreciated and unloved. Instead she'd slept with Val. And now Val was here and already expecting something she wasn't willing to give. "I'm going for a walk," she whispered, pulling away.

"Shall I come along?"

"No. I need to be alone."

Val sighed. "I shouldn't have come."

"If you hadn't, you'd probably be dead by now," she whispered back, pulling on her boots.

Kat was at the top of the hill and heading to the spot where Arwen had created the wormhole when she saw the raven. It was flying high above the forest, its caw making the hair on the back of her neck stand up. The sun was not yet up and there was a stillness to the air, the sky pale with streaks of gray and salmon pink, the hint of a beautiful day within the tinges of color. She squinted and shaded her eyes, hoping it was Bran and at the same time dreading it. Her mind stilled and suddenly she was Hummingbird, tiny wings propelling her upward. Below her the landscape stretched out in strange rippling colors. And then the black shape that was Raven loomed up in front of her.

She danced around him, wings whirring as he peered at her out of sad eyes, his wings positioned to keep the wind from carrying him away. As a hummingbird there was little Kat could do but signal her delight with her wings. Somehow this shiny black bird made her happy. When Raven flew off, she followed him, but when he rose higher and disappeared into a cloud, she couldn't keep going. The air was too thin.

When she landed back on Earth and shifted, her eyes immediately filled with tears. "Why did you do that?" she screamed, staring at the sky.

"Do what?"

Kat turned to see Val climbing the hill, his eyes swirling in confusion.

"Raven was here," she murmured, wiping her eyes.

"Bran was here? Where is he now?"

Kat shrugged and shook her head. "I tried to follow him as a hummingbird, but he flew so high I ran out of oxygen. Something was very wrong."

Val reached for her and pulled her close. "If he came once he'll be back. Maybe he just wanted to check that you were here and okay."

Kat wriggled away and peered into the distance. "Maybe when he saw you, he decided to leave."

Val frowned. "I never saw the raven. I only saw you standing up here crying. Please don't make me the reason for your unhappiness."

"I'm not unhappy—I'm worried. That's all."

"We all are. If I could go back to Alfheim I would, but right now I think I'm safer here. And maybe I can be of some use."

Kat glanced at his distraught face. "I'm sorry—of course you can be of use. You have more magic than any of us."

Val scoffed. "Not so sure about that. Your mother told me some stories about Mior. She's made something for breakfast—it looked like rice."

Kat gazed toward the sun rising in the distance. "It grows in the meadow. It's not bad if you add honey." But her mind was not on food, it was back with Raven and wondering why he'd been here. And why he'd gone.

16

yrddin lifted himself off the ground and whirled through a thicket of prickly bushes, landing on the other side with a thud. He was out of breath, annoyed at his ineptness and feeling vulnerable about how close he'd come to being found by his mother. His magic was strong, but hers was stronger, especially because she used it every day. He had been lax with his, becoming complacent with his simple life.

He was still searching for a hideout and it was looking as though he might have to leave Otherworld to find one. His mother knew too much about this place, and despite closing off his mind, he was sure she was managing to worm her way in. He felt it in the mornings when he woke to the sense that he'd been invaded. He heard her voice echoing in his memory— the woman and mother she'd been. Her name was Hunnith back then. This version wasn't the same person.

It was time to seek out his father. *A thousand years later*, he laughed to himself. If his father was human, he would be long gone, but the wizard doubted that he was; Myrddin's magic was legendary, and despite how strong his mother had become, his powers did not originate from her. He leaned against a tree and closed his eyes, searching through the past.

It took days for Myrddin to find what he was looking for, his impatience growing as the hours passed by. When he finally found his father, Myrddin saw him in a castle somewhere amid snowy mountains, in a world encased in ice. It had to be in the Norse realm of Nifleheim. He smiled to himself, ready to transport to the coldest region he knew.

Myrddin's thoughts drifted as he traveled. He had countless misgivings that he didn't want to contemplate, but with time on his hands they reared up unbidden. He stumbled over a rock hidden in the snow, staring about him at Nifleheim's bleak landscape. Dark stone and ragged peaks covered in ice appeared in the distance, disappearing into the clouds.

Sleet was drifting over him, leaving a freezing gray sheen on his cloak which he pulled closer, pushing onward; his repelling magic wasn't working as it should. He'd tried several times to thrust himself through the ether, another of his abilities that was absent for some reason. And then it came to him. The witch had risen from her dark prison into the Norse world. Her dark magic had already infected the entire realm.

Memories he'd hidden from himself began to rush back; his life flashed by in stark imagery. He'd loved the goddess

Nimue, an enchantress who, among other things, had managed to seal him into a cave, angry for how he'd spurned her. His time in this cave was hazy, but he knew he'd been there for a very long time. He deserved what she did to him and he accepted his fate without complaint. But when she didn't come back to release him, he'd grown angry and that anger was what had finally given him the strength to escape. And now he was on his way to where Nimue had resided all those years ago. Had his father been there then? For some reason he had no memories of him at all.

The thought of the god who fathered him filled his mind with confusion. Why hadn't he shown himself and why hadn't his mother ever told him who he was? A moment later he was filled with a kind of frenzy, whirling through the frigid air as he recalled that time in the past. He pictured Nimue's features contorted in anger, her magic grown strong because of his instruction. How ironic that his teachings were what allowed her to do what she did; he'd taught her his most intricate spells. But instead of being wary, he pictured her bright golden hair, the thought of her soft curves bringing long-forgotten sensations. He shook his head, telling himself no. Now was not the time for such things.

But later that night, after he'd managed to conjure a fire and done the exercises that loosened his physical body, the memories returned. He'd been young, so young. He prided himself on his lack of emotions, his ability to move through life without becoming attached. But with Nimue he'd been besotted, not himself at all.

It was at that moment that he became aware of her

watching him. Was Nimue part of the darkness that lay over the land like a shroud, or was she still pure of heart? He chuckled at the term *pure of heart*, for how could a goddess pure of heart be so cruel to leave him imprisoned like that? And yet that's how he'd always thought of her. He trudged on, aware of his heart thudding, and the weakness in his limbs. Nimue's charms were already affecting him. He had to shut her out.

17

Bran returned to human form feeling odd and off balance. He was in Otherworld in an unfamiliar area. Somehow, he'd managed to become Raven again and had flown to Earth. He'd seen her below, and when hummingbird had flown to greet him his heart had done several somersaults. It was when he spied the Fae man that he'd realized the folly of what he was doing. Kat was with him now.

Without Kat what was the use of anything? At least if he were a god, he'd be strong enough to help defeat the fucking witch. But even that thought did nothing to make him feel any clearer. In truth all he wanted to do was crawl into a hole and sleep for a thousand years. When he found a deep hollow within the roots of an enormous oak, he wriggled into it and curled up, closing his eyes.

'Bran, my sweet boy—what has happened to you?'

Bran heard the familiar dulcet tones, his heart beating a little faster. It had been centuries since he'd heard his mother, but even so, he would know her voice anywhere. 'Mother? Where am I?'

'You are lost, my son. Lost to yourself and who you are. You must

seek me and your father out and decide now before it is too late!'

'Too late for what?' But his mother was gone.

Bran woke wet and shivering, a cold rain dripping from his hair, his clothing soaked through. The dream remained in his mind, the sight of his beautiful mother making him yearn for a time that was long past. She was in a realm far away—a sun-filled valley where the sea met the fresh water that ran down from the mountains. He sat for several moments, remembering, before he pushed himself to standing and set off in the rain, his heart a tiny bit lighter.

But when he tried to shift to make the trip go faster, nothing happened. It seemed that his last power was gone for good. He had the sense that the witch had bled him dry. He still didn't know how he'd managed the flight to Earth, but maybe it was the last gasp…like a car running out of gas.

Bran walked for weeks before he spied the two mountains he remembered from so long ago. They were covered in yellow and purple, lush with the flowering heather and gorse. He was suddenly impatient and began to jog, and then he was running.

As his feet pounded along the familiar trails his memories returned, the childhood and early years he'd forgotten coming back in sharp detail. But when he finally reached the top of the hill where the view of the castle was the best, there was nothing there but trees. The sea still lapped against the rocky shore, but as far as a castle, out buildings, or any sign of habitation, it was as if no one had ever lived there.

Shadows were creeping by the time Bran made it to where the castle had once stood, the encroaching darkness adding to his somber mood. He searched the land and the surrounding forest, finding little of what had once been a kingdom fit for a god and goddess. Perhaps Iwerydd and Llyr had both returned to the sea and let the castle crumble away. But his memories were all from the castle where he'd been raised with his sister, Branwen. He let the memories go and began the long climb down to the shore.

The sand was cold on his bare feet as he walked the shoreline. Longing for his childhood rose up, his eyes welling. The moon was rising when he settled on the sand, stars winking into existence. He heard his sister's laughter as he chased her along the sand, his mother's call of warning, "Watch out for the sea monster!" There was no monster. She was only trying to keep them from roaming too far.

"What is your purpose here?"

Bran jerked in surprise, turning to see Llyr rising from the water, shaking off droplets, his dark eyes trained on Bran.

"It's me, Bran. Your son," he managed to say, rising to his feet.

Llyr's craggy face broke into a wide smile as he came forward, wet arms encircling Bran's shoulders. "It has been so many years I did not recognize you." He pulled back to stare at Bran. "And you are much changed," he said, frowning. "What has happened to you?"

The question everyone seemed to be asking, Bran thought to himself. He shivered from the cold seawater seeping into his clothing. Instead of answering the unanswerable, he asked, "What happened to the castle? Why is there a forest covering our kingdom?"

"It was destroyed years ago. You would have known if you'd ever bothered to visit."

Bran hung his head. "I'm sorry."

"Why have you come now, when the entire scenario is about to play out again?"

"What scenario?"

"The witch, my son, she is here again."

Bran eyed the dark trees, the enormous blocks of rock that now rested on the sand. "Are you saying she was here before and did all this?"

"That is exactly what I'm saying. I have sent the message through the forests, letting the trees and the animals and birds know what is coming. It took five-hundred years to reclaim life the last time she was here, and we were never able to rebuild."

"Where is my mother?"

Llyr's eyes narrowed as he gazed into the distance. "Iwerydd is in hiding."

"But she's a sea goddess—why are you in the sea and she is not?"

"Your mother must tell you why that is. As you must remember I married a human after your mother left. Penarddun gave me two sons. But her mortal life was snuffed out in no time. I was foolish to put myself through such pain."

"I recently dreamed about my mother. She told me I had to make a decision. That's why I'm here—to figure out how to get back what I've lost."

"You willingly gave it up, my son. Now you will have to

prove to the gods that you're worthy."

"How is it that everyone knows my predicament but no one can tell me how to reclaim my power?"

"Because you have not committed. Can you tell me that you wish this beyond a shadow of a doubt?"

Bran gazed at the sea, riveted by the ribbon of silver cast by the moon. He wanted to float there in that light, to be bathed in it and cleansed of everything he'd ever known and been. "Myrddin said if I wanted my powers back they would appear. Now you're saying I have to prove myself to the gods?"

Llyr laughed. "Myrddin is a demigod. He should not be handing out opinions about things he knows nothing about. But with the witch on the rise it would behoove you to have your magic. I suggest you make up your mind quickly."

"You're a god—why can't you help me?"

Llyr scoffed. "I have little to do with the gods these days. Your mother will help you. She is more equipped in this area."

"Then I'll have to find her," Bran mumbled. "I dreamed about her once, she'll come to me again.

Llyr turned and headed away, his wide-shouldered form a shadowy blackness as he strode toward the water. "Where are you going?" Bran called out.

Llyr stopped to look back. "If you want to find your mother you must search deep in the forest. She lives in a cave." He pointed vaguely in the direction of the mountains.

"Where?" But by that time, Llyr had disappeared beneath the surface without a sound.

Bran watched the bubbles rising from where his father

had been. A memory flashed by of strong arms holding him, laughter as Llyr tossed him into the sea. Now Llyr could barely spare five minutes with his son. He exhaled and headed for the trees to find a place to spend the night.

Bran was gone before dawn, struggling through bracken and around trees packed too close together. His mother had come to his dreams, leaving him with a map in his mind of how to find her. He'd had no food or water, his throat dry, his stomach growling. He felt as though he was going in circles, his equilibrium off, making him wonder if the witch had poisoned him. Raven was no longer a part of him, the bird's absence like a wound in his chest. He was now fully human, a mortal who would die like every other mortal.

There were several landmarks he was supposed to find, none of which had appeared. He finally gave up and sat beneath a thick-limbed tree and promptly fell into an uneasy sleep.

"Bran? Come with me." Bran felt the hand that took his, rising as she tugged him to his feet.

"I'm sorry, mother. I should have come sooner. I didn't know about the…"

"Hush," she whispered, her finger to her lips. *"These woods are not safe. We will talk when we reach my cave."*

Bran woke blearily, his eyes hazy with sleep. When he looked around, he was no longer under a tree. He was in a cave, and a woman with her back to him was bustling around a firepit.

She turned when he stirred. "You're awake. I have tea made and I'm warming the bread."

"Mother? How did I...?"

She smiled, the flame of many candles lighting up her ruddy face. Her hair was as he remembered it, thick and red-brown, her eyes sea green and clear. "I found you and brought you here."

Bran gazed around the cave. Herbs hung from the ceiling, peppermint, sage, thyme, rosemary, and others he couldn't identify, and a pot hung over the firepit. She'd placed a sleeping mat in one corner, a blanket covering it. "My father is living in the sea and you're alone in a cave? I know he married another, but it seems that you two would reconnect after Penarrdun died."

"Your father...he...well, he's no longer the god I fell in love with." She laughed. "But after more than a thousand years, who would be?"

Bran glanced at the spindly trees outside the cave entrance bending in the wind, feeling the chill air that blew around the damp stone walls. "But why here? This is so...bleak."

She smiled and brought him a mug of peppermint tea, waving a hand that closed the entrance with a wind-proof spider-web-like material. Warmth from the fire finally reached him.

"My desires have changed over the years. I am more of a hermit now and I like simple things. The sea is too vast, too open. When I decided to leave, I asked your father to come with me, but he'd grown used to the underwater life. Land no longer interested him." She poured another mug of tea and came to sit next to him. "With the witch on the rise things are rapidly changing. I am glad you heeded my call."

"Can you help me reclaim my god status?"

"Yes, Bran, I can and I will. In these trying times you must be able to protect yourself. But first tell me—what prompted you to give up your power?"

Bran sipped the hot tea, his thoughts scanning back to the first time he met Kat. Her face loomed into his mind. He'd never been in love until he met her—not even to the woman who bore him two children so many years ago. He put his mug down and began to recount the long story.

"So, in truth you never knew what was happening to you?" she asked after he'd talked for a while.

He shook his head. "It didn't happen all at once. It must have been the physical effects of falling in love."

Iwerydd nodded. "If this Katel is your first real love, I would say you are correct. And being on Earth was more than likely part of it. Where is this demigoddess now?"

Bran looked up. "She's with another and it's all my fault."

18

at spent the next weeks plotting with her father, Mior, and Val about how to prepare for the witch. She wanted to exclude her brother, but he refused to be left behind, his shining eyes brightening whatever dark conversation they happened to be having. No matter what they talked about he found a way to lighten the mood, adding his unique views and his infectious energy. When the moon was full Kat danced with him, her parents and Val joining in as the silver orb rose higher. Mior chanted, and when she asked, he taught his sister the Sanskrit words and their meanings.

"But how do you know this?" she asked in astonishment.

Mior shrugged his narrow shoulders. "It is the language used by the gods," he told her. "The only language used solely for devotion."

Kat wondered how he even knew what devotion meant, but Val motioned for her not to question the boy further. "He is touched by the gods," he whispered. "There is no logical explanation for who or what he is."

Dagda nodded his agreement as he pulled Siobhan

close, cradling her within his arms as she held the baby to her bosom. In these special moments Kat was overcome with an emotion she couldn't name. As though all of her life had led to these magical seconds in time. The preciousness of where she was and what she had, rolled over her in waves, sometimes making her cry. Bran's absence made it even more bittersweet, her heart contracting with loss whenever she thought of him.

But all was not sweetness and light as they pondered the future. Mior assured them that Jormungand was his to command, but it was hard for anyone to believe as they regarded the creature stretched across the sky. But they had to admit that the dragon *had* put out the fire.

As the weeks passed and weather began to change there were other things to consider. Like how to survive the coming winter. Siobhan was working hard to gather nuts, berries and dry the herbs and vegetables they'd managed to grow, but someone had to hunt, a job no one wanted to participate in. "Dad?" Kat said one morning, "you don't have many chores. Why don't you kill and skin the animals? You certainly have the expertise."

Dagda frowned from where he sat next to Siobhan, watching her feed the baby. "I don't have a bow or any arrows. I have no sword."

"But you have a gun," Kat reminded him.

"No shells," he muttered, glancing at Val.

"I can steal some from those men," Val said. "All you have to do is tell me what kind of gun it is."

"That's dangerous," Kat said staring up at him.

His eyes swirled. "Not for me."

Kat watched him for a moment before nodding.

"Okay—Val will steal shells and Dad will hunt for the rabbits and squirrels."

"What about deer?" Dagda asked.

Kat's eyes clouded. "They're too beautiful to kill."

"But they will provide food for the winter. I know how to dress them and I know how to use every bit of what they have to offer. One deer will provide..."

Kat raised her hands. "Okay, okay."

"What about the witch?" Mior asked suddenly.

Kat turned to where he sat cross-legged behind Siobhan. "What about her?"

"She's coming," he said, his eyes darkening.

Kat felt her insides turn over. "When is she coming, Mior?"

"Soon," the boy replied, his eyes opaque and unfocused.

They all exchanged looks before Dagda asked, "Do we have time to hunt?"

Mior nodded slowly. "But hurry."

"Guess I'd better go and steal those shells." Val headed out the door without looking back.

The baby let out a wail as Siobhan pulled her away from the breast. "How do we prepare?" No one spoke.

"Arwen's coming first," Mior muttered into the silence. "He's showing her the way."

Kat glanced at her father. "We have to destroy that wormhole." When he nodded his agreement, she grabbed his arm and helped him to his feet.

It wasn't hard to find it again. The energy was still strong, and when Kat attempted to approach, she was thrown backward. "Crap," she said, rising to her feet to dust herself off.

"You have powers, Katel. Use them," her father ordered. "Arwen is just a boy."

"A boy with some of Carmun's dark energy, Dad."

"And you have Danu at your beck and call, as well as that priestess. You're a goddess—act like one."

Kat glowered at her father who frowned back at her. "I wish I could say something mean like I used to when you were still a god."

"Don't waste your breath. I'm nothing now but an old man. But I know what *you* are."

Kat examined the downed trees, the others that were dead from burning—charred limbs and ash was all that was left. An enormous swath lay around the wormhole, bare of life. "Danu, if you can hear me, I need your help," Kat whispered.

"You don't need her help!" Dagda roared. "For fuck's sake, Katel, do what you were born to do!"

"Like what, Dad? Send lightning bolts like you used to?"

"Try it."

"All that would do is burn down the rest of the forest. I need to destroy Arwen's ability to get back here."

"And the doors? Can you stop him opening one of those?"

Kat took in a breath and let it out. "He doesn't have that power yet. So, if we can close this breach…"

"Carmun can get him in."

Kat frowned. "Why are you being so negative? Why are we even here if there's no way to stop him?"

"There's a way to stop him," Val said, arriving from

under the shadowy trees. He held out a box of shells and Dagda pocketed them. A moment later he waved his hands around, sending sparks flying and flinging the shimmering energy upward. "Water needs to be thrown over this entire area. It will purify and close the opening." Val looked around. "And we need Mior to chant over it before we use it."

Kat took off through the woods and down the hill, leaving the two men to watch over things until she collected Mior and a pan in which to collect water from the stream.

"What's happening?" Siobhan asked when Kat arrived out of breath.

"We need Mior and I need a pan for water, Mom."

Mior…water…what for?"

"It's to close the opening Arwen made."

"Mior is in the meadow. Shall I join you?"

Kat gazed at the baby sleeping in her arms. "No, Mom. Stay here and take care of Tus Nua," she said, grabbing the pot her mother held out.

Kat ran for the meadow, hardly noticing the dragon's eye watching her or the scales gleaming like spun gold in the sun.

By the time Kat and Mior had gathered water and hurried back to the wormhole, the sky had turned nearly black.

"Chant, Mior," Val ordered, conjuring a magical circle around them. "A chant for erasing negative energy and healing and closing the place where it's been."

Kat squinted nervously through the branches as Mior chanted, his voice echoing into the ominous silence. No birds sang, no crickets chirped. "What's happening?" she whispered, glancing at Val.

"The witch is watching and the creatures can feel it. The sooner we get this done the better."

Mior stopped chanting and waved his hands in strange circles. He reached for the pan of water and threw it over the area, droplets scattering in all directions. The water hissed and spit, a pale mist rising into the air. A second later the sky cleared, and the sun blazed down again.

"What is a Valkeer...?" Mior asked.

"A Valkyrie?" Dagda asked him.

Mior nodded, frowning.

"What did you see?" Val asked.

"They were there—in the sky. But I didn't know if they were good or bad."

"In the sky?" Kat asked. "Just now?"

Mior looked confused. "They were in here," he explained, pointing to his head.

Kat and Dagda exchanged a look.

"Are they coming, Mior?" her father asked.

"I...I don't know—they might be bad—they looked bad."

"They are fearsome," Val said gently, "but they're actually female spirits who help Odin."

Kat let out a heavy sigh, wondering what was next. "Are they part of Ragnarok?"

He nodded. "They will help Odin in battle and choose who lives and dies."

Kat thought about that for a second, wondering if they'd been taken over by the witch. It seemed logical, considering that the Valkyrie were all dead. They were the perfect foil for her dark magic. She turned when she heard her mother calling. "We'd better get back—who knows what will happen now that we pissed off the witch."

The next morning was when they decided it was time to find a more hidden shelter. The house was too exposed, too easy to target. "I wish Bran was here to help," Kat murmured, her fingers going to her neck where her pendant used to hang. "He's good with this sort of thing."

Dagda watched her, a scowl appearing on his face. "Where's the pendant?"

"It burned—didn't I tell you? Bran's burned too."

"Some kind of ritual burning you two conjured up?" Dagda asked, his scowl deepening.

"No, Dad. It happened after he came back from the Underworld. He almost died. The pendants saved his life."

"That pendant had enough magic within it to take on the witch, Katel—and you used it to save that fucking idiot? The reason he almost died was because he gave up being a god!"

Kat glared at him. "I didn't do anything but watch them burn!" she shouted. A second later she was running toward the meadow with tears streaming down her face. She and Bran were connected, not only in this life but in many others—the pendants had proven that. He should be here. Where was he?

When she noticed her father heading toward the forest, her anger rose. But at the same time, she knew that the biggest reason her father was so down on Bran was because of his own loss. Dagda was unable to imagine giving up something so priceless for the love of a woman. But Bran had. His absence was because of her. She'd barely defended him against Dagda, and also ignored his needs.

19

Bran followed Iwerydd along the trail, uneasy about the deepening gloom of the forest. "Where are we going?"

"I know a druid who can help bring back your god-powers. He lives in a cottage not too far from here."

"A druid—how can a druid help?"

"Druids are far more powerful than anyone knows. Taliesin was found injured on a distant shore by Myrddin, who saved his life. Myrddin named him and nursed him back to health, not knowing who or what he was."

"Myrddin? The wizard?"

His mother nodded. "Have you met him?"

"Yes. I spent weeks with him hoping he could do something about my powers. But in the end he said it was up to me to decide. I guess I'm still conflicted."

His mother nodded. "Taliesin will find a way to bring back your magic, Bran. He helped me years ago when I was so despondent that I thought of ending it all."

Bran didn't say anything, afraid of what part he might have played in his mother's grief.

Ten minutes or so later they stopped by a stream to drink water and eat the flat breads his mother had thought to bring along. "Taliesin enjoys my bread," she said shyly.

"Are you in love with this druid?"

Iwerydd glanced at him, a faraway look in her eyes. "I wouldn't say so, but I am very fond of him. He brought me through a very bleak time."

But the expression on her face belied her statement.

It was nearly dark by the time they reached the section of woods where Taliesin lived. "Will we stay here tonight?"

His mother smiled. "I certainly hope so. He will need time to find his way through your issues, Bran. Your problems cannot be solved in an hour."

The house was as dark as the woods; the only thing distinguishing it from the press of trees were the candles burning in the tiny windows. Iwerydd went ahead and knocked three times on a door that could have been the trunk of a tree. When it opened the man standing there looked like a tree himself, tangled gray hair flowing down his back, and eyes set deep within a face that looked like weathered bark. He wore a green hooded robe that matched the forest, and from his posture it was obvious that the body under it was strong and muscular.

When he spied Iwerydd, his mouth moved into a smile. He pulled her into his arms. "Did you bring my bread?"

Iwerydd nodded and stepped back, her fingers tucking in the strand of hair that had pulled loose from her chignon.

Her cheeks were flushed when she turned to Bran. "This is my son. Bran was once a god and needs to become one again. I have brought him here to seek your help."

Taliesin turned to peer at Bran, his gaze searching. "You are not certain this is what you want," he said.

Bran felt invaded and uncomfortable, his gaze going to the ground. "It *is* what I want," he mumbled.

Taliesin was silent before stepping away from the entrance to allow them to walk past him. "Come inside where it's warm."

The inside was rather like the outside, with green things growing out of pots, and vines coiling, their tendrils circling the small room. Lit candles were the only thing standing between them and utter darkness. Three stumps served as stools in front of a small fireplace, the pot over the flames emitting scents of herbs and spice.

"Please sit," Taliesin invited. "I have tea made since I knew you were on your way." He smiled at Iwerydd, raising one eyebrow. "I can heat the bread, if you like," he offered, reaching for the basket she carried.

Bran gazed around the dark almost womb-like space, wondering about the man who was now carrying mugs their way.

"Jasmine and cinnamon," the druid said, staring hard at Bran as he handed him the mug. "Good for annoyance, anger and depression. And cinnamon is good for the brain and relieves stress."

Bran felt a flush of heat as he took the mug. Was it that obvious how depressed and confused he happened to be? And right now, he was angry with himself and annoyed by his inability to make a decision regarding this entire process. After everything he'd gone through, he still didn't know what he wanted.

It was late when Taliesin pointed to a ladder that led to a loft. "You will sleep up there," he told Bran. "Your mother and I are old friends and will share my bed down here."

Bran nodded, feeling like a small boy as he climbed the ladder into the dark space. He stretched out on the thick mat and pulled a blanket over himself, wondering if he would find sleep. The candles were snuffed out one by one, after which he heard the murmur of his mother's voice and then Taliesin's deeper tones. The bed creaked as they lay down, their whispering continuing until a silence descended. Bran was afraid of what he would hear next, not sure that he wanted to witness what his mother was up to with the aging druid, but before he could worry about it too much, he fell asleep.

But instead of being restful, his sleep was filled with images of Kat being chased by shadows as he tried to reach her to help. He heard her terrified screams, realizing that there was nothing he could do but watch her being ripped apart by the demonic forces that had caught up with her.

He woke then, his entire body shaking. Below him he heard the rhythmic creak of the bed, the soft murmurs that indicated pleasure. He rolled over and tuned into his breath.

When Bran woke in the morning, he heard his mother's voice below, her laughter bubbling over. And when he peeked over the edge of the loft, she was wearing only a thin shift, her hair tangled around her face as she bent to rekindle the fire. Taliesin stood behind her, wearing only loose trousers. His face seemed years younger than it had the night before as he pushed her hair aside to kiss her neck. Bran coughed to alert them that he was awake and lowered down the ladder, not at all sure what the day would bring. He hoped it would be resolution to his fevered mind and would put a stop to all the emotions that refused to leave him alone.

"Good morn to you!" Iwerydd called, smiling. "Taliesin has fresh eggs from his chickens. Would you like some?"

"Yes," Bran answered, his feet landing on the dirt floor. He padded to where his mother held out a mug of tea, trying not to envision what their night had been like. But it was obvious from his mother's glowing skin and the brightness of her eyes that they'd enjoyed each other. "What will we do today?" he asked Taliesin.

When Taliesin didn't answer his mother said, "Taliesin has the means to determine what it is you want. But in order for that to happen you must give yourself over."

"Give myself over?" Bran glanced at the druid.

"You must trust and allow me to look into your soul. It is only there that I will find the answers you seek."

"My soul. My soul is linked with Kat's soul."

"That may or may not be so. We will determine that later, after we have broken our fast and walked to the well."

An hour later they left the small house and headed toward the impenetrable forest. The woods were dark, thick with oaks and beech trees, hazelnuts in between. No birds sang, no creatures rustled. The druid led the way in silence, Bran following and his mother behind. As they moved ever deeper under the trees, Bran began to sweat, strange images of supernatural creatures catching his eye. But whenever he turned there was nothing there. "Where are we?" Bran finally asked, his heart pounding with nerves

"This is still the visible world, but soon we will be in the invisible world where the spirits dwell. This forest is enchanted and holds the secrets from the old ways. Respect is needed, as the beings who live here can become agitated if they feel their realm is being invaded by those who do not belong. It will not be long before we reach the well."

"The weather is different in here…it seems warm, but then again it also seems cold."

"It is neither warm nor cold. We are coming to the separation of everything, but also where everything is connected. It is all sacred."

Bran turned to his mother who was looking around in awe. "Have you been here before?"

"Oh yes. Taliesin has taken me to the well many times. It is a magical place."

It was another fifteen minutes of walking before they came to a small glade surrounded with oak trees. Oaks were the sacred tree of druids and the beautiful moss covered well of stone imbued the grove with numinous power.

"Come, Bran," Taliesin beckoned. "You must drink the waters."

Bran moved forward, his gaze going to the ancient well. When he leaned over the well, his worried face peered back at him. He scooped water into his cupped hands and drank, the cool liquid soothing his throat as he swallowed.

Taliesin nodded. "Good. Now we can proceed. Look at yourself again, and tell me if you see any differences."

Bran bent to look, surprised by the ripples that still remained from the disturbance of his hands. The face he saw was not familiar. "But...that's not me," he muttered, staring at the raven-haired man with the sharp features and high chiseled cheekbones. "I have light hair and I don't have..."

"It is your raven self in human form," Taliesin told him. "The Raven you gave up. Now we will learn what it is that keeps you from knowing who you are."

"Are you saying that I really look like that?"

Taliesin didn't answer as his hands went to the sides of Bran's face. He held them there with his eyes closed for what seemed like many minutes. When he finally let go, he stood back, a frown on his face. "You are conflicted because of the love you have for this half goddess. You mistakenly think that you will lose her if you take back what is rightfully yours. But the opposite is true."

"What about the pendants—our soul connection?"

"Pendants?"

"We both had Celtic pendants—silver. That's how we knew we belonged together. But they burned and turned to ash."

Taliesin narrowed his eyes. "Both pendants burned."

"Yes. They saved my life."

"Without your god status you are unable to move forward. Why would you wish to remain mortal?"

Bran glanced at the druid's scowling face, afraid for a second. "I...I don't know, other than what you said earlier. I'm afraid of losing Kat."

"This is about *you*!" Taliesin shouted. "It is *your* life we are dealing with here. Until you decide who you are, you

133

will not only be lost to her, but also lost to yourself! The witch has taken your soul, Bran. You've been stripped, robbed of the last vestige of who you are. She poisoned you."

"How do you know about that?" Bran asked in shock.

"I can see it here," Taliesin replied, reaching to touch Bran's chest with one long finger. "What she has done has left you defenseless. Is this what you want, to go through life with no center or understanding of who you really are? To have to ask others for things that you used to know for yourself? You have contacted many in your search, and yet you are still undecided and afraid."

Bran had backed away from the druid's harsh tone when he felt his mother's hand on his arm. "He is trying to help you, Bran. Trust him," she whispered.

"What should I do?" he asked, meeting the druid's scowling gaze.

"What do you want to do?"

Bran's thoughts skipped backward, to what he'd seen as Raven the last time he'd become that part of himself. Kat was with Val. Val was the father of her child. He'd been searching for over a year, unable to come to terms with anything. He was either a god or he wasn't. "What the witch did to me…is it fixable?"

"Her spells are powerful and some of the poison has been left inside you to rot from the inside out. You will die from it."

Bran knew that he didn't want to die. That was a given. "I want to live."

Taliesin nodded. "And do you want your god powers back?"

Bran gazed unseeing into the distance. He hated what he'd become—weak, ineffectual, afraid. Kat was gone. And even if they were still together, he had nothing to offer her. To fight the witch, he had to be a god. And he did want to fight the witch—he wanted to kill her. "Yes, I do."

Taliesin peered at him, dark eyes narrowing before he pointed across the clearing. "See that path over there? It will take you to a high cliff next to a void. You will not be able to see the bottom. You must jump off that cliff."

Bran thought of Raven. Without the bird he would drop like a stone.

"You must risk death to discover who you are," Taliesin said, sensing his thoughts. "But if you decide not to risk, your death will be assured. Which is it to be?"

Bran gazed into the dark eyes for a moment before he turned toward the path in the distance. Uncertainty sat heavily on his shoulders as he walked across the grove and headed into the thicket of trees.

The felling of the supernatural grew with each step. Instead of being calming, the silence was ominous. Limbs bent toward him as he walked under them. Whispering took his attention but when he turned there was nothing there. The air felt electric, setting his nerves on edge.

He didn't know how long he'd been walking when he emerged from under the heavy trees. He let out his held breath, glad to see the light again. When he glanced back, the forest stood as still as stone, not a leaf moving. He held his breath, afraid to make a sound. It was as though time stood still. Ten feet away a ravine loomed into view, the other side luring him with its sunlit woods and wide rolling meadows. But there was no bridge—no way over that impossible drop into nothingness. And when he gazed into the abyss, he couldn't see the bottom, only the floating cold mists that wafted upward.

When he moved closer, he heard the heavy roar of a waterfall. It split the silence, making him jump. He breathed in and out trying to calm his fast beating heart. But when he saw Kat's face in the mist, the terror was back. He loved her, had always loved her. His entire focus had been on her, even when it became clear that she no longer wanted him. Now he was lost to himself, no good to anyone. And with the witch's poison inside him he would die anyway. What did he have to lose? Whatever happened here would signify a new beginning, either in death or as a god. It didn't matter which one it was.

He moved to the edge, took in a deep breath and jumped.

20

K at gasped. "Something's happened," she muttered, turning to Val beside her. The two of them were in the woods searching for a suitable hiding place for a family of six. The caves and hollows were small, but Kat was hopeful that once they reached the rocky formations higher up, they'd discover a larger one.

"Something with Arwen or Carmun?"

Kat stared through him. "I don't know. It's like a shift just happened."

Val frowned. "I hope to hell Arwen hasn't gotten in deeper with the witch."

Kat scoffed. "Our son is about as deep as he can get, Val. I don't know why you keep acting as though he hasn't already been consumed by darkness. If he could, he would kill us where we stand."

"No. He wouldn't do that. There's a part of him that..."

"What part? You did see what he did here...those people he killed? They may not have been very nice, but they didn't deserve to die that way."

"But he didn't hurt any of us."

"Not yet, but if he comes back, I fear for all of us. He's certainly been taken over. Even as a toddler he had this strange side to him."

"We all do. It's part of being Elven."

Kat scoffed and headed off to climb the hill. "How come I've never seen your evil side?" she asked over her shoulder.

"Because I control it," he answered.

Siobhan looked skeptical when Kat and Val returned and explained what they'd found. She shifted the baby to her other hip. "How far away is it?"

"About a half hour?" Kat said, gazing at Val for corroboration.

"Yes, I would agree," he answered. "It's a deep cave and the ceiling is high. And there's a stream of fresh water running through it."

Kat and Val had spent almost the entire day trudging through the mud and rocks of the higher hills. Kat sat on a stump her father had recently dragged inside, helping herself to a mug of the tea brewing. When she looked up Val was staring at her with an all too familiar look in his swirling eyes. She frowned and shook her head. She was too busy worrying about the future and trying to form a plan to be interested in sex. It seemed wrong to indulge in pleasures of the body when the world was about to come crashing down.

"I think we need to find joy wherever we can," Dagda

said, as though reading Kat's mind. "Because who knows how long we'll be alive?"

"Dad!" Kat yelled, widening her eyes as Mior peered up from where he was playing.

Mior smiled. "Jormungand will keep us safe," he stated before returning to the game he was playing with the small stones he'd gathered.

"Your joy might have left me with another baby to deal with, Dag," Siobhan muttered.

Dagda put his arm around her hunched shoulders. "If your suspicions prove true, I will welcome another child with open arms."

"Easy for you to say," she grumped, pulling away and handing him Tus Nua. "I have to use the wonderful facilities you recently provided."

When Siobhan left the house, Kat followed her.

"What's with the baby talk?" Kat asked, when they reached the freshly dug pit.

"I may be pregnant again," she whispered, lifting her skirts.

"You're way too thin to conceive. That's why you aren't bleeding."

"It's not any different than the last time—I didn't bleed for months and got pregnant anyway. Sometimes I think your father is still a god." She tried to smile and failed as she stood and pulled down her skirt.

"This is like the worst time for it."

"Don't I know it—I just wish he'd think about what he's doing. He should have stopped himself. But then again, I let him, didn't I?"

"Both of you are responsible, Mom. But from what I

know about Dad, god or not, he doesn't hold back. Maybe you should have discussed this at some point."

"I've tried to bring it up but he always says the same thing: If loving you brings another baby, then it's meant to be.'"

"Bastard," Kat muttered. "You have to get stronger, Mom. Don't let him control you."

Siobhan sighed. "I'm from another generation and living like animals hasn't changed that."

"I've been worried too, trying to stave off Val."

Siobhan nodded, waiting for Kat. "He loves you. How do you feel?"

"With the witch about to descend on us? Are you kidding?"

"Life goes on until it doesn't."

Kat chuckled, stepping over the pit to rearrange her clothing. She kicked some dirt in before she joined her mother. "That's true. I just haven't been interested in sex. I don't know if it's Bran, or fear of getting pregnant, or what."

"Do you think Bran will be back?"

Kat shook her head, her mind going to the man she thought she was pledged to for all eternity. "I think Raven saw Val that last time he flew over. He probably thinks I'm with him."

"But you're not."

"No, I'm not."

It was later that day that they made the move onto higher ground, finding their way to the cave Val and Kat had discovered.

"This isn't as bad as I thought it would be," Siobhan said, heading through the narrow opening. "It's definitely big enough—there's fresh water and it's close to the spring where we bathe."

Dagda and Val were exploring deeper, their echoing voices bouncing off the stone.

"I think your father prefers Val to Bran," Siobhan murmured, listening.

Kat held her lit candle up to examine another passageway that headed off into darkness. "I think so too. He loves that Val is powerful."

Siobhan scoffed. "He's a funny one, your father. Impressed with things that mean nothing to me."

When Mior let out a scream they both turned. "The sky is black!" he yelled.

There was no light in the sky at all, the trees barely visible in the suffocating gloom. "Dag!" Siobhan shouted.

He reached her a few seconds later, his face red from running. "What in hell is happening?"

Val moved to the opening and peered out. "The witch is here."

"What do we do?" Siobhan whispered, her voice shaking.

"We go as deep into the cave as we can," Val said, turning to Kat. "Can you draw a circle around us? My one will not be enough."

Kat nodded and grabbed Mior's hand. "Let's go," she said, tugging him into the tunnel.

They went as far as the passage would allow before crowding close together. After Val moved around them waving his fingers and chanting, Kat drew the circle, the priestess who lived inside her at the forefront of her mind.

Once she set the boundaries they waited, listening to the screeching and the howl of what sounded like animals being ripped apart. "What is she doing?" Siobhan whimpered. When the baby let out a shriek, she tried to feed her, but Tus Nua refused the breast, her screams echoing in the small space and setting everyone's nerves on edge.

"She's searching for us," Val whispered. "I hope the circle holds."

"How did they get here?"

"Either Arwen can open doors now, or Carmun broke thought the barrier's we put up at the wormhole."

Dagda lit a candle, the flickering flame revealing all their frightened faces. "We need more than a circle," he mumbled.

"If I was outside, I could command Jormungand," Mior said in a small voice.

Kat listened to the shriek of trees being uprooted, the scream of the wind and the squawk of the birds Carmun had with her. "I'm glad we're all safe in here."

A few moments later there was a gust of wind and one of the enormous birds was upon them. It had red eyes, and a beak that could cut easily through flesh and bone. But when it tried to breach the circle it couldn't get through. It let out a deafening screech that reverberated off the stone, staring at them malevolently.

"It's calling to Carmun," Val whispered. "We need to move, even if it means crawling. If she and Arwen find us, their combined power will certainly breach the circle."

Once the bird flew off, Kat led the way on her hands and knees.

"Hurry," Val whispered from behind her.

"Why the fuck can't one of you use magic?" Dagda hissed from behind Siobhan and Mior. "If I was still a god, I'd kill the bitch."

No one answered as they struggled forward, hands and knees cut and bleeding from the sharp stones. The baby was quiet now, asleep inside the tattered scarf Siobhan had slung over her shoulder.

They heard the witch enter the cave, heard her scrabbling around, her voice ordering the birds off in all directions. "Arwen? Find your father," she said, her cackle sending shivers up Kat's spine.

"I can feel them," they heard Arwen mutter. "But it's so dark in here."

"If you don't find them, you know what happens."

Val grabbed Kat's arm. "She's torturing our son," he whispered in her ear.

"He chose it," Kat whispered back, crawling faster. The passage had narrowed and now they were nearly on their bellies. She wondered how Siobhan was managing with the baby. It was a few moments later when she reached forward to put her hand down and there was nothing there. Val ran into her from behind and nearly shoved her over the edge.

"There's a drop-off of some sort here," she muttered as softly as she could. "I'll figure out what it is." She squirmed around until she could put her leg out. "Hand me a candle," she hissed.

A candle was passed forward and Val lit it with his fingers and passed it on to Kat. She held it out and peered into inky blackness. Steps had been carved into the rock. A second later Mior let out a shrill scream.

"Mior!" Siobhan yelled, attempting to turn.

"Mama!"they heard him call, his voice fading into the distance.

Siobhan let out a terrified scream, shouting to her son, but he didn't answer. "You can't get to him, Siobhan," Dagda whispered, trying to quiet her.

"But he's my baby! We have to go after him!"

"We can't. If we do, they'll capture all of us. Remember, Mior is half god."

Siobhan broke into noisy sobs. "How did they get to him? He was in front of you!"

"He must have fallen behind when the passage widened. It was dark and I didn't know he was there."

"This is your fault, Dag!"

"Siobhan, please. I didn't know. You have to be quiet!"

Meanwhile Kat began to descend backward down the steps.

Nimue found him on the trail, her fingers tracing lightly down his arm. "You didn't know I was here," she said softly. "That's not the Myrddin I remember."

Myrddin was tongue tied for a moment, his gaze traveling her body, a dull ache in his lower belly as he felt her hands on his skin. "I was preoccupied. I knew you were close, but I was lost in the past."

She cocked her head to stare at him out of her almond-shaped eyes. "You should be more careful. There are dark forces everywhere now. I take it you are seeking out your mother? The castle is only another mile from here."

"Do you know her?" he asked, looking at her sideways.

She smiled sweetly. "Of course, I *know* her. Don't you remember? I met her when we were young."

"She is much changed, Nimue."

"As are we all," she murmured, her fingers moving through his gray hair.

He frowned and moved a step away. "My mother is dangerous. Is she here?"

Nimue looked up at the branches forming an arch over them. "She was, I think. But she may have left by now."

Myrddin grabbed her by the shoulders. "Do not fuck with me. If this is a trap…"

She pulled out of his grasp. "Are you afraid I'll seal you into a cave again?"

"The thought had crossed my mind."

She let out a tinkling laugh. "I'll keep you safe from your mother. Apparently, you've lost your powers?"

"I have not lost…"

"Shush," she said, placing her finger on his lips. A second later she pressed her mouth to his.

God damn it, he thought as his tongue entered her mouth. The kiss was long and deep and Myrddin's body was ready to burst when it was over. "What are you trying to do to me?"

"Why, nothing, my love. It was only a kiss. You seem a bit…pent-up? Is that the correct word?"

He frowned and turned away. "I was hoping to find my father."

"Your father? Have you ever met your father?"

"Well, no, but it is his castle, is it not?"

"From what I understand, yes. But I don't think he's been here for many years. Pity you never met him."

Myrddin was angry now, tired of being taunted and ready to fling her down on the leafy detritus and rip her clothes off. If she didn't stop baiting him, he might lose all control…

She laughed. "I can see your thoughts, you know. I would really prefer it if you didn't rape me. I think we can come to an agreement, don't you?"

He let out a long breath. "Yes, I would like to bed you, Nimue. You've always had that effect on me. But I would like it to be consensual."

"Oh, it will be. I have not lost my taste for your prowess in that regard. But I want it to happen on a comfortable bed with a fire in the fireplace and where we might have wine before and afterward."

"And where might that be?"

"The castle, silly. I've been a guest there many times."

"But you just said…"

"It was many years ago that your mother gave me her permission to come and go as I please. I guess it made her happy when I sealed you up in that cave." She chuckled and moved ahead of him on the trail.

Myrddin was seething as he tried to block his thoughts. He wanted her badly but he refused to play her games. And if what she said was true, there was no finding his father and no talking with his mother. Carmun wasn't here and he was beginning to believe that he would never discover the identity of the man who sired him.

"I cannot believe you still don't know who fathered you. How is that possible, my love?"

"It's a mystery to me as well. I'd hoped my mother would tell me, but we haven't communicated much this past few hundred years."

"Well, I am a sorceress with much power. Perhaps I can help you discover your origins."

"I am also quite powerful, Nimue. And as I remember I taught you everything you know."

"Not quite," she said, looking over her shoulder. "There is much you do not know about me."

Myrddin felt a shiver, his earlier worries about her connection with his mother rising to the surface of his mind. "That's true. We have not been together for a very long time."

She moved to walk beside him. "I've missed you," she murmured as she linked arms with him.

He pulled away and strode ahead, trying to ignore her snort of derision.

The castle loomed into view, gray stone and high turrets covered in snow. It looked lonely—abandoned. "Who keeps it going?" he asked.

"There are still servants there. They light the fires and do the cooking if guests come. It is a stopping off place for those who wish to climb the higher peaks—the ones who want to reach the other realms."

Who would be stopping off here? If they were traveling to other realms why would they want to spend time in Nifleheim where the ice and cold were unrelenting? Perhaps they wished to visit Mimir's well and bargain for a favor. But other than that, he couldn't fathom it at all. He scanned the familiar fortress, the snow-covered grounds around it and the trees which had grown huge in his absence. He'd left at a young age, and had not been back. "She never would tell me," he muttered.

"Tell you what?"

"Who he is or was."

Nimue pulled her hood up, hiding her hair. "I have some ideas but I refuse to have a conversation out here. I'm freezing and it's beginning to snow."

Myrddin looked up to see tiny white flakes sifting

through the branches. He pulled his cloak closed, unsettled both in mind and in body. A part of him wished his mother was here. She certainly wouldn't kill her only son. At the very least he'd learn the secrets of his past.

Nimue hurried by him, rushing for the entrance to the castle. Her hood fell back, golden hair loosening from its pins and white from the snow, her cheeks red. "Hurry up slow-poke!" she called out, her voice bright in the silence.

Merlin was a boy again, his heart racing as he ran to catch her up. When he reached her, they both slipped, falling into a tangled heap in the thick snow around the entrance. He grabbed her, their cold cheeks pressed together, his chest pressed against the bodice of her dress. He could feel her heartbeat, hear her gasping breath and smelled the lavender in her hair. The words *if only*, rang through his mind. He had the power to turn back time, but before he could think about it further, he was caught up in the now, his fingers in her hair, his mouth searching for hers.

"Too cold," she grumbled, pulling away. He watched her rise to her feet and run for the door. A second later she had disappeared inside. He sighed and hurried after her.

Nimue was naked and straddling Myrddin on the enormous four poster bed when the heavy oak door burst open and slammed against the stone wall behind it.

"I had to see if what that idiot peasant downstairs told me was true," Carmun rasped, her black dress swirling around her. Her eyes were onyx, her hair tangled and as dark as raven feathers. She looked young and vibrant. "My son here in the castle? How could that be? And Nimue too, I see. Seems you two have settled your differences?" She let out a cackle. "Finish up and get dressed and meet me in the great room. I have a surprise for you." She pulled the door closed, her footsteps receding.

Myrddin met Nimue's gaze. "Well, that was a total cockblock."

Nimue made a moue of annoyance and scrambled off, her skin flushed with the effort of what they'd been doing. "Not exactly what I would call an aphrodisiac, no. And the worst timing!" She grinned slyly. "She did say to finish up, though. Should we do what she ordered?"

Myrddin chuckled and grabbed her. "I might manage to come back to life," he mumbled, pulling her close.

"Yes, I would say that you might," she whispered, her eyes going wide.

It was forty minutes later when Nimue and Myrddin arrived downstairs to see Carmun pacing, a frown between her brows. "Took your time, didn't you?"

"You did say…"

"I know what I said!" she shrieked. "But I don't have time to waste!"

"What's this surprise you…" Myrddin was in mid-sentence when he noticed the boy sitting on an upholstered chair. "Who are you?"

"He's the former god, Dagda's, son. He has powers, powers that are far beyond what any of us would have guessed." She gazed at the boy, a greedy expression on her face.

"And why is he here?" Myrddin asked.

"This boy is going to help us bring it all down. He's the key to everything."

"I won't help you," the boy muttered.

Carmun let out an amused chuckle. "You will do whatever I tell you to do, Mior."

Mior scowled and looked away.

"Mother, what have you done? He's just a child! They will come after him."

Carmun smiled. "I certainly hope they do."

"My sister will kill you," Mior muttered.

"Katel? I highly doubt it," Carmun murmured, pleased with herself.

Nimue left to get wine, her wide gray eyes signaling her dismay at the turn of events. Once she was out of the room Myrddin turned to Carmun. "It's time you revealed the identity of my father."

Carmun's eyebrows lifted. "You still don't know?"

"How would I know?"

She chuckled and glanced at the boy who sat with arms crossed. "I was sure *someone* would tell you. After all, it has been centuries!"

"Don't make this into a game—just tell me."

"It's Loki, dear boy. We had a moment."

It all made sense, the pieces clicking into place like a puzzle. Loki was a trickster, a wizard, really. Loki was father to Jormungand, which meant that the dragon was Myrddin's half-brother. He could see Loki and his mother together—they were cut from the same cloth. "And is he involved in your scheme to end the world?"

"Your father is part of what's to come, yes."

Nimue arrived and placed a bottle and three glasses on the table. "What has happened?" she asked, looking from Myrddin to his mother.

"I just found out who my father is."

"Well? Who is it?"

"Loki."

Nimue went pale, her eyes widening in alarm. "Loki…is a monster!"

Carmun laughed. "And your lover is his progeny."

Myrddin felt suddenly ill. Both his parents were monsters. When his glance met Mior's, there was look in the boy's eyes that Myrddin found startling—as though he knew a secret that he could barely keep to himself.

When Nimue poured wine and handed him a full glass, he drank it down in one gulp. "So, what happens now?" he asked, refilling his glass.

"Now we wait for Mior's rescuers."

"They won't come," the boy said.

Carmun smirked. "Oh yes, they will. I have seen it."

Myrddin saw it too, a vision of a dark-haired woman and a Fae man. They were already on their way. But there was also a shadow that he couldn't make out, as though the future was not entirely formed. "There's a prophecy," he muttered.

"Indeed, there is. Katel and I will battle for the future of the world," his mother said. "She is my nemesis and I am hers."

"Who wins?" Nimue asked.

22

Kat placed her foot on solid ground. She didn't
know where it was coming from, but it was
light enough to see the dim shapes of the
stunted trees and bushes.

"Where are we?" Siobhan asked, her voice shaking.
She'd been crying for an hour, her sobs echoing as they
made their way carefully down the steps.

"I don't know. And I can't figure out how this could be
here after what happened with the earthquakes."

"It's an underground world," Val said, looking around.

"Unfortunately, the witch now knows about it. We
won't be safe for long," Dagda muttered.

Kat took hold of Val's arm. "Will you come with me to
find Mior?"

"Of course. Do you want to go right now?"

She shook her head, glancing at her mother and her
father, the exhaustion etched into their features. "We need
to find out what's down here and make sure everyone's safe
before we head off again. I'm hoping you can conjure a
door?"

"To where?"

"I haven't figured that out yet."

"And how do you plan to do that?" Dagda asked.

"I don't know, Dad. I'm hoping something comes to me."

"We know who took him," Val mused. "But where did she go?"

"That's the question. I fear she's taken him into the Underworld."

"Please find him," Siobhan sobbed, "before they kill him."

"I don't think she wants to kill him, Mom. Mior is powerful and she knows it. She wants to use him."

"My poor baby."

Dagda put his arm around her slumped shoulders and pulled her close. "Mior is smart and canny, my sweet. We must think positively."

Tus Nua chose that moment to let out a cry. "I have to feed her," Siobhan muttered, searching for a place to sit.

After the baby was fed, they moved on, peering into the shadowy distance. It wasn't long before small round dwellings materialized out of the gloom, the silhouettes of people milling around them. It looked like a real village. "Dad—remember what Mior told us when this first happened, about all the people being underground? I think this is it."

Dagda squinted ahead. "Odin's Ghost," he muttered, his eyebrows rising in astonishment.

As they drew closer frightened faces turned their way. "We aren't here to hurt you!" Kat called out, raising her hand to swirl positive energy.

"We thought that exit was sealed off," a blonde woman in her thirties said, coming close to stare at them suspiciously.

Kat looked her over, noticing the threadbare dress, her bare feet and pale skin. She was thin to the point of emaciation. "It nearly is," Kat answered. "We had to crawl. How have you managed all this time? How many of you are there?"

The woman peered behind her to the man who approached with a frown on his face. "I'd say at least two-hundred, maybe more—wouldn't you say so, Clive?"

Clive looked less than friendly, a hatchet in his hand as he eyed Kat and the others. "What are you doing here?"

"We were in the cave above, and..."

"The witch was after us," Siobhan blurted as the baby let out a little cry.

"What witch?" Clive asked. "We've been safe down here since the earthquakes. Don't tell me there are witches now."

Kat glared at her mother before turning back to Clive and the woman. "Things up top are not as safe," she said carefully. "We've had more storms just today. It's why we found our way here. Seems as though you've been surviving quite well. How are you growing things? There isn't much sunlight, is there?"

"We punctured through to let in the sun, but you're right. We may all have vitamin deficiencies." He let out an uneasy laugh. "We thought everyone up top was dead. It's why we never attempted to go back."

"Come see our village," the woman invited, pointing

toward the cluster of many dwellings that disappeared into the gloom.

"I'm Kat and this is my father, Dagda, my mother, Siobhan and my baby sister, Tus Nua. And this is…" She glanced at Val's ears, his swirling eyes. At least his hair mostly covered the ears, but his eyes… "my friend, Val."

"Your *friend?*" Val frowned.

"We have a child together," Kat amended.

Clive glared at them without speaking before walking away. "Don't mind him," the woman said. "I'm Carol, by the way. Clive is my man, but he can be difficult."

When she turned, Kat and the others followed her.

The houses were rudimentary at best, built with bricks from the former buildings and wood from the trees that apparently still grew underground. They had plots where they grew vegetables, spindly, but at least sustenance. There were chickens running around, a goat or two. And a few sheep. "How did you end up here with all this?"

"It was as though the earth opened up and swallowed us whole. And thank our good lord it did. The buildings came with us and some people were crushed, but along with the bricks and the wood and everything else that had been stored in the houses, we had enough food to last us a year or more. The death count was high, but it was a miracle that any of us survived. God is our savior who led us to safety." She pressed her hands together and looked upward.

"My boy, Mior, told us there were people living underground. But we didn't believe him," Siobhan said, moving close to examine one of the houses.

"Where is he?" Carol asked, looking around.

"He…"

Kat grabbed her mother's arm to stop her from speaking. "He's still up top. He's watching over things while we're gone."

Carol nodded and led them over to a group of people who were whispering and staring. She introduced the two men and three women before moving along a dirt path that led between houses. "We've been making due, but none of the women have been able to conceive. It's worrisome. Perhaps we have made God angry?"

"It's the lack of light and possibly you're not getting proper nutrition," Kat said, glancing toward a woman whose face was covered in sores.

"Now that we know about you, we should move up top. We thought everyone had died up there."

"That might not be a good idea," Dagda said, joining the conversation. "The storms are raging again. We heard them from the tunnels."

"And you left your boy up there? That doesn't sound very wise."

"He has access to the passage," Dagda assured her quickly. "He'll be fine."

"We don't have an empty cabin where you can stay," Carol said. "But I can give you bedding and you can bunk over by the trees. How long do you plan to be here?"

Kat glanced at Val. "Val and I may have to leave soon. We have work to do. But my father and…"

"Siobhan and I will stay for a while, if that's okay," Dagda interrupted.

"Of course," Carol said, smiling for the first time. "I'll

show you to a spot where you can bed down. If you want to make a fire it's allowed, as long as you're close to one of the sun holes so the smoke can escape."

Carol found blankets and led them to a small copse of trees. "There's a sun hole here and you will have privacy. If you need anything find me in the morning."

By this time most of the people had headed off to their houses, darkness sifting down from the 'sun holes'. A few stars were visible in the slice of night sky they could see. "I can't believe this," Kat whispered once Carol had gone. "They aren't healthy, but they're alive."

"We must be careful what we say," Dagda muttered. "We could have a problem if they learn the truth."

"They seem very suspicious," Siobhan whispered. "Especially the men."

"They've been living down here for several years now with no news. It makes sense that they'd be distrustful," Kat said.

"Why wouldn't they check?" Siobhan asked. "My goodness, it's been a long time since those first earthquakes struck."

"Fear," Dagda answered.

There was a long silence as they all digested that. A few minutes later Val stood and dusted himself off. "Should I conjure a door?"

Kat nodded. "I think it's time."

"Where, Kat? Where are they?"

Kat gazed up at him. "Somewhere snowy. It reminded me of Nifleheim."

"Nifleheim is a large area."

"Is there a castle there?"

"There are several."

"I saw a turreted castle standing on a hill. There was forest all around it. Big trees covered in snow and enormous roots heading in every direction. Mimir's well is surrounded with roots, isn't it?"

"Yes, the well is beneath Yggdrasil, and the third root goes to Nifleheim. Perhaps it is Myrddin's castle you saw."

"Myrddin? The wizard?"

"His mother and father once lived in a castle somewhere close to Mimir's well."

"Who are his parents?"

"His mother's name is Hunnith, I think. No one seems to know who his father is."

"Why would I have a vision of *that* castle? Myrddin isn't evil, is he?"

"He can be, but it's not so much evil as devious and clever."

"Do you know him?"

"Only by reputation."

Kat watched her mother sag against Dagda. She looked utterly drained. "Mom, are you okay?"

"Not really, dear. But I'll survive."

"I think I would know if something bad had happened to Mior."

Siobhan nodded but she didn't look convinced.

Dagda pulled her close. "You two should go. We don't want to spend too much time with these people. And the air isn't good for your mother."

"The air?"

"Didn't you notice how stale it is? If she's pregnant she needs to be in the light with fresh water and food."

"Mom, do you really think…?"

Siobhan nodded. "I'm almost certain."

Kat jerked her head from side to side, disgusted with her father. How could he blithely make her pregnant with the way things were? Siobhan was already overtaxed with the one she had.

"Come back as soon as you can," Dagda muttered, his worried gaze going to Siobhan's pale face.

Kat nodded, leaning down to kiss her mother's cheek. "Don't worry—we'll find him."

"To Myrddin's castle?" Val asked, grabbing her hand.

"Yes, but not in it, please. If my vision is telling me where to find Mior, I don't want to run straight into the witch."

He nodded and a second later there was a shimmering door standing open. On the other side was a mass of dark trees covered in snow. A gust of freezing wind hit her in the face, making her shiver. She glanced back at her parents and then she and Val stepped through.

23

Bran strode confidently through the forest, his
vision clear. He would kill the witch and when
that was completed, he would rid the world of
all the evil she wrought. When he breathed in, he felt the
power flow through his body, every thought imbued with
the knowledge of what he was. He was a god again with
the foreknowledge and ability to take on the darkness.
He laughed, his voice deep and resonating as it echoed
across the chasm where he'd fallen to his death. But he
was alive now, his recent past just a hazy memory that he
didn't wish to recall. The druid was right—he was
nothing without his god status. He let out a snort of
derision. His mother would be proud of him now, his
father too. He knew exactly what he was doing and
where to go.

It was during these musings that the vision came. A
woman with long dark hair and sad eyes seemed to be
calling to him. Who was she? He shook the images away,
putting his mind on the task at hand. *I'm on my way to kill the
witch*, he thought, his hand going to the pommel of his

sword. She didn't have a chance against him. *I'm invincible,* he muttered, puffing out his chest.

Kat and Val were hidden beneath the trees when she looked up to see a raven-haired man striding toward them. Shining black hair hung on either side of an angular face with high cheekbones. He looked dangerous with his tattoos and snug-fitting dark leather armor, his arms bare aside from the silver armbands circling his muscular biceps. She backed into the shadows.

"Do not bother hiding. I know you are there. I'm a god and I can easily see you."

"Who *is* that?" she whispered to Val.

Val gave her a look and turned away, letting out a heavy sigh.

"I am not here to harm you," the man continued. "I have come to battle the witch."

The cadence of the voice was familiar, although nothing else about him rang any bells. "How do you know about the witch?""

"I am a god and I know these things."

"Do you know *us*?"

"Of course," he snorted. "You are Dagda's daughter and the man you are with is the Fae, Val." He moved closer to their hiding place, peering at them curiously.

"Before you come any closer, who are you?"

"I am Bran, the blessed. We have met before, Katel. You came to me in a vision."

Kat frowned. "Bran? You don't look anything like the Bran I know."

Bran laughed. "Because I'm *not* the same Bran. I have returned to what I was meant to be."

Kat turned to Val. "Who is he?"

Val shrugged. "It is Bran. As far as how he looks, I have no explanation."

"He doesn't act like Bran," she whispered, watching him flip a dagger from one hand to the other.

"Shall we go see what the witch is up to?" Bran asked, squinting through the trees toward the fortress in the distance. He stuck the dagger in his boot, his hand going to the hilt of the sword hanging from his belt. He pulled it out and ran a finger along the blade, testing the sharpness.

Kat raised her eyebrows. "Are you thinking of rushing in and chopping off her head? Don't you think we should have a plan in place before we storm the castle? My brother is in there."

"Your brother…" Bran's eyes narrowed.

"My brother, Mior. Carmun kidnapped him."

Bran's frowning gaze went into the distance. "That changes things."

Val peered at Bran for a moment before heading toward the trail. "I'll do some reconnaissance before we decide how we want to handle this."

"I'll come with you," the god said, turning to follow.

But before he could rush off Kat grabbed his arm. "Let Val go. I want to talk to you. Alone."

Bran stopped in mid-stride, confused. "Isn't it better if I help, Kate?"

"You two hash things out—I'll be back," Val called out, disappearing under the

trees.

"First of all, why do you call me Katel? You've always called me Kat."

He shifted his weight and folded his arms. "All right, Kat, if that makes you happy."

When he glanced at her she tried to find some trace of recognition in his gaze, but his expression was alien and emotionless. "Do you remember how our twin pendants saved you from the Underworld?"

"Pendants?" Bran scowled and ran his fingers through his hair. "That isn't a memory I have."

"How did you become what you are now?"

"A powerful druid helped me reclaim my god status. Why do you ask?"

"Because you aren't the man I knew, nor are you the god I knew." She peered closely at his arms. "Where did you get these tattoos?"

"I am the god of ravens, Katel. Perhaps Raven placed them there."

"What do the runes mean?" she asked, bending to look at the simple line designs.

Bran frowned and turned to look at them. "Forgetting and barriers is the closest interpretation."

She gazed up at him, wishing she could see any remnant of the Bran she knew. "What do they signify?"

He shrugged. "How should I know? If Raven put them there, ask him."

"Kiss me."

Bran scowled. "What? Why would I do that?"

"Because we used to love each other."

"Love? Gods do not love mortals."

"I'm half goddess, Bran. If you kiss me maybe you'll

remember something." She waited in front of him, determined to have him remember her, even if he looked like a total stranger. The way he was acting made her cold all over.

He stared at her for a full minute, his expression bewildered. He was still thinking about it when Val returned.

"Myrddin is there with his mother and a goddess I didn't recognize. I saw Mior sitting in a chair. He looks fine."

"Scared?"

"Not really."

Kat shuddered as she thought of Mior stuck there. "What should we do?"

"I should walk in there and kill her," Bran muttered. "It's easy enough."

"Val is Fae, Bran, and he's not even as powerful as Carmun—not anywhere near. If you entered that castle, she'd kill you before you'd taken a step."

"I'm a god. I am fearless and strong beyond measure. How could she kill me?"

Kat gazed at Val. "How can I explain?"

"Apparently you have little memory of your life before," Val began, gazing at the frowning man. "Gods do not hold as much sway as you seem to think. And this witch is grown strong from forces we know nothing about. You must follow our lead."

"Your lead?" He let out a snort.

Val moved his fingers in a spell. "Yes, Bran. Our lead."

Bran's frown softened. "When do we go?"

It was night before they'd come up with a potential plan, Val and Bran conspiring together and leaving Kat out of the conversation. "I don't appreciate this," she finally hissed. "I have powers too, you know."

Bran turned. "You're a woman and not strong enough to do what we have in mind."

"Using force against a sorceress rarely works," she replied calmly.

"I have a sword, Katel, and I know how to use it."

"Swords are useless against Carmun."

Val shook his head and pulled a hunk of bread and cheese out of his pack. "While you two bicker I'll eat."

Kat turned away from Bran's angry scowl and reached for a hunk of cheese. "I need to go alone," she murmured, trying not to look at the dark-haired stranger staring at her. "Carmun will not harm me. I've had a vision of our interchange."

Val frowned. "You want to die, Kat?"

"Wasn't it you who told me that the witch and I are connected? She knows this as well as I do. I want to talk to her, Val. Find out what her motives are."

"Her motives are to destroy everything," Bran muttered darkly. "She's in league with Loki and they wish to bring Ragnarok sooner rather than later."

"Loki's the god of chaos," Kat said, gazing at the new version of Bran. "And his son is the creature Mior claims to have befriended."

"You don't think I know who Loki is?" Bran let out a belly laugh. "As far as your brother goes, Jormungand is not his friend."

"If you remembered Mior you wouldn't be saying that," Kat hissed, ready to slap him. His arrogance was beginning to grate on her nerves.

Val yawned. "We need to wrap this up. The fire is nearly out and I'm ready for sleep. If you want to chance this crazy idea, Kat, I'll support you. But I plan to be there as back-up." He glanced at Bran. "With you with me, I hope."

"I am loathe to go along with this foolhardy plan, but I will allow it to play out. But if I see any sign of trouble, I'm going in. The witch needs to die, not be cajoled by a conversation that has no apparent meaning."

"It has meaning. The Bran I knew understood the subtleties of warfare. He would never rush in ready to chop an enemy's head off, especially an enemy who could kill him with a flick of her little finger."

"I'm a god!" he roared at her, anger coming off his body in waves. "I have no memory of this person you speak of, but he sounds weak and ineffectual."

"Can you two stop arguing and try and get some rest?" Val asked in an irritated tone.

Bran glared at him before he turned toward the trees. "I'll stand watch. I'm a god and I don't need to sleep."

Kat watched him go and then followed Val to the hollow he'd found. She let him pull her down next to him, shifting around to get comfortable on the roots and hard ground.

"I don't trust him," Val muttered, "but he is brawny and he has a sword."

Val began to snore immediately but Kat couldn't sleep, her gaze on the dark shadow leaning against the tree. When she closed her eyes, she had a vision of her Bran superimposed over the one sitting about forty feet away. Was he still in there? She extricated herself from Val's arms and walked quietly toward him.

"Thought you'd come," he said, without turning. "If you want me to kiss you, I'm ready to do it."

Kat moved closer, pulling the wool cloak around her shivering body. The fire had gone out an hour before and the air was icy. "Why now?"

He turned to her. "I got used to the idea."

She sat next to him. "I can't believe you don't remember me. We loved each other, Bran. We were bound to each other for all eternity. When you were Raven, I was Hummingbird. Do you remember that at least? The druid must have used sorcery on you. There's no other explanation."

Bran gazed into the dark. "I don't remember Hummingbird. And the druid did not use sorcery. I died and I was resurrected."

Kat let out a gasp. "You died?"

"I jumped off a cliff—what did you think would happen?"

"You...this druid made you kill yourself?"

"He didn't *make* me do anything. He only convinced me to restore my powers and told me what I had to do."

"But...that isn't the way it should happen. You're not supposed to *die* to regain your god status."

Anger drew lines across his forehead. "And what do you know about it?"

"You were already a god."

"I gave it all up—if we were close once you must know that."

"If you died and came back to life you began again, from scratch. Why didn't you go to a god to help you? This druid sounds suspicious to me."

Bran seemed confused for a second, his forehead

wrinkling. "It was my mother who suggested Taliesin. She would only want what's best for me."

"Maybe so, but perhaps she doesn't know this druid very well."

"They're lovers," he mumbled.

"You were wonderful just the way you were. The Bran I knew was sweet and loving and funny and capable of incredible magic. I fell in love with you way before you gave up your powers. I'm not sure there's any coming back from this," Kat whispered sadly. She was rising when he put his hand on her arm.

"Do you still want me to kiss you?"

Kat glanced at him, feeling utterly bereft. This was not even the same man. "It won't help you remember us."

Bran rose and bent to take her face in his hands. He moved his thumb lightly across her lips before his mouth found hers. The last thing Kat remembered was the thought, *at least he knows how to kiss.*

It was just before dawn when Kat woke up, her body wrapped up tight in her cloak. Another layer of some material was on top of that, keeping her warm. She gazed around, realizing she was no longer lying next to Val. And that's when she remembered the kiss and what happened after. He'd lifted her and carried her to the spot where she was now, his heat like a magnet that refused to let her go. He wasn't Bran, and yet there was some essence that called out to her—the strangeness of him and also the deep familiarity. Her body registered what they'd done together as she sat up.

"There you are," Val said, walking toward her. "Why are

you sleeping here?" He glanced at the cape lying across her, reaching down to lift it off. "Where did this come from?"

Kat shrugged. "I don't know. I think I sleep-walked. I had this strange dream."

"It's time to think about going, Kat. The sun is nearly up." He looked around. "Where's Bran?"

"I don't know. Last I saw him he was keeping watch over there." She pointed at the tree in the distance. Where the kiss had happened.

"You're flushed. Are you feeling all right?"

"I'm fine." Kat pushed up to sitting, but when she began to unwrap the cloak, she realized she was completely naked. "I took off my dress last night because the buttons were cutting into me. Do you see it anywhere?"

Val searched, coming back with her dress and the heavy hand-knit sweater she wore over it. "Not sure how you managed last night without clothes, especially without my warmth. It was freezing cold."

Kat grabbed her dress and sweater, pulled the cloak around her and hurried under the trees to dress.

24

"Why is everyone standing around?" Carmun shouted. "It's time to get moving. We want to be ready for her when she gets here, don't we?"

"I didn't appreciate being woken at the butt crack of dawn, *Mother*." Myrddin frowned and ran his hands through his thoroughly knotted hair.

Carmun sneered. "Not getting enough beauty sleep, are we? And where is your lovely lady this morning?"

"She chose to stay in bed, a decision I should have made as well."

"Go and get her, Myrddin. She is part of this too. We want to put on our best unified face for Katel when she arrives."

Myrddin glanced over at Mior sitting in the same chair. "Did you make the kid sleep in the chair all night?"

"Of course not. He has a bed." She clapped her hands. "Bring in breakfast!" she called out to the servants milling about. "It is time!"

"And why do you think I'm on board with this fiasco you're pulling?"

"Because you're my son. And because I say so. Your wizardry will soon come in handy, but today won't be anything more than a meet and greet. Nothing to concern yourself with. Now go get Nimue and be quick about it."

Myrddin turned to the stairs. He was tired of his mother, tired of her constant plans that seemed ridiculous and over the top, and concerned for the boy. He wanted to be left alone with Nimue. His mother being here had taken his libido and thrown it out the window. God damn her and her vile schemes. He would not participate in whatever plot she was about to enact. He reached the bedroom and opened the door, wishing he could barricade himself inside with Nimue and ignore all of it.

"What now?" Nimue asked sleepily when she saw him.

"Kat will be here soon and Mother is going ballistic. She wants you to come down."

"Why? What do I have to do with anything?"

Myrddin gazed at the fire, feeling its warmth and thinking of the peace he'd felt for the one second he and Nimue had been alone. "You know how she is, Nimue. Everyone has to take part."

Nimue sighed and climbed out of bed. He feasted his eyes on her naked body before she turned her back to get dressed.

It was an hour later that the knock came. Carmun looked around, nodding in satisfaction at the array of food and the people seated around the table. Mior had been given a pillow to sit on, his head lower than the others, but it worked. "Answer," she ordered, waving at a servant girl.

The girl was probably fifteen years old, wearing a pale green dress Carmun had conjured for her. She wore a white cap, her hair pinned up neatly underneath, an apron over the dress. Carmun was dressed all in black, which seemed to suggest widow's weeds. But there was nothing widow-like about the low-cut bodice or the layers of gossamer material that swirled about her shapely legs. Aside from that, the entire scenario reeked of gentility. That is until you realized who Carmun was—and then it all went to shit.

The door opened, revealing Kat wearing a simple brown wool dress that hung to mid-calf, a wool cloak over it. It had a ragged hem and her boots were covered in snow and mud. Her hair had not been brushed, and was filled with bits of twig and leaf. Her eyes were dark with rage. She looked ready for a fight. "Come in, come in!" Carmun invited, hurrying over and pushing the servant girl out of the way. "We have breakfast ready. Please seat yourself anywhere."

"You expected me?"

Of course, dear Katel. I can see everything that is about to happen. I prepared breakfast in your honor." Carmun ushered her inside and gestured for the servant to close the door.

When Kat noticed Mior she rushed toward him and pulled him into a hug. "Are you okay?"

He nodded and winked, a smile lighting up his pale face.

"You've greeted your brother and seen how he thrives in my care." Carmun smiled at her and gestured toward the man and woman seated at the table. "And this is my son, Myrddin and his lover, the goddess Nimue. You may have heard of her, but I doubt it. She's a lesser goddess." She turned to Kat. "But you have left your protectors outside. Wouldn't they enjoy some breakfast as well? It was a cold night last night."

Kat looked around the table. "I...they weren't planning on it."

"Of course, they weren't, but things change. I will call to them and see if they'd like to join us."

Carmun opened the door, "Val and Bran, please come join us! It's a shame to waste all this lovely food!"

After a few moments when nothing happened, she closed the door. "If they want to freeze out there and starve, I suppose it's up to them," she said brightly. "And how are your plans to defeat me coming along? Have you come up with anything?"

Kat moved to sit by Mior, lowering herself carefully into the chair. "I was hoping to talk to you about that. Why do you want to destroy the world?"

"Well, because I can, my dear. There is no one to stop me, now is there?"

"But what does it do for you? There won't be anything for you to have power over if there's nothing left."

Carmun smiled as she sat at the head of the table and began to pass the covered dishes. "Oh, there will be a lot of things left. I'll have my birds and those who champion me. It is true, it will be dark, but I can make it light if I wish it. And the souls..." she shivered in delight. "the energy from all those souls will come into me. Can you imagine how that will feel? It is almost orgasmic."

Kat stared at the dish of eggs, feeling like she might have to retch. "I'm not very hungry," she said, passing it on to Myrddin.

"You will be there, my dear. It will be you who unleashes the last of it. It has been foretold."

"How will it happen?" Kat asked.

Carmun laughed. "That has not yet been decided by the fates. We have to have a little mystery, don't we? But rest assured it will be you who brings it all down."

"Mother, why do you keep bringing up this prophecy business? I've heard nothing about it."

"You've been hiding in a cave, Myrddin. How could you hear anything? Your part in it will please you, I'm sure."

"And what is his part?" Nimue asked, nibbling delicately on a piece of toasted bread.

"That would be telling."

"And do I have a part?" Nimue asked.

"Oh no, my dear. You will be long dead by that time."

Nimue's eyes went wide. She dropped her toast and pushed her chair back, and ran for the stairs.

"Why do you insist on terrorizing her?" Myrddin asked, frowning. "She doesn't deserve it."

"But she's such an easy target."

"Are you saying she won't die?" Kat asked.

Carmun's eyes narrowed. "I'm not saying that at all."

Kat watched the interactions between Myrddin and his mother, wondering whose side Myrddin was on. From what she'd heard about the wizard it was hard to imagine him aiding his mother in destroying the world—unless Carmun had some hold over him. His dark eyes flipped from one side of the room to the other, always scanning, as though his thoughts were scanning too. Could Carmun read him like she seemed to be able to read everyone else?

"Mior is coming home with me," she announced into the lull.

Carmun turned her gaze away from Myrddin. "Mior is staying here, Katel. He will help me destroy the world."

"I won't help you," Mior said, his arms crossing in front of his chest.

Carmun laughed, gazing at Kat. "If you want Mior to remain alive you will stay out of my way. Any retaliation and he dies first—do you understand?"

Kat frowned. When she glanced at her brother he was smiling as though he knew something she didn't. If only she could read his mind. For some reason neither Danu nor the priestess were available to her here. "Do you really think I'm going to stand by and let you destroy everything I love?"

"Your precious Danu and that other entity who serves you haven't told you the truth?"

There it was. Carmun had just read her mind.

"Our breakfast is over," Carmun said, rising from the table. "Time for you to go."

Kat pushed her chair back and went to hug Mior. "I'll find a way to rescue you."

He looked up at her. "This is where I'm supposed to be."

Kat straightened. "I doubt that," she whispered.

"Come along now," Carmun said, impatient. "I have work to do and you are getting in my way. Remember what I told you about your precious brother. He will not last long if you plot against me."

Kat headed toward the door, her heart feeling squeezed. She did not want to leave Mior behind. A servant opened it and she walked through. It slammed behind her, the sound reverberating in the silence. She stood on the steps for a few seconds, scanning for Val and hoping Bran was with him, but when neither of them appeared she hurried down the rest of them and ran for the gate.

Kat was in a daze as she left the castle, her mind on the scene she'd left behind. Carmun must have some humanity if she was taking care of Mior. But Kat still didn't know what her motivations were. Why would someone want to destroy the entire world—what possible benefit would that give her? There was still no sign of either Bran or Val outside the castle.

It began to snow on her way back to their little camp. She shivered when she felt the cold flakes on her face. The cold was inside her, in her heart and in her tangled thoughts. It felt like Carmun was in her mind snarling everything into a confused mess. The sky was charcoal, the darkness a symbol of the despair she felt. Carmun could read her thoughts and had her brother in her clutches. She felt defeated before she'd even begun.

She was close to the camp when Myrddin materialized out of the ether. She started, her heart thudding against her ribs.

"Sorry," he said, "but I had to talk to you."

25

Bran stopped his frenzied dash through the forest, his gut twisting in agony. He grimaced, bending to grab his stomach. A moment later he'd pulled off his leathers and was squatting in the snow, his insides cramping as his bowels violently emptied. What was happening to him? Gods didn't experience this sort of sickness.

He lay in the snow for a while, his thoughts moving from one scene to the next. A vision rose up in his mind of Katel's body pressed against his, her hair soft against his cheek, her murmured *Bran* as he entered her. He'd called her Kat, saying it with tenderness, as though...as though he cared about her. He grabbed his head, letting out a tortured scream. A second later he was on his knees and retching.

Katel had bewitched him. There was no other explanation. He was a god and gods did not feel like this or behave the way he'd behaved. It was her fault that his insides twisted, making him curl up in a tight ball. She was a witch, just like the one in the castle.

He watched the snow falling softly all around him. He didn't feel the cold. He was immune to it. Then why was he so sick? He let out a bellow that echoed, leafless limbs swaying from the power of it. When he shook his fist, the trees bent away from him. *That's more like it*, he thought. But when a vision of Kat appeared in his mind a second later, he was up and squatting again, and this time it was worse. He shivered; his naked body was unable to keep the cold from invading every part of him. He lay down on his side with his arms around himself, hoping this was the last of it.

It was after he'd slept for a while that he shifted into Raven, wings lifting him up through the dark snow-covered branches into a charcoal sky. He soared in the falling snow, letting his wings catch the wind and propel him into the clouds until he no longer felt anything.

Kat saw the Raven and heard the troubled caw that burst across the still forest. She turned back to Myrddin who stood silently beside her. "That's Bran," she said, pointing.

"I have met the man. He came to me about his love for you. He couldn't determine whether or not he wanted to be a god. Did he decide?"

"Apparently, yes. He went to a druid who helped him kill himself and then come back to life. He's changed, Myrddin. He bears no resemblance, either physically or mentally, to the man I knew, or even to the god he used to be."

Myrddin frowned. "Not the proper way to handle things. I told him, but he wouldn't listen. He is stubborn, that one."

Kat nodded, watching the raven soar. "He...we... connected last night. I'm sure that's why he's up there. What happened between us didn't fit with his new persona."

Myrddin nodded as though he understood. "If he is changed as you say, he is a new god, one who does not have the capacity to deal with, um, complications."

"Like love?"

The wizard nodded again. "I can help him, but he must ask first."

Kat scoffed. "Good luck with that. He seems to think he can do anything. He's arrogant and clueless."

Myrddin chuckled. "A new god who has no idea of his own limitations."

Kat was impatient now, ready to get on with things. "Why did you want to talk with me? I'm sure it wasn't to do with Bran."

"No, not about the young fool. I needed to let you know what my mother is doing. Whatever disturbing thoughts you've had since that fiasco back there, she is responsible. She's messing with you. I can teach you how to keep her out of your head."

Kat gazed at him, trying to decide whether to trust him or not. "I would be very grateful for that."

"You can trust me, Kat. Believe me, I'm not in league with my mother. Just the opposite."

Kat leaned close to peer into his worried eyes. "I believe you."

He nodded before his eyebrows drew together in concentration. And then he showed her two simple mudras and spoke words that made no sense. "Do these gestures and speak the words every morning when you meditate."

Kay scoffed. "Meditate?"

Myrddin's eyes narrowed. "Meditation is the only way to stop your fears and thoughts and allow what you really *know* to rise to the surface."

His intensity moved through her. "I used to know this," she whispered.

"When chaos takes over, what we know often disappears."

She listened to his calm voice, her pulse slowing a little. "Okay," she said hesitantly, "I will. But how do we stop your mother?"

"That's the question, isn't it?"

Kat practiced what he'd shown her, saying the words with the same inflection and emphasis he used. When he was satisfied, he nodded. "I must go. I stopped time in the castle, but the spell is wearing off."

"But if you can stop time, then…"

He gave her one last penetrating stare, waved his hand in the air and was gone.

Kat gazed at the place he'd been, aware of the fine mist that he'd left behind. *Another ally*, she thought to herself. And a powerful one. She realized that the snow had not found her while Myrddin was with her, but now it soaked her cloak, leaving a white coating that chilled her to the bone.

When Kat arrived back at the camp, Val jumped up from where he sat in front of the flames. "Where have you been? I saw you leave the castle an hour and a half ago."

"Myrddin found me. He wanted to teach me how to keep my thoughts clear of the witch."

Val's eyes swirled. "I wouldn't trust him."

"I do trust him, Val. He has no reason to hurt me. And he helped Bran a while back."

"Speaking of that arrogant bastard, where is he?"

Kat shrugged. "I don't know."

"Did something happen between you two?"

Kat stared into the distance. The snow was getting heavier, coating limbs and drifting in the wind. It was beautiful in the woods, a fairyland of white.

"Kat?"

Kat turned. "We talked is all."

Val was instantly wary. "And what did you talk about?"

"I don't know—this and that? Nothing important," she lied.

"Is this *talk* you had the reason I found you naked out here this morning with his cloak over you?"

Kat scowled at him. "If you choose not to believe me, I can't do much about it. You haven't even asked about Mior. Isn't he more important than Bran?"

"I know what happened in there. I listened. Mior is staying."

Kat turned away. "We need to go back to Earth."

Val glared at her and bent to gather his things. He dowsed the fire and a second later a door was standing open. The Fae man stepped through and Kat hurried after him.

"Where have you been?" Dagda shouted as soon as they appeared in the underground village.

"Dad, you know where we were. It's only been a couple of days."

"No, Kat, it's been many weeks. Don't you understand how time works here? Your mother lost the baby while you were gone."

Kat's mouth fell open. "Is she okay?"

"Barely. She's hanging on but she is not at all well. We need to get out of this sunless hell where you left us."

"And you blame me."

"If you'd been here, I'm sure you could have helped her. Maybe she…"

"Dad, you're the one who selfishly got her pregnant without any regard to the state of her health or the fact that she was trying to take care of Tus Nua!"

Dagda barely registered her outburst. "Where's Mior?"

Kat let out a gasp of exasperation. "He's still with the witch. I couldn't get him. He acts like he knows some secret, like he has a secret weapon or something."

"This news is going to kill your mother."

"If you don't do it first," Kat muttered. She looked around, realizing that their argument was being witnessed by a group of hollowed-eyed men and women.

A woman with thinning hair and a pale face covered in boils came forward. "No one can carry a baby here. That's why she miscarried. The Lord is angry with us but we don't know why. Perhaps they are angry because you are here. Are you believers or not?"

Dagda grimaced. "And that's another reason we need to leave," he muttered, staring at Kat.

Val was behind him, his fingers pointing toward the woman when Kat hurried away, searching in the dark for her mother. "You are witches!" Kat heard the woman scream a few moments later. There was a shout and her father's angry roar before Dagda hurtled toward her. "Get ready to get us the hell out of here," Dagda hissed.

But Kat was bending toward her mother who seemed utterly diminished, her skin drooping and gray.

"I've stopped them for the moment," Val said, appearing next to her a second later.

Kat glanced up at him. "Mom is…"

"Your mother needs to heal, Katel. If you'd come back when you said you would things wouldn't have reached this point."

It was true. Siobhan was very weak. But worse than that she was utterly despondent. The loss of the baby and Mior's continuing absence had exacted a heavy payment on her psyche. "I don't want to live anymore," she confided when Dagda was out of earshot. "What's the point of it? The witch is about to take everything we have. We'll all be dead in a month anyway. I am terribly afraid for Mior, Kat. I'm not sure I can survive any more stress."

"Mom, it isn't a done deal that the witch will win this fight. The wizard Myrddin is on our side now, the gods are on our side. We have Val. And Mior has a secret. I think he's our secret weapon. And the witch isn't treating him badly. Honestly, I think she likes him."

"You met her?"

Kat nodded. "And Bran was there."

Siobhan gasped. "Bran is with the witch now?"

"No, Mom. He found Val and me where we were camping. He said he was there to help. You wouldn't recognize him. He's buff, with tattoos all over his arms, and his hair is black. He's arrogant, not at all like he used to be."

Siobhan stared hard at her daughter. "And what aren't you saying?"

Kat gazed into the lightless distance. She let out a sigh, turning back to her mother. "I know this sounds weird after what I just told you, but we made love. I still haven't wrapped my mind around what happened between us."

"I knew it," Val said, stepping out of the shadows.

Kat stepped back, fearful of the look on the Fae man's face. "I didn't tell you because I didn't want to upset you."

"It upsets me even more that you lied. That man isn't even close to the man you knew—how could you do it? You've been keeping me at arm's length and you decide to fuck a complete stranger?"

"Okay," Dagda said, taking hold of his arm. "This conversation should be held in private."

Val shook off his arm and a second later a shimmering door appeared. He was gone in a flash of blinding light.

Dagda held out a candle, frowning at his daughter. "What in holy hell have you been doing? I thought you went to Nifleheim to save Mior."

Kat turned when she heard shuffling feet and saw the lanterns held high.

"You'd best get back to where you came from," a man's gruff voice said. "If you don't, there may be a lynch mob after you. We don't allow witches here."

Dagda glared at Kat. "And now you chased away our means of escape. Thank you, daughter, for all you've done for us."

"You bastard!" Kat yelled, all her anger rising to the surface at once. "This is your fault, not mine!"

"And how is it my fault that you're a whore?" he shouted back.

Siobhan grabbed his arm and pulled him away from the angry crowd. "Dag, you know that isn't true. She loves Bran."

"This isn't Bran, Siobhan. This is a newly formed god who doesn't even know her. In my eyes that's the behavior of a slut."

"Whores are sinners!" someone shouted. "Where did that man go?" someone else screamed. "He's a witch! You are all witches! You will die!"

Siobhan's eyes went wide. The mob was moving toward them, lanterns held high, coiled ropes in hands.

Kat picked up the sleeping baby and grabbed her mother's arm. "Follow me."

She took off running toward where she remembered the steps to be. Behind them there were angry shouts as the mob followed.

Once they were on the steps, the crowd halted. "Do not come back here!" a woman's voice yelled out. "If you do, we'll string you up!" a man's voice added.

Kat pushed her mother in front of her on the steps and hurried after her. Dagda lumbered behind, cursing.

their house was gone, uprooted trees scattered across the landscape like toothpicks thrown by a giant. Boulders had tumbled, rocks everywhere. Kat could hear her mother crying, Dagda's soothing murmurs. The baby began to wail, as though even Tus Nua felt the change in energy.

"I'm going to check on the spring. We can rebuild up there if the pond still exists. It's the most sacred spot I know and will keep us safe."

Dagda waved her off, his arm around Siobhan.

Kat trudged up the hill, aware of the changes she felt in herself. The energy here was bad but she was in control again, as though all her anger had been caused by dark forces. Val was gone and it was time to take Myrddin's advice.

The pond remained but the trees around it had been toppled. When Kat took a seat on a downed trunk the sun appeared from behind a cloud, warming her and bringing with it the light of hope. This was home, and despite the devastation, they could rebuild. She dared the witch to try it again.

She closed her eyes and let her breathing slow. When

visions of her night with Bran rushed into her mind, she let them float by. She could revisit that later. And she would. Her breath deepened, the awareness of her body drifting off. She was in a place of nothingness. A void. She stayed there, even the awareness of breathing disappearing as the minutes went by. It was twenty minutes or so into it when she heard Mior calling to her. "I have the answers! I know how it ends!" She saw him in the castle, his eyes bright. Behind him the witch moved like a shadow, listening. "Don't tell me," Kat whispered. "Keep it a secret."

Mior turned suddenly and the witch grabbed him up, smiling as though she could see Kat through the ether. Kat withdrew, saying the words and arranging her fingers in the mudras Myrddin had taught her. The witch looked angry just before she disappeared.

Kat drifted in empty space, visions appearing and disappearing. Bran loomed up in front of her, his skin pale and sweaty, his eyes dark holes of pain. She tried to empty her mind again, tried to find the void, but the vision stubbornly remained. The void was where the answers lay. The answers she needed in order to prevail over the witch. Kat felt a presence and opened her eyes.

Bran was standing there, a look of utter surprise on his sickly and sweaty face.

"What are you doing here?"

"I have no idea. One minute I was Raven and then I was here." He looked around. "Where am I?"

"This is Earth. You spent months here with me. You don't remember?"

He glanced at the downed trees, the pond of clear water. "A sacred spring?"

"Yes."

"Maybe that's why I'm here."

"Are you sick? You look sick."

He wrapped his arms around his stomach, grimacing. "Yes, I am, but I'm a god and gods don't…"

"…get sick. Yes, I know. What caused it?"

"You!" he yelled, backing away. "You bewitched me. That's why I'm here—to have you undo the spell you cast."

"I didn't cast a spell, Bran. I'm not a witch. I'm half goddess."

Bran began to undress, removing his leathers carefully and placing them down on a log. He took off his silver arm bands and placed them on top of the pile of clothes. Kat rose to examine the tattoos lining his arms. They were Celtic in nature, an endless knot, a serpent or dragon, intricate vines and the spiral symbol of the triple goddess. A snake. The two runes etched into his upper arm were separate and distinct from the others. "What do the runes really mean?" she asked, tracing the strange lines with her finger.

Bran jumped at her touch, turning to see what she was talking about. "Why are you asking about these again? I told you before when we first met. Together the two runes signify some kind of barricade and an absence of some kind."

"The absence is us, Bran. You have forgotten me and what we had together. Last time I asked, you said something about Raven. Do you and Raven share memories?"

"How the hell should I know?" He grimaced and bent to grab his belly. "Can we talk about this later?" he moaned.

Kat shook her head, confused. "Raven is you and you are Raven. How is it possible that you don't have the same memories?"

He ignored her as he stepped into the water. His long dark hair floated like a curtain as he closed his eyes and let himself sink.

The priestess was inside her, waiting. But would he allow her to touch him? "I can help you heal."

His eyes opened and widened in alarm. "Who are you now? I guess as a witch you can turn into anybody?"

"I'm not a witch. There is a priestess who comes when I need her. She seems to think you need my help."

Bran frowned. "Go away and leave me alone. I only came for the waters."

"This is my spring, Bran."

He didn't answer as he ducked beneath the surface, dark eyes peering at her from under the water. She took off her clothes and climbed in.

Kat stayed as far from him as she could, allowing her thoughts to float away with the mist rising from the warm spring. She felt him watching her but she did nothing. He was like a wild animal and it would take him a while to trust her.

A few minutes later he rose with a splash. "Well? Are you planning to help me or what? My belly hurts."

Kat opened her eyes. "Can I touch you? Because I have to in order to heal you."

He winced and then grimaced, closing his eyes against the pain. "I think I'm dying."

"Gods don't die."

He glared at her. "Do what you need to do."

Kat moved close, her hands reaching for his lower belly. At first when she touched him, he shuddered and moved away, but when she moved her hands in clockwise circles he began to relax. She continued the motion, encouraging his intestines to move whatever was bothering him down and out. She closed her eyes, concentrating on bringing heat to his digestive system, seeing the poison that had invaded him. "Let it go," she murmured. "Let it travel out."

Bran moaned. "I don't want that again. It was terrible."

Kat continued what she was doing, chanting softly.

"Oh gods!" he cried, leaping out of the spring. She watched him hurry behind a log, listening to him groaning. "What did you do?" he moaned.

"Wait a minute or two. You should be feeling much better."

Kat relaxed back against the pond's edge, every muscle letting go in the warmth. When she heard a splash, she looked up. "Are you better?"

He frowned. "I guess I owe you a debt."

"This is what I do. I'm a healer, Bran. You used to know that."

"What caused it? I want to know so it will never happen again."

Kat gazed at his handsome face, the expression of innocence that seemed incongruous with his stature and build. "It was something you ate combined with what happened between us. You turned what we did into something terrible instead of what it was. And it made you sick."

"And what was it?"

Kat didn't answer as she rose from the water and reached for her wool dress.

"Tell me, please."

She glanced down to button the bodice. "It isn't for me to tell—it's for you to discover." She left him there and headed down the hill to where she'd left her parents.

"I guess we're sleeping in the cave tonight," Kat said later. "The spring is okay, but with the downed trees it's not a good place to shelter."

"You've been gone a long time…what have you been doing?" her father asked, annoyed.

Kat turned, trying not to get angry with him again. He was baiting her. "Not that it's any of your business, but I meditated at the spring and then Bran came and I healed his upset stomach."

"What?"

"Bran arrived when I was meditating. I think he instinctively knew where to find me."

"You told us that he isn't *our* Bran. How would he know?"

"For someone who hated him, you sure are interested, Dad."

"Will you two please stop bickering. It's making my milk turn sour," Siobhan muttered, attempting to get the baby to nurse.

Kat turned away from her father. "As soon as she's fed, let's go. It's nearly dark."

"And what are we to eat?" Dagda whined.

Kat's annoyance rose. "Am I the one who has to do

everything around here? You have two good arms, Dad. Why don't you search for greens? Or perhaps there's a fish in the spring. I'm sure if you looked, you'd find some sort of critter that escaped the damage."

"Fish in the spring? Not likely, Katel. Is your precious god still there or did he leave?"

Siobhan rose from the log and grabbed Dagda's arm, pinching him until he cried out. "You will stop heckling our daughter. If you don't, you will sleep alone."

Dagda rubbed his arm. "All the gods in Otherworld, woman. I was only talking."

Siobhan glared at him and headed for the hill, the sleeping baby in her arms.

Kat smiled to herself and hurried after her. Despite her down mood her mother was feeling spunky again. "Let me take Tus Nua for a while, Mom. She's heavy and we have a hill to climb."

Siobhan smiled gratefully and handed her over.

The weather had become unpredictable, clouds racing by as the though the goddess of the wind was right behind them. There were no longer discernable seasons—according to her calculations this should have been late fall. But instead the temperature fluctuated from cold to hot on a daily basis.

Kat stumbled on a rock and righted herself, looking up at the cave. How long would they have to shelter there before they could build again? She glanced back at her father and Siobhan arm and arm, struggling around the downed trees and boulders. They both looked pale and wan. This next week was going to be difficult, what with trying to find food, building another shelter and making a plan regarding the witch.

They were settled in the cave in front of the fire Dagda had managed to coax into existence when Dagda muttered, "Why doesn't she just get it over with? I'm sick of wondering when she'll attack. This latest one took out the life we'd established here. What is the point of building again if it's to be destroyed as soon as it's finished?"

Siobhan nodded her agreement, tears welling.

Kat gazed at her father sitting on his heels in front of the flames. He looked old and dejected. She knew now why he'd been so bad-tempered and curt with her. He felt vulnerable, unable to keep his family safe. His wife had just miscarried and their son was being held captive by the witch. Her heart softened. "She's gathering her forces. I don't know what else we can do aside from wait."

His bleary eyes met hers. None of them had slept well for the few days they'd been living inside the cave. The ground was hard and they had nothing to keep them warm but the fire. And so far, they'd had only water, any animals scarce and seemingly impossible to find. "Why isn't this wizard you mentioned here to help us? He told you he was on our side."

"I don't know, Dad. Maybe he's planning something of his own."

"Like a bunch of sitting ducks," he mumbled, staring morosely at the fire.

It was before dawn the next morning when Kat discovered

two dead rabbits lying at the entrance. They'd been skinned and were ready to cook. It had been three days with only water and a bit of green algae that grew in the stream that ran at the back of the cave. She scanned the area and listened, but there was no sign of anyone.

By the time her mother and Dagda arrived outside, she'd made a fire and the meat was nearly cooked.

"Thank you, daughter," Dagda mumbled.

"I didn't do it, Dad. They were here when I woke up."

Dagda frowned and looked around. "If this is the witch's doing, they could be poisoned."

Kat peered out across the hillside that was now bare of conifers. "The witch didn't leave these. It was Bran."

"Of course," Siobhan murmured, settling in front of the fire. "Please thank him for me," she said, picking up one of the skewers.

Kat sat next to her to share the meat. "I will if I ever see him again."

Dagda scowled as he picked up the second skewer. "I might actually like this version of that halfwit."

"Of course, you would. He's a god."

Dagda looked up. "I feel better knowing he's lurking about. But why is he here?"

Kat shrugged. "I have no idea. I just hope he keeps supplying us with food."

"I do too," Siobhan muttered, wiping the dripping juices off her chin with the sleeve of her dress.

Kat watched for Bran as she and her mother searched for the blankets and the other supplies that had been scattered during the storm. They found a pot or two, but no clothing and no blankets turned up. And as far as Bran, Kat never saw him. The small ready-to-cook rodents continued to be delivered on a daily basis. It didn't matter what they were, only that they were meat and would keep them from starving.

Kat and her mother were in the meadow resurrecting the herbs they'd been growing, when the temperature abruptly dipped, the sky turning an ominous purple. Within the thick clouds she could see the silhouette of the witch. "It's Carmun," Kat muttered, grabbing the baby. Her mother's eyes went wide. "What do we do?"

"We have to get into the cave before that storm hits." Kat held the baby close and ran for the hillside.

They were halfway up when it began to hail. Wind whipped their hair back, the gusts so strong they could barely move against it to climb. Lightning struck all around them, a few of the downed trees catching fire. Through the slanted rain Kat saw her father racing toward them, wet hair streaming behind him, his mouth open trying to tell them something they couldn't hear. Lightning struck the ground less than two feet away, singing Kat's hair.

Her mother had stopped to wait when Dagda reached them, his head turning to look up at the sky. "Siobhan!" he shouted. A second later lightning streaked down and he launched himself over her, sizzling electricity illuminating everything in garish detail as the strike hit his back and his clothing caught fire.

Kat screamed and tried to run toward him, but the wind

kept her back. "Dad!" she shouted, but it was too late. Siobhan twisted from under him unharmed, but Dagda was dead, his charred body unrecognizable.

27

"My Papa!" Mior murmured, turning to gaze at the wizard sitting next to him. "What is it, Mior?"

"The witch killed him." His eyes filled with tears.

Myrddin frowned, a savage expression on his face. "She's on Earth?"

Mior nodded, his hands over his face as he sobbed.

Myrddin was up and pacing. He'd thought his mother was merely on an errand somewhere to gather poisonous herbs or meet up with the cadre of dark spirits she was aligned with. "I thought she would wait to do this," he mumbled. "Has she hurt anyone else?"

But Mior was unable to respond as he whimpered and sobbed.

"What's happened?" Nimue asked, arriving in the room.

"Mother attacked and killed Mior's father. If I had known her plans, I could have done something to stop her, or at least protected Kat's family."

Nimue went to Mior and pulled him into her arms. "She knows, Myrddin. Carmun knows you're working against her."

Myrddin nodded. "I thought I could keep her from seeing into my mind, but I was wrong."

"I want to go home. Can you take me?" Mior asked, wiping his face. "I can talk to Jormungand. He'll help us."

Myrddin glowered at the boy. "The dragon? He's not on our side, Mior. He's aligned with Loki and my mother. He's Loki's son."

Mior shook his head. "He's my friend."

"I can get you to Earth, but are you sure you want to be there with my mother still on the rampage?"

Mior wiped at his red eyes. "Mama's there and Kat and Tus Nua. What if the witch kills them too?"

Myrddin gazed at the child, trying to see into the future. It was murky and fraught with changing scenarios, as though nothing was solid. He saw Kat's distraught face in his mind, and Mior's mother, but where they were was hard to determine. "They are alive as of now, but that's all I can see."

"Can you save them?"

"With help, perhaps, but alone I cannot prevail against the witch."

Mior ran for the door. "Can we go now, please?"

"What about me?" Nimue asked when Myrddin strode toward the door.

"You need to leave here, Nimue. Get as far away from the castle as you can. I'll come find you."

Nimue rushed toward him and threw herself into his arms. "You know I love you," she whispered, tears flooding her eyes.

Myrddin grabbed her shoulders, and leaned down to kiss her. "I love you too." He gave her one last lingering look before he grabbed Mior's hand and whirled away, disappearing into a gray mist.

Earth was covered in darkness. There was no longer any sun, moon or stars. It was as though all light had been sucked away, leaving a void filled with an impenetrable blackness. Mior gripped Myrddin's hand, gasping as they arrived on solid ground. "Where are we?"

Myrddin could barely see the boy next to him in the murk. He let his eyes adjust, shocked by what he knew had happened. "I thought of where you lived, Mior. I'm as close as we can get."

Above them clouds swirled, lightning brightening the landscape every few minutes. "I know where we are!" Mior cried. "But I don't see anybody."

Myrddin pulled his cloak tight. His mother was in those clouds, her enormous shadow stretched from one side of the sky to the other. "It seems we need to look for them."

"Maybe they're in the cave?" Mior tugged the wizard forward, heading in a zigzag line across the boggy ground.

Trees and scattered rocks had them stumbling, the wind screeching and grabbing at their clothes. When the hail started, they ran, slipping and falling and getting up to run again. "Can't you take us like you did before?" Mior shouted, trying to be heard.

"Not with my mother close by. She saps my magic."

"Is she here?"

"Yes, Mior. The lightning is not natural nor is the wind. She's destroying your home."

Mior let out a little moan. "Mama," he whispered.

Myrddin caught a glimpse of the hill and tugged Mior

forward. "We'll find them—I know they're still alive." He didn't know any such thing since his senses had been shut down by his mother's powers, but there was no reason to scare the boy. He raced for the hillside and dragged Mior with him, hoping they would make it to the cave before his mother sensed his presence.

"There!" Mior yelled. He pointed at the cave mouth where the dimmest of light could be seen.

They hurtled toward it and fell in a heap inside just before lightning struck the spot where they'd been a second before. "That was meant for me," the wizard muttered.

Siobhan rose to her feet and scooped up her son, showering him with kisses. "My sweet boy," she murmured, her tears landing on his soft head.

"Papa?" Mior asked.

Siobhan began to sob.

Kat appeared a moment later, the baby clutched against her. She bent to pick up a lit candle. "We need to move deeper into the cave," she muttered urgently.

"There are several passages up here," Kat said over her shoulder. "We've already explored one, which led us underground. Maybe we should take another this time. If Carmun decides to come after us we're basically sitting ducks." Kat began to cry. They were the exact words her father had said only a few days before.

"Are you taking us into the one where we left his body?" her mother asked querulously.

"No, Mom. He's in the one that heads off to the left—

this one goes to the right. Hurry," she urged when a gust of wind whistled by them. "Myrddin, can you put up a magical barrier once we find a suitable spot?"

"I can try. It depends on how far away I am. She controls me if she gets too close. Has your Fae man abandoned you?"

Kat drew in a deep breath. "Yes." Luckily Myrddin didn't pursue it, but Kat could hear his thoughts whirring.

Once the passage widened out and they'd settled on the floor, Myrddin moved his hands in specific configurations and muttered incantations. "That should do it," he mumbled after a few minutes, lowering to sit next to Siobhan.

Kat lit another candle and placed it on the floor, hoping the gusts wouldn't put it out. "What's her end game?" she asked, glancing at Myrddin's shadowy face.

"I wish I knew. This is a side of her I've never seen. Perhaps she's under a spell herself."

"Who would put a spell on her?" Siobhan asked.

"Loki is the one prophesized to start Ragnarok. Perhaps he's using her."

"She attacks but never finishes the job," Kat mused. "And what about my part in it all? According to Carmun, I'm her nemesis. And Val said that I'm the dark goddess, the one they call the destroyer."

Myrddin looked up from where he'd been staring at the candle flame. "You? The destroyer?"

"That's what I've been told. You heard her tell me that I'm the one who unleashes it all."

"It doesn't mean what you think it means."

Kat turned to him, feeling as though the weight of the world was sitting on her shoulders. "If you can explain it, I'm all ears."

"The dark goddess is the destroyer of evil. I would have thought your Fae man would have explained this."

"Maybe he did," Kat muttered. "I can't remember half of what he told me. It's as black as pitch out there now and the witch is turning Earth upside down. She's already won."

"And yet you are all still alive."

Siobhan began to cry. "Not all of us. Dagda died saving me," she whispered, breaking into sobs.

Kat moved next to her and placed the sleeping baby in her mother's arms. "You have a part of him here in Mior and Tus Nua," she murmured. "And we will all remember that selfless act. He was many things, but in the end, he showed his true colors."

But Siobhan could not be consoled, all the pain of losing the man she loved etched into her face as she continued to cry.

Hours had gone by when they heard the whisper of footsteps moving quietly down the tunnel. Kat was the first to see the witch standing just outside the circle.

Her eyes were dark with rage, hair eddying around her head as though being blown about by the wind. "You think you're safe from me?" she cackled. "You have no food, no water. You will die in here, just as your precious former god died." She laughed and pinned Myrddin with her furious gaze before gathering her dress around her and vanishing into a smoky cloud.

"That's my mother," Myrddin said. "Always goes for the dramatic."

"She's right, though. We will die if we can't get water or food," Kat muttered, trying not to wake Mior who lay sleeping in Siobhan's lap.

"There's water up ahead," Myrddin assured her, pointing into the dark. "And Mother will not hang around long if there's no action. She gets bored easily."

"I hope you're right."

There was no way to tell night from day as the hours moved slowly by. They were all parched by now, and Siobhan's milk production was being affected by the dehydration. There hadn't been any more sign of the witch. "I'll scout ahead," Myrddin announced. "Find water at least. Stay here until I get back."

Kat nodded, gazing at the candles. They were stubs now—nearly gone. The idea of being in utter darkness did not appeal. Hunger had her thinking of the rabbits she was sure Bran had provided, wondering where he was now. She'd never seen him in all the time she searched. And then she was caught up in a reverie about the night they'd kissed and the dreamworld he created afterwards.

She remembered it in dreamlike scenes: his alabaster skin glowing blue-white in the moonlight, the exquisite feel of his hands on her body as he undressed her. His dark tattoos and onyx eyes. He was nothing like the Bran she knew. This Bran was rougher, lost to himself as he devoured her. He seemed wild, untamed, as though he was new to sex and had no control over his body. And she had surrendered to it all, meeting his wildness with her own as they came together. And at the end they'd both cried out at the same time.

"Kat?"

Kat turned to see her mother frowning at her. "I called your name three times. Where were you?"

"Never mind. What is it?"

"I have to pee."

Kat laughed. "Go anywhere, Mom."

"Can I leave the circle?"

Kat nodded, holding out a candle and watching her mother disappear down another tunnel.

"Water," Myrddin muttered from the darkness, arriving a second later with a bowl brimming with liquid. He held it out.

"Where'd the bowl come from?" Kat asked, taking it. She drank deeply.

He waggled his eyebrows. "My secret."

Kat chuckled and handed the bowl to Mior.

As soon as Siobhan was back, Myrddin made sure she drank, holding the bowl for her. For just a second it seemed like a normal outing, smiles on their faces as they gazed around at each other. But they all knew what was to come. The witch was an ominous presence that hung over them like a heavy cloud.

28

Bran sat cross-legged under a tree contemplating the situation. He'd fought against the witch, stopping some of what she'd planned, but alone he wasn't strong enough to do much good. He didn't have much memory of the Dagda, the all-father god, but somewhere in his mind he knew of his power before he'd been thrust onto Earth as a mortal. It was sad to see him die like that—sacrificing himself for a woman.

When he thought of Katel his eyes watered, confusing him. His body felt odd, as though his muscles had turned to water. In the pool her touch had sent shivers all over him. The experience with her in Nifleheim had seemingly caused the sickness. But despite that, he'd wanted to see her again—to be with her in the same way. He shook his head, disgusted with himself for his wayward thoughts. He was a god now. Sex was fine, but *feelings* had no place. He would think of her in this way—as an object to be used. He smiled, but a hard knot settled in the pit of his stomach.

As a god he would plead his case to the gods. He'd expected to be stronger than he was—invincible. Instead this sickness seemed to have weakened him. The less he was around Katel the better. *She* weakened him and he couldn't afford it.

Bringing meat was the only way he could think to say thanks for what Kat had done for him. But now they depended on his supply. If he left Earth they would starve. He rose and stretched out his muscles, heading off into the early dawn to hunt. The witch had retreated for the moment, but who was to say when she'd be back? Carmun's son was here now; the wizard had brought the boy back to his mother. If Taliesin, who was merely a druid, could bring Bran back from the dead, surely the wizard could defeat his own mother.

It was mid-day and a cold wind had come up by the time he finished his hunt. He sat on a downed log and skinned and prepared the rabbit and the squirrel, giving thanks for their sacrifice. Once they were ready, he set off for the cave.

He was nearly there when the wind turned into a gale, cold snow landing on his neck. He looked up to see the shadow of the witch, dark eyes glowing as she stared down at him. Behind her Jormungand watched, a quiet presence. Bran sprinted for the cave, entering quickly to leave the meat before racing out again. A second later he was Raven, flying home to Otherworld to consult with the gods.

"Did you hear something?" Kat asked, staring toward the cave mouth.

"No, but I can smell blood," Myrddin said.

Kat smiled and left the circle, hurrying to the cave mouth. Sure enough, a skinned rabbit and another creature had been left just inside. When she glanced out, the wind was raging, snow eddying in wild circles. It was so cold she could barely take in a breath. Before she could move away from the entrance, something sharp hit her neck. Stumbling backward she staggered down the tunnel. She let out a cry before she fell, the meat dropping to the ground as she lost consciousness.

"Kat?"

Kat opened her eyes to see Myrddin staring down at her. When she reached for her neck, the wizard grabbed her hand. "Don't touch it."

She let out a yelp when she tried to turn her head.

"Stay still," the wizard said. "She shot you with a dart. I got it out but the poison was already in your system."

Kat winced. "Is it fixable?"

His eyes darkened. "I'll do what I can."

Kat smelled the meat cooking, saw smoke wafting toward the cave opening. It burned her eyes. "He brought meat."

"Yes," her mother said, appearing next to Myrddin. "Your new Bran is looking out for us."

"I hope he doesn't get himself killed," Kat muttered as a wave of dizziness went through her.

"He's gone now," the wizard said. "I saw him fly away."

"Gone?" Kat tried to sit up before Myrddin pushed her gently back. "The more you move around the more the poison will spread."

"Where did he go?"

"Home to Otherworld."

Kat closed her eyes.

It was a short time later that she awakened to heat on her neck. "Lie still," Myrddin said, leaning over her. "I'm using hot compresses to draw the poison out. That and some magic."

He closed his eyes and held his hands over the wet rag he'd torn off his cloak and soaked in the hot water. When he began to chant Kat entered a place filled with light and warmth. Her mind stilled and she drifted away.

"The fireflies can help," Kat heard Mior say sometime later. She was far away and couldn't seem to open her eyes.

"She's very near death," the wizard whispered. "Do you think the fireflies are still around?"

Kat heard her mother crying, felt the somber atmosphere. She left her body and lifted into the air to see the pallor of her skin, her shuttered eyes. Her mother held her hand, weeping, and Myrddin looked hopeless.

Mior had tears running down his cheeks. "I can try," her brother said.

I can't die, she thought to herself. If I die how will I connect with Bran again? But then again, if I die maybe the witch will stop. Maybe this is how I save everyone. She let go.

Raven landed by a tree and shifted, his heart beating fast. The woman...something had happened to Katel. How did he know? And then he saw her. She was a phantom, a wraith, her body insubstantial as she gazed at him. *"I came to say goodbye."*

He reached for her but his hand went right through. A

second later her lips brushed against his, a feathery softness that he wished he could feel more than he did. "Katel, I...I'm sorry."

"I love you..."

The words drifted in his mind as she turned into mist and dissipated. His knees buckled and a second later he was on the ground. His chest ached, his belly hollow. His eyes watered non-stop.

Siobhan sat by her daughter's still body, numb with shock.

Mior was chanting, calling for the fireflies, but so far, they had not arrived.

"She's gone, Mior," Myrddin whispered, putting a hand on the boy's shoulder. "It's time to stop."

But Mior shook him off and raced for the cave entrance. He gazed into the snow and thought of the fireflies. They had to come. They always came when he called them. The world was so quiet, as though Kat's death had stopped the fighting. He could feel it. Carmun had done what she'd planned. The witch was gone and Kat was dead. "No!" Mior yelled, his voice echoing through the quiet. He sat cross-legged and held out his arms, strange words rising up to spill from his mouth.

The chant went on and on as Mior repeated more verses, tears falling from his eyes. He felt the words as though they were tiny bright beings with wings, saw them drift from his lips and fly away behind him. Fireflies. It was sometime later when he heard the wizard shouting. When he opened his eyes, the wizard was running toward him.

"She's alive! Kat's alive!" The wizard grabbed his hand and tugged him to his feet.

"You saved me, Mior," Kat murmured, reaching for him. She gathered him into her arms and held him tight.

"It was the fireflies. They came a different way this time, but I know it was them."

Myrddin glanced at the child. "That chant was the language of the gods. How do you know it?"

Mior shrugged. "It just came to me. The words were fireflies."

"Do *you* know the chant?" Kat asked the wizard.

He shook his head. "But I have heard the language." He glanced at Mior. "And Mior is right—there were fireflies all around you."

Siobhan sat on the other side of Kat, the baby in her arms. She was unable to utter a word as tears traced silently down her cheeks.

"The witch thinks you're dead," Mior said. "She went away."

Kat felt weak, her body heavy and sore. "Will she come back?"

Myrddin pressed his lips together and raised his eyebrows. "We'll know soon enough."

Kat frowned. "Bran is gathering the gods together to fight."

"How do you now that?" Siobhan asked.

When Kat turned to her mother, she felt a pinch in her neck. But when she touched the spot, all she felt was a small raised bump. "I went to say goodbye."

Her mother's eyes widened. "You mean…after you died?"

Kat nodded, her eyes filling. "I told him I loved him."

"*Do* you love him? I thought he wasn't the same person."

Kat scoffed. "He isn't, but…" she shrugged, glancing away. "I can see the old Bran in there. It's hard to explain."

"And he told you what he was doing?"

"No, but I could read his thoughts. He didn't say it, but…he loves me too."

"And now he thinks you're dead."

Kat grimaced, trying not to envision what that might mean for the future. "Is there any meat left?"

Later, after her belly was full, Kat thought about the interchange between her ghost self and Bran. Bran didn't know what love was or even how to recognize it in himself. He was an innocent, unaware of what his bodily sensations or his emotions meant. She was lying when she said he loved her. He didn't even know the meaning of the word. Why had she felt compelled to tell her mother and Myrddin that he did?

Two days had gone by since her 'death', and Kat was out in the snow, finding wood for the fire and hoping to discover something to eat. Bran's offerings were long gone. Mior ran to where she crouched in the meadow. A pile of sticks was stacked neatly next to her.

"Loki's coming!" he yelled.

Kat stood and shaded her eyes against the glare of the sun. "What?"

Mior nodded excitedly. "He's coming. The witch knows you're alive!"

"Here? Are they coming here?"

Mior frowned, thinking. "I don't know. I saw him. He's a giant with fire hair!"

Kat stared into the distance. "Not sure how to combat Loki *and* the witch."

"We still have Jormungand."

"Mior, you need to stop thinking he's on our side. He's Loki's second child."

Mior made a face. "He's bigger now," he said, pointing up at the sky. "He's formed a circle around us. He doesn't like Loki because Loki isn't nice to him. He's protecting us."

"If he's protecting us, why did he let the witch destroy our home?"

Mior pouted, his bottom lip jutting out. "He doesn't want her to know he isn't on her side."

Kat let out a frustrated sigh and headed off to search for something besides greens. Since Bran's departure they'd all grown thin. "Take the firewood up to the cave!" she yelled over her shoulder.

When she glanced at the place where their house had once stood her thoughts went to her father, a sharp pain moving through her chest. None of them had recovered from his death. Siobhan moved like a zombie now, all her energy gone as she mourned. They had done nothing with his remains but store them in the cave. They needed to have a ritual to send him off. They needed closure.

But when she spoke to the wizard about it, he shook his head. "If we expose ourselves like that the witch will come."

"Mior said she's coming back and Loki's with her. We need to have this ritual before they get here."

He frowned, glancing away. "She will feel us, Kat. You forget how well I know her."

Kat frowned. "Mom needs to say goodbye. And Mior too."

"I understand, but can't we do it in the cave instead of up at the spring? With all the trees gone we'll be completely out in the open up there."

Kat scowled, trying to envision a ritual in that lightless place. "We need to have a ritual fire—he needs to be burned. And after that we need water."

"Water?"

Kat let out a sob. "His ashes—I thought we'd scatter them in the spring."

Myrddin shook his head. "The spring is our only source of drinking water, Kat. That won't work. And as far as burning goes, the smoke will be seen for miles. You don't think my mother won't swoop down during something like that?"

"Are you sure she knows I'm alive?"

"If Mior said that Loki is coming, she knows. And if Loki's with her, things will be even worse. Trust me."

The sun had been out for several days and the snow had mostly melted away. They were beginning to relax. And it was then that the witch came, and with her was Arwen, dressed all in black, his eyes glowing just as Carmun's did. An enormous giant lumbered after them with hair the color of flames.

Mior saw them first, his shrill cry alerting them. Siobhan ran for her son, her eyes wide with terror. Myrddin stayed behind as Kat, Siobhan and Mior raced for the cave. Kat glanced over her shoulder to see the wizard waving his hands in the air, lightning streaking toward the witch as she moved toward him. "Hurry!" Kat shouted, grabbing Mior's hand. But Mior jerked away from her, his face turned up toward the sky.

"Jormungand!" he cried. "Help me!"

The giant serpent stirred, his enormous head swiveling toward Mior. But before anything happened, Kat scooped Mior into her arms and ran with his wriggling body struggling against her.

Once they were in the cave, she let him down, surprised by his frown and bright red face.

"You ruined everything!" he shouted. "He's my friend!"

Kat took hold of his sleeve as he ran past her. "Wait, Mior. What if he's coming to see his father?"

"He hates his father! I told you that. Why won't you believe me?"

Kat looked outside, peering up at the sky. The creature was just as he'd been before. But when she glanced down the hill, Myrddin had disappeared.

"Look, Mior. Jormungand isn't doing anything."

"That's because you took me away!" Mior was sobbing now.

Kat scanned for the witch, wondering where they'd all gone. "We'd better get inside," she said, grabbing Mior and dragging him behind her. A second later the earth rumbled and bucked as the first earthquake struck. Siobhan fell and cracked her head against the cave wall, Tus Nua tumbling with her. Kat struggled to stay upright as she rushed to pick up the screaming baby. When she looked behind her Mior had disappeared.

Just as she was helping her mother up another earthquake thundered through, nearly knocking them both down. "We have to get into the back," she urged, trying not to look at the bleeding gash on her mother's head. Siobhan looked dazed and was barely able to walk. Kat put an arm around her and moved as quickly as she could away from the entrance, watching in horror as the walls tumbled, rocks dropped on top of each other to seal them inside.

29

Bran was in conference with the gods when he felt it. He put his hands up to his head as the sounds reverberated.

"What is wrong?" Lugh asked, staring at him worriedly.

"The witch is on Earth."

Lugh, the sun god, glanced around the conference room. The marble floors and walls gleamed in the low light, vines dripping with purple flowers trailing around the pillars. Birdsong could be heard in the lush gardens surrounding the structure.

"It is to be expected," Taranis, the god of thunder said bluntly.

Bran was angry with how unconcerned the gods seemed to be. His hands turned into fists. "The witch is doing great damage!" he bellowed.

Taranis fixed him with a cold stare. "You are here to petition us for help, but you have waited too long. By the time we are decided this half goddess and her family may well be dead. This is your fault, not ours."

"Dagda threw his body over his wife to save her from a

lightning strike. He sacrificed himself to save her."

The gods looked around at each other. "The Dagda did this willingly knowing he would die?"

"Yes. I saw it with my own eyes."

"And you did not stop him?"

"How could I? It was done before I knew it. I have been hiding from them, not sure what my role should be."

"Your role, as you put it, is to be the god you are meant to be. We are all pleased with your decision to reclaim your powers. In your haste to reinvent yourself, you have forgotten the rules here."

"The rules are not clear about the witch," he said, changing the subject. "If she is a goddess and is doing harm without your permission, you should want to stop her. If we don't do something soon, she…"

"We sense your impatience," Taranis interrupted, "but what you have presented to this court will take some time for us to ponder. We do not insert ourselves into the affairs of humans."

"And yet Carmun is poised to take down not only Earth, but the Norse world as well. And I've heard that Otherworld is also on her radar. She's aligned with Loki."

"Loki?" Morrighan glanced toward the others.

There was a heavy silence.

"This child, Katel, is my ward," Danu said a few moments later. "I have taken her under my wing. She is special and has an important part to play in this unfolding drama."

Camulos, the war god, gazed at her thoughtfully. "Is it your desire to help her, Danu?"

Danu nodded. "I am there if she calls on me—always."

Bran gazed without expression at Danu. "Katel is dead."

Danu gasped, staring at him wide-eyed.

"She came to me to say good-bye." At this he felt a slight choking sensation in his throat.

"If Katel is dead, why are you asking for our help?" Lugh asked.

"Because it will take more than Danu to save the rest," Bran muttered.

Taranis turned his shaggy grey head toward Bran. "And how would you know? You are newly reborn, a neophyte."

Bran glared, anger twisting inside him. "I just *know*," he said. He had every right to be here. He was a god, and they should respect that.

"And were you in love with this woman just as your previous incarnation was?" Morrighan asked.

Bran felt as though she'd stuck a knife into him and twisted it. "What I feel is of no consequence since Katel is no longer alive."

Low murmurs erupted through the room before Danu began to speak, her voice carrying as she rose. "I have just had a vision. Katel is most certainly alive. Her brother, Mior, has done something extraordinary to help her. And there is something else...something that I cannot see. It is hazy—hidden." Her eyes opened wide to gaze around. "Whatever it is will have to remain buried for now."

Bran let out a shuddering breath, something heavy lifting from his chest. He reached behind him for a chair and sank into it. "When she came to me, she wasn't solid. I could barely see her."

Danu gazed his way. "Yes, I see that she *was* dead. To bring her back to life would take a tremendous amount of numinous energy."

Taranis frowned and waved his hand in the air. "Enough! Leave us. We will discuss your proposal and make our decision."

Bran forced himself to his feet, making his way unsteadily toward the open-air entrance. Had none of them ever felt anything for humans? But then he wondered: why was *he* so concerned? When he stepped into the garden, he saw her in his mind's eye, across from him in the spring. He remembered the feel of her hands, shivering just as he had then. He gazed upward into the clear sky. His body felt light, buoyant. He would see her again.

After he walked the gardens, he became impatient, tracing his steps back to the hall. But they were not finished arguing. He could hear them from the portico. He hid behind a pillar to listen.

"This Bran does not resemble Bran, the blessed. Is he truly Bran or is he some interloper sent by this witch everyone keeps talking about?"

There was a collective muttering before a deep voice intoned, "Whoever he might be, he is asking us to do something we have previously voted against. How do you see this, Airmid? You were heavily involved with the last disaster regarding Earth."

"I have not personally spoken with this version of Bran. The old one was my friend and it was more than likely my advice that sent him off to Myrddin to reclaim his god status. But I am unclear as to how he would reappear with dark-hair and tattoos covering his arms. He doesn't even have the same build as the Bran I knew. My question is, how did he come to be this way? Until he has explained himself, I hesitate to give him our support."

There was a long silence and then a goddess said, "I tend to agree with Airmid. None of us recognize him. Why have we listened and not asked this important question?"

"Well, then, our answer is no. Earth is on its own as it has been for millennia. The gods do not entangle themselves in human affairs."

"I fear that if we say no, this Bran will do just the opposite," a goddess in the back said.

"And if he does, he will be banned from Otherworld for all eternity," Taranis replied.

Bran drew in a deep breath, a hard knot forming in his belly. He placed a hand there, wondering if it would lead to the sickness. He waited for the sudden need to run for the bushes, but nothing happened. He moved from behind the pillar and approached the room filled with gods and goddesses, swallowing whatever it was that had suddenly invaded his throat. "You want to know how I came to be this way?" he called out.

Heads turned and then Taranis, who seemed to have taken over the proceedings, nodded. "Come forth and tell us."

After Bran relayed what he remembered about his death and resurrection, a whisper went around the room. After a few moments of this Taranis raised his hand. "Anyone who has questions, please pose them now."

"Why would you think this Taliesin had your best interests in mind?" Lugh asked.

"My mother, Iwerydd, believed in him. She told me that druids are as powerful as the gods."

An annoyed murmur went around the room before Taranis raised his hand again. "Let us hear him out before we rush to judgement." He turned to Bran. "Go on."

"He seemed to know what he was doing. But I don't

remember much of the time before I jumped off the cliff. It is as though my earlier identity disappeared in the moments that lay between that life and this one."

Taranis's dark eyes bored into him. "And what is Iwerydd's relationship to this druid?"

Bran stared into the distance as shadowy memories crossed his mind. Laughter, murmuring, a kiss. "They are lovers."

Taranis stared at the floor. "This is what I feared. She has broken the rules to lie with a druid and has included her son in her deception. I am sorry to hear this. This is disturbing news since it means that you have been altered in ways that are not in keeping with the laws that bind us together. And because of that we will not be able to assist you in this endeavor."

Bran turned and strode out of the hall without looking back.

"Bran! Wait!"

Bran paused as Airmid rushed after him. "Do you remember me?" she asked, placing a hand on his forearm.

He peered at her and shook his head.

"Not at all? We…"

"I heard what you said in there. I have some memories of before, but they are shadowy—unclear."

She gazed at him, frowning. "You don't look the same, but there's something—in your eyes. I see you in there."

Bran pressed his lips together. "Good for you, but that does me no favors. I suppose I am destined to be the Ronin of gods."

"Ronin? How do you know that term?"

Bran shrugged. "It just came to me that I am to be a

lone wanderer—not that I care."

Airmid smiled. "That's what the Bran I knew might have said. He detested the hierarchical nonsense that goes on here. I think it's partly why he allowed his powers to drift away. He went against them for her."

"What do you mean?"

"You fell in love with Kat, and you kept it a secret from the gods."

Bran stared at her, wishing he could remember that Bran and not the one he was now, simmering with rage and unable to do anything about it. He wondered about the depth of what he was feeling, his inability to let it all go.

"What will you do now?"

"Alone I cannot go up against the witch and her cronies. But I heard what you said in there. You are not inclined to help me either."

Airmid regarded him with a frown. "But you did explain yourself. You told them what happened to you. I was concerned that you might be a creature conjured by the witch."

Bran listened, nodding. "Perhaps we can form a team. And since Danu is dedicated to Katel, she might be willing to help. Are you interested?"

"Yes. Yes I am."

"Good. I have to get back to Earth now and find out what's happened. Can you speak with Danu and if possible, find others willing to go against the so-called rules here?"

"I'll do what I can."

"Where do I find you?"

"The spring—my healing spring. Do you remember it?"

"No, but possibly Raven does."

"Meet me there."

Bran nodded and shifted into Raven, dark wings lifting him into the pale sky.

"What were you discussing?" Taranis asked, glowering at Airmid as he exited the conference hall.

She gazed at him blandly. "Bran says he feels like the Ronin of gods—a wanderer."

"And so he is. He should go back to that druid and kill him for what he did. Bran is nothing now."

Airmid didn't answer.

Raven was over Earth when he saw the smoke, the tumbled rocks and the fires. His wings stilled, allowing him to soar downward. And when he reached solid ground he shifted. A twisting sensation worked through his gut as he gazed over the wasteland the witch had left behind. He searched for any remnant of Katel or the others, finding no one. And when he climbed the hill to where the cave had been, he discovered what the witch had done. Rocks and rubble covered over any remnant of the cave entrance.

They were sealed inside, and she'd made sure that her magic would keep anyone from being able to dig them free. He sat on the stripped and empty dirt, wiping at the water that flowed from his eyes. A sound came out of his throat that scared him—between a whimper and a howl.

30

Kat found the candle stubs in the dark and lit them, using her fingertips. At least she was still able to do that. Her powers seemed to have withered of late, either that or stress prevented her from accessing them. Even Hummingbird had been sadly absent, her ability to shift seemingly lost. The last time was when she flew to meet Raven and then watched him fly up and away. She took a breath and turned to face the others.

"We should check and see if the steps are still there. At least the people underground have food." When she glanced at her mother, Siobhan's face seemed leached of all color, her eyes filled with pain.

"I can't go there again," Siobhan whispered.

"We have to, Mom. We have nothing to eat."

Siobhan cried silently, tears rolling down her gaunt cheeks. "Where is Myrddin? Did he get left out there?"

Kat crouched in front of her mother. "He's Carmun's son. He knows how to deal with her."

"And what about us?" she asked pitifully.

"Mom, I have some abilities left, and Mior..."

"I don't want Mior anywhere near that entrance! If something happens to him, I'll…"

"Nothing will happen," Mior said, moving from his place by the wall. "They're gone, but there's someone else out there."

Kat stared at her baby brother. "Who is it?"

"It's a man with tattoos all over his arms. He looks like a warrior!"

"That's Bran, Mior. He looks different now, but he's the same inside." *Even if he doesn't know it*, she thought to herself.

"Can he dig us out?"

"He's the god of prophecy, so I doubt that's one of his talents. Judging by how it happened, I'm sure it was done with powerful magic."

"But he's Raven, and Raven is powerful too. He's a messenger between the worlds, isn't he? Bran is really strong—he has big arms," Mior continued, frowning.

"Yes, Raven is sacred and this Bran is very strong. He's bigger than the one we used to know. But as I said, he can't move a mountain of stone that's had a spell put on it."

"Maybe Myrddin is out there too," Mior whispered, looking scared for the first time.

Kat gathered him close and kissed the top of his head. "Before we make assumptions, we need to explore the back of the cave. If there's a way out of here we'll be fine."

"No," Siobhan sobbed, "we won't. Have you forgotten what happened?"

Kat remembered all too well as she pulled her mother to her feet and took the mewling baby out of her arms. But what other choice did they have? "Let me check your head before we go, Mom. Blood's trickling down your back."

The cut was superficial but it was oozing a lot of blood. Kat held the baby on her hip and pressed the fingers of one hand there to cauterize it. Afterward her mother reached up, a surprised expression on her face. "You closed the wound?"

She smiled. "I do have some talents."

"You have lots of magic, Kat," Mior said, an infectious smile lighting up his former grimace. He skipped away, heading down the dark passage.

Kat picked up a candle. "Do you want to carry Tus Nua or should I?"

Siobhan shook her head, downcast. "I don't have the strength for anything right now. And I doubt I have the milk to feed her."

"Mom, don't say that. You've been doing fine."

Siobhan met her gaze. "And now your father's gone and we have no food and we're sealed inside a lightless hell. How much oxygen do we have? I would like to lie down and die."

Kat made a face and pressed her lips together. "Please do not say things like that when Mior is around. You have two small children. How do you think they would feel if you weren't here anymore?"

Siobhan sighed and nodded, following Kat.

When they walked past the place where they'd stowed Dagda's remains, Kat stopped. They needed to have a ceremony before it rotted and began to stink. But when she held the candle out to look for him, his body was gone. In its place were only a few burned rags.

"Kat?" Siobhan was right behind her, looking down. "Where's your father?"

"I...I don't know. Do you think animals got him?"

"There are no animals in here. This is a dead zone."

Kat crouched down to examine the clothing left behind. "He was wrapped in these. I did it myself. He was badly burned, but there was at least enough left to bury."

Siobhan clamped a hand over her mouth. "This is horrible. I'd hoped we could bury him and say a few words, and now..." She let out a sob and bent to retch, her face contorting.

Kat let a few minutes go by, hoping her mom could manage to get it together. "We have to go now," she finally said to the white-faced woman. When the baby woke and began to wail, Kat handed Tus Nua over, hoping the distraction would snap Siobhan out of her funk.

Siobhan took the baby and dutifully opened her shirt, her unfocused eyes in the middle distance. But a second after the baby began to nurse, her little face wrinkled and she screamed. "I don't have any milk left," she whispered. She handed the baby back to Kat and moved away like a zombie as the baby's pitiful cries reverberated off the stone.

Kat held Tus Nua close and tried to soothe her, even sticking her finger in the baby's mouth. It worked for about thirty seconds before the howls began again. She hurried after her mother.

Kat and Siobhan were on the floor crawling when Mior reappeared. "I found another way out," he said, pointing into the darkness.

"Where does it go?" Kat asked.

"It doesn't go underground. It goes somewhere else."

Kat sighed, knowing that further questions were useless.

Maybe the earthquakes had opened up another exit? But with the witch in charge, it seemed remote at best.

Mior led them down a wide passage that headed off to the right. It felt good to stand upright again. The candle stub had now burned out and Siobhan had not stopped whimpering. Thankfully the baby had finally fallen asleep. It was a long while before Kat noticed faint light in the distance.

"That's the end," Mior announced with great glee.

Kat heard voices. "Who's down there?" she hissed.

"It's Myrddin!" Mior suddenly yelled, taking off at a run.

"Myrddin is here?" Siobhan asked, sagging against Kat.

"And someone else, Mom. There are two people."

"I don't care who it is—if Myrddin's with them we'll be okay."

"Unless it's his mother," Kat muttered darkly.

But Siobhan had moved by her and was nearly running now. Kat cradled the baby against her chest and hurried after her, wondering why it was that her mother trusted a wizard to save them, but not her own half goddess daughter.

When Kat emerged from the passage, the sky was filled with magenta and gray streaks, beautiful after the utter blackness they'd been suffering through. Siobhan was smiling, standing next to Myrddin, and Mior was...hanging on to Bran's hand as though they were best buds?

When Bran caught sight of Kat, he rushed toward her before stopping himself, his cheeks reddening. "I thought you..."

She smiled. "So did I. How did you end up here?"

"Myrddin told me about the far side of the mountain where we might find a way in. We were just about to come looking for you."

Kat gazed at Myrddin who had his head bent to her mother. "Myrddin? How did you survive the earthquake?"

He grinned. "I wasn't here when it happened. You know I can move through the ether rather quickly, don't you?"

Kat laughed. "I'm very glad to see you. And you as well," she said, turning back to Bran who was staring at her.

"I went to the gods and they refused to help. I knew something bad had happened here. Airmid said she'd help me. But now she won't need to."

Kat glanced at the wizard. "Do you think this is it, Myrddin?"

"It? You mean the last of my mother's treachery? Hell no. She won't stop until you're dead."

Kat pressed her lips together. "That's what I figured. We may need Airmid's help after all."

"The gods can't do much against Carmun," Myrddin warned, his eyes suddenly dark.

"Bran's a god!" Mior shouted, dancing around him. "He's stronger than the other one!"

Kat laughed, watching the bewildered expression that arrived on Bran's face. When she glanced at the bare hills, she registered the lack of birdsong. The silence spread across her senses like the shadows that would soon bring the night. "We have to find shelter," she muttered. She pointed toward the cave. "We may have to sleep in there."

"I'm hungry," Mior whined.

"There is nothing left," Bran told the boy. "All creatures are either dead or gone."

"Hazelnuts?" Siobhan asked.

Bran lips pressed together. "The witch has scoured this land."

"Dad's body is gone," Kat said, gazing at the wizard.

"Gone? From the tunnel?"

She nodded. "What does it mean?"

"I could speculate, but I hesitate to say anything. I *can* tell you that my mother had nothing to do with it."

"I didn't think she did. But we planned a sending off ceremony and now there's no body to send off."

Siobhan had turned pale again, tears welling. And then Tus Nua opened her eyes, and feeling the hunger in her belly, she let out a cry that would have startled the birds, had there been any. Siobhan stared at Kat. "What can we do?"

"You need milk?" Myrddin asked.

Kat and Siobhan turned to him at the same time.

A second later there was a goat bleating in front of them. He held out a container. "Which one of you wants to milk her?"

Kat took the bowl and settled cross-legged on the ground. She'd never milked an animal before but it seemed second nature. When the bowl was full, she turned to her mother. "Now how do we get her to drink it?"

Siobhan tore a strip from the bottom of her skirt and soaked it in the milk. She took the baby from Kat and pressed the rag into the crying baby's mouth. Tus Nua's angry face settled as she sucked. When the rag was dry, Siobhan repeated it. "I knew having a wizard around would be a good idea," Siobhan murmured, smiling up at Myrddin.

His eyebrows rose suggestively. "Are you flirting with me?"

Siobhan looked horrified. "No, of course not! I just lost my husband."

Myrddin laughed. "I didn't mean to shock you. I was only teasing."

Kat glanced at the wizard, her intuition telling her that he wasn't teasing. She'd seen the way he looked at Siobhan. "I guess we're all having milk for dinner," she said, moving to milk the goat again. "Is she a magical goat with an endless milk supply?" she asked as her fingers tugged.

Myrddin smiled. "A conjured goat is always magical, Katel."

It was deep night when they moved into the cave, Myrddin's abilities coming in handy as he conjured wood for a fire and lit it with his fingers. The goat came in with them and settled on its forelegs. They'd all had the milk the goat provided; their bellies were full for the first time in days.

Myrddin lit several candles which he placed here and there. The light and being together again brought smiles for the first time. Kat settled with her back against the wall, her gaze straying toward Bran. When their eyes met her stomach did a little flip-flop. His gaze was unreadable, his eyes dark, a slight frown between his brows. She turned away, trying to put her mind on more important things, like how to stop another attack.

"I'll stand watch first," Kat said a while later, rising to her feet and heading for the entrance.

"No need," Myrddin told her. "I need very little sleep. I will keep watch, especially because I know what to expect."

"I can spell you," Bran offered.

Myrddin shook his head. "Get some sleep. Tomorrow will be worse."

Kat decided not to ask what he meant, heading back to her spot against the wall. It was very cold and she was missing her cloak. Siobhan, the baby, and Mior moved further back into the dark. Siobhan cradled the baby against her, her other arm around Mior who ended up with his head in her lap.

Kat was drifting in a half sleep when she felt a presence next to her. Bran put his cloak over her and sat with his back against the wall next to her. She glanced up at his bare arms crossed over his chest. "Won't you be cold?"

He gazed down with narrowed eyes. "Gods don't get cold."

Kat smiled and closed her eyes.

When Kat opened her eyes it was early dawn, the sky outside the tunnel brilliant orange and rose. She was lying next to Bran, his body curled around hers from the back. His arm lay across her and their hands were clasped together. He was still asleep, lashes dark against his pale skin. She snuggled into him, feeling his warming heat, hearing his steady heartbeat. A feeling of peace settled over her like a familiar blanket.

A scream broke the silence. Siobhan was up and running, her eyes wide with terror. "She's here!" she shouted as she clutched the baby and disappeared into the shadows.

Bran pulled away from Kat and stood hurriedly. There was no one at the entrance. "Where is the wizard?"

A moment later the wind began to howl, followed by the dawn sky being snuffed out as though a light had been switched off. Kat reached for a candle stub and lit it with her fingertips, scanning the tunnel. "Where's Mior?"

"I don't see him," Bran said.

"Did he go somewhere with Myrddin?"

Bran's dark eyes met hers. "Last I knew Myrddin was sitting at the entrance and your mother was with Mior and the baby. I fell asleep, Katel. I should never have done that."

Kat grabbed his tense arm. He was like an animal poised for flight. "This is not your fault." She could feel him fighting the urge to pull out of her grip. "Maybe he followed Mom."

A second later there was a high-pitched screech and lightning struck the cave entrance, narrowly missing the two of them. Bran dragged her backward. "She's after you." He headed toward the entrance, a dagger in his hand.

"You can't fight her," Kat hissed, rushing after him to grab his arm. She felt him shudder, his body trembling all over.

"What is it? What's wrong?"

"I feel that sickness, not the stomach, but inside. I don't know what it means."

But before she could respond, another strike hit and shattered the opening, sending rocks tumbling. "Not again!" Kat shouted.

Bran smashed his fist into the rocks and sent them flying. "She will not seal us inside this cave," he muttered, pulling rocks out of the entrance and hurling them away. Kat closed her eyes against the shimmering light that suddenly appeared. When she opened them again Val was standing in front of her.

31

K at stared at the Fae man in surprise. "Why are you here?"

He glared at her, his normally swirling eyes as dark as night. He didn't look like himself. But when she heard her mother scream Kat left him there and took off running.

The darkness was like a suffocating blanket, her hands in front of her to keep from running into walls as she hurtled on.

"Mior isn't here!" she heard her mother shout.

She hurried toward the voice, feeling for her mom in the dark. "Myrddin's gone too."

"Myrddin isn't here?"

Kat couldn't see Siobhan but she could hear the anguish in her voice. "He'll be back," she soothed. "I bet Mior's with him. He loves the wizard."

Another screech split the silence followed by a roar that sounded like hurricane force winds. "The witch is conjuring a storm! Stay here!" Kat left her mother and ran, hoping Myrddin and Mior would be there when she reached the entrance, but instead, a streak of lightning revealed Val and Bran outside facing each other. Another lightning strike lit up the pulsating ball of energy Val held in front of him and the gleaming spear in Bran's hand. What in hell were they doing? The pulsating ball lit up the darkness, swirling colors spinning as it moved in a straight line toward Bran. A second later the bright spear hissed through the air.

Kat was riveted to the spot, watching in horror as the ball hit Bran's chest and exploded, shimmering crystals flying in every direction. When she ran toward his sprawled body, lightning bolts glittered and crackled all around her. Ten feet away Val was lit up, his pale hair electrified, his arms in the air as lightning burst from his fingers, sparks flying.

A funnel cloud materialized, picking up the dust and pebbles and churning them in a sickening wild circle. It was roaring, enormous, spinning menacingly toward the ground. Kat ran for the cave, only looking back when she'd reached the safety of the rock. Out of the maelstrom she saw Myrddin emerge carrying a wriggling Mior. Kat couldn't form words, gibbering as she tried to point out Bran as Myrddin rushed toward her.

"I was in the clouds!" Mior shouted, his eyes as big as saucers. "I was with Jormungand, but Myrddin wouldn't…"

"He was about to be eaten!" Myrddin yelled. "I had a hell of time getting him away from that monster."

Kat pulled a crying Mior into her arms. "Bran's hurt," she told the wizard, trying to suppress the sob that rose into her throat.

Myrddin peered into the murk outside the cave. "For all that is holy," he muttered. A second later he was gone.

Kat held Mior tight, trying to see, but when it began to hail and the lightning strikes increased, she had to back away from the opening. And amidst the madness and turmoil she could hear Tus Nua screaming at the top of her lungs.

By the time Kat returned with her mother and the screaming baby Myrddin had carried Bran inside.

"Where's the goat?" Siobhan yelled, her attention on the unhappy baby held in her arms.

Myrddin looked up from where he kneeled next to Bran. "An animal that is summoned only remains so long."

Siobhan noticed what he was doing, her eyes going wide. "What happened to Bran?"

Myrddin glanced at Kat. "Apparently Val and Bran had a duel over your daughter. Bran lost."

Kat was about to respond when she saw something moving out of the corner of her eye. A surging wave of water was headed straight for the cave entrance. "Run!" she screamed, giving Siobhan a push. Her mother did not hesitate, running as though the hounds of hell were after her. "Myrddin!" she shouted.

He waved his hand in the air. "I've got Bran—get the hell out of here!"

But it was too late. The wave hit with a sickening roar, bursting through the opening and lifting Kat off her feet and carrying her away.

Sounds, eerie and muffled. Banging, echoes. Screaming. Numbing cold. Voices murmuring. Darkness. Pain.

Kat opened her eyes, but in the darkness it was though they were still closed. She felt around her but all her hands came into contact with were sticks, small pebbles and mud. She was wet through and shivering, her body aching from where she'd been slammed against the walls. "Is anyone here?"

No one answered. Fear took her, its hands clutching her stomach while it sat on her chest. Her heartbeat got faster and faster. Her breath panted. She couldn't think, could barely breathe. Visions tore through her mind. Knowing she was going to drown, crashing into walls as the water slammed her along. Colors and the feel of others drifting by. Had everyone drowned?

"Katel?"

"I'm here!" she shouted. "Follow my voice!" She heard the slosh of boots, the stumble and a muttered oath.

"Bran…is that you?" she asked in a hoarse whisper.

Something touched her, a hand a foot, she didn't know. She reached out and grabbed hold of a muscular arm. "Bran," she sobbed. "I thought you were dead."

A hand touched her cheek. "I thought I was too. But it doesn't mean I'm not injured." He felt around and sat next to her.

"Have you seen anyone?"

"Haven't heard a sound other than your voice. Last thing I remember was that energy ball hitting me. I woke up underwater."

Kat leaned into him, and found his hand, twining her fingers through his. "Where are the others?" Kat finally asked.

"They either drowned or they're further up where we can't hear them."

"I hope it's the latter. Maybe we should try and find them."

Kat could see him nod in her mind, her internal sense showing her things that she couldn't perceive with her eyes. There was a glow around him, illuminating his face. *Like Mior's fireflies*, she thought. *Maybe they are in me now.* He had bruises on his cheek and forehead and deep cuts on both his arms. When she touched one, he winced. "That looks bad."

Bran frowned. "You can see me?"

Their eyes met. He could see her too. "What's happening?" she asked, wondering abut the magic of seeing in the dark.

Bran continued to stare at her, a pained look appearing on his face. His hand went to his stomach before he leaned toward her, his mouth finding hers.

The scent of his special pine and sweat permeated her senses. Strong arms held her tightly as their lips met and clung together. She tasted him, felt his heart beating, her body responding. When he pulled away there was a long silence.

"The sickness," he muttered. "The sickness goes away when I kiss you."

"And when I woke up and you were sleeping next to me? Did that make it go away too?"

He smiled sheepishly. "What does it mean?"

Kat smiled. "It means you love me, Bran."

He shook his head. "Gods don't love. Even Taranis said that. Even caring is wrong between humans and gods."

"How many times do I have to tell you that I'm a goddess? My father was a god."

His dark eyes met hers again. "I don't know what love is."

"It's this," she said, pointing to their clasped hands. "And it's this," she said leaning forward to kiss him lightly on the mouth, "and it's this," she continued, putting her fingers gently on his wound. She closed her eyes and sent heat surging into the deep cut, asking the skin to come together. When she opened her eyes a few minutes later the wound was still red but the skin was beginning to knit together. "How is the place where the energy ball hit?"

Bran opened his soggy leather jerkin and showed her the mottled angry redness on his chest, the shards that still remained. Kat was shocked into silence. When she looked up at him, he was watching her. "Val tried to kill me. Is his love for you the reason? Love doesn't seem like a good thing."

"Val didn't seem like himself. He didn't look like himself either. He might love me, but I don't feel the same for him. I did once, but it's changed now. I've changed. You had a spear, Bran. Where did you get it?"

Bran chuckled awkwardly. "That spear was suddenly in my hand when I needed it. I have no idea where it came from."

Kat reached for a shard, tugging at it until Bran let out a groan and grabbed her hand. "Stop."

"I can't get them out without causing a lot of pain."

"They're poisoned. It's why I feel so weak."

"Poisoned?" Kat was suddenly furious. "That bastard," she muttered. "He knew…he knew…"

"Knew what?"

"He knows I love you! In hurting you he has hurt me and any chance he ever had of us being friends. If he's alive I'll kill him with my bare hands." Kat returned her attention to the bright shards. "If they're poisoned, I shouldn't pull them out."

"Myrddin can help."

"But where is he?" Kat looked around desperately. "Where's anyone?"

"We need to search," he said, pushing up to standing. He reached for her hand and tugged her to her feet. Together they headed into the murky darkness.

"Are you serious?" Airmid stared hard at Morrighan, the goddess of war.

"Yes, and I am livid about it. That bastard led me on. He took me to his bed whenever he was here and I never knew of his deception. He got what he deserved."

"And now they will undo the former decision? Why?"

"I guess they decided that one act of selflessness made up for all his bad behavior. And in their next breath they inform Bran that they can't help him against this evil goddess who is destroying Earth." Her eyes narrowed dangerously as she paced in front of Airmid's spring. "And their reason was that Bran was put back together by a druid! What has that got to do with anything? He certainly looked godlike to me—in fact way more godlike than the former Bran."

"He is rather striking, isn't he?" When Morrighan raised her eyebrows suggestively, Airmid laughed. "Bran wanted us to help and I told him we would. Would you be interested in joining us? So far, it's Danu, myself and Rhiannon."

Morrigan's eyes brightened. "I'm in."

"To prepare shall we take a dip in the spring?"

After the two goddesses pinned up their long hair and stepped into the healing waters, Morrighan twisted to look at her. "Hope the gods don't get wind of our plans."

"I don't care if they do or don't," Airmid responded, her eyes closed.

32

Bran and Kat hobbled slowly along the passageway for what seemed like hours. The cave walls closed in, the smells of rot and muck fouling the air.

"Did you hear that?" Bran whispered, pulling her to a stop.

"What?"

"Voices. There are people up ahead."

"I can't hear them but I'll take your word for it." Kat tugged him forward, trying to go a bit faster.

It was another ten minutes before Kat heard the murmur of voices. "Hello?" she called out.

"Kat!" Siobhan shouted. "Hurry. The baby..." her voice drifted off.

When Kat heard her sob, she let go of Bran's hand and took off running. She felt her mother before she reached her, Siobhan's normally pale blue aura filled with black flecks. "Where's Tus Nua?"

Siobhan broke down, her sobs reverberating off the dark stone. She pressed the still form into Kat's arms. "She isn't breathing."

Tus Nua was limp and cold with no heartbeat. "How long has she been like this?"

"Maybe two or three minutes? She was fine and then suddenly she wasn't."

"Is Mior with you?"

"No…I don't know where he is!" Her mother let out another sob just as Bran caught up.

He grabbed the baby out of Kat's arms, his aura fiery red and purple as he breathed air into the child's mouth. He took off his vest and placed Tus Nua on it and kneeled over her, his hands on the region of her heart. And then he leaned to breathe into her mouth again. It looked like he was doing CPR, but Kat knew it was much more than that. It was only a few seconds later that the baby let out a high-pitched scream and began to cry.

"Oh my god!" Siobhan cried, holding out her arms. Bran placed the baby there and stood back, his aura fading into a pale greenish blue.

Kat reached for his hand. "Thank you," she murmured.

"I don't know how I did that," he muttered, surprised.

Kat squeezed his hand. "Healing powers. As I recall, the old Bran didn't have those."

"Maybe it's Fae magic from the shards. I'm filled with poison."

"And you can't heal yourself?"

"This is not the same affliction. It was done with evil intent."

Kat thought about that for a moment. "That does not sound like the Val I know," she muttered.

Siobhan was sitting on the floor attempting to feed the baby, tears still flowing down her chapped cheeks. "I think she's getting something," she whispered hopefully.

"Tell me what happened, Mom."

"The wave came over us and I let go of Tus Nua."

Kat heard the anguish and guilt in her voice and reached to touch her shoulder. "You were being carried away by a force that took all your energy. You shouldn't feel guilty."

"And where is my boy?" Siobhan murmured.

"Mior is fine. He's got powers none of us can even guess at. He and Myrddin are probably somewhere up ahead working on some magical plot to get back at the witch."

"I suggest we search for a place of safety," Bran said, his hand shaking as he reached for Kat. "If she sends another one of those water waves, or whatever you call them, we might not be so lucky."

When Siobhan rose to her feet the baby continued to nurse, her aura bright with contentment.

"Let's go," Bran urged. "I'm getting weaker."

Kat put an arm around his waist, unnerved by how much Bran leaned against her. "The healing sapped your energy," she whispered.

Bran didn't answer as he stumbled along, his breathing labored.

"Is there any way to stop the witch?" Siobhan asked in a small voice as they struggled through the thick mud.

"Mior says we have the support of the dragon. But I'm not sure whether I believe him," Kat answered.

"He did put out the fire," Siobhan reminded her.

"That's true, but why does Jormungand watch as the witch attacks and attacks? She's already killed…"

"Don't say it," Siobhan whispered.

"Sorry, Mom. It hurts me too." Kat stared ahead, her eyes welling. Bran's breathing had turned into a wheezy rasp, his weight leaning heavily against her. They had to find Myrddin—and soon.

They'd been walking silently for some time when they heard Mior yell. He was lit up from behind as he raced toward them, Myrddin's silhouette following.

"Mior!" Siobhan shouted, her aura brightening into shifting streaks of violet. She held the baby on her hip and bent down to catch her hurtling son.

"We found the way out!" he yelled, rushing into her arms.

"My sweet boy," she whispered. "I was so worried."

Mior laughed and twirled around them, his hands out to touch them all as he wove between them. "It's a new world!"

"What?" Kat asked, grabbing his arm to stop his manic flight.

"Tell them, Myrddin. Tell them what we found!"

Myrddin caught up, muddy fingers pushing the filthy gray hair behind his ears. The light revealed his tired eyes, the bruises on his face and the mud that covered him from head to toe. He smelled worse than the air. "This is a new one for me," he said. "I have no idea where we are."

"We aren't on Earth?"

His eyebrows came together. "Not the Earth I know."

"Where is Val?" Bran asked, moving into the light.

Myrddin gazed at him, seemingly surprised to see him alive. "Val disappeared."

"Wait till you see!" Mior yelled, rushing around them in circles

"It is rather a surprise," Myrddin said. "Not anything I would have expected."

"Myrddin," Kat said, touching his arm. "Bran is seriously injured. The energy ball left pieces in his chest and apparently they're poisoned."

Myrddin frowned and ran his fingers lightly over Bran's chest. "And you can't help him?"

"Those spikes need to come out. I thought perhaps with your wizardry you could make them evaporate, or…"

Myrddin made a sound in the back of his throat. "I may be a wizard but some things are beyond even me. All the gods be damned," he muttered when Bran removed his jerkin to show him the wound. "This will require magic I haven't attempted in a very long time." He glanced at Kat and Siobhan. "For your own safety I suggest you take yourselves out of here. Mior can stay."

Mior came close, his dark eyes focused on Bran's chest as he reached to touch a shard. "They're cursed."

"You are correct. The curse acts like poison," Kat heard Myrddin say as she and her mother walked away. "As soon as you take them out the curse spreads and kills. What do you suggest, young wizard? I had thought to use a spell to dissolve, but that might make things worse."

Their voices receded as Kat and Siobhan reached the opening. "You love him. I can see it in your eyes," Siobhan murmured.

Kat nodded, trying hard not to cry. "He's not the same Bran, but there's an essence that remains."

"And Val?"

"Val did this to him. How could I ever have feelings for him after that? Even if I didn't love Bran, what he did is despicable."

"Bran tried to kill Val too, didn't he?"

Kat shook her head. "Bran was defending himself." She turned when she heard Bran let out a howl of pain, unable to stop herself from racing back.

"Stay back!" Myrddin shouted when he saw her. "These crystals are alive and they are not benevolent!"

The crystals had become a fiery reddish color and it was obvious that they were burning Bran's chest. Bran's eyes were closed, his lips twisting. Mior chanted as the wizard waved his hands in ever smaller circles, muttering an incantation.

"What can I do?" she whispered.

"Send energy. Send him love."

Kat closed her eyes and imagined Bran cocooned in golden light. She held the image in her mind, letting go of all other thought. She heard a gasp and a sucking sound, opening her eyes to see Myrddin extracting one of the crystals. It turned to ash in his hand. "One out," he muttered, his fingers moving over the rest. "Keep up the golden light."

Kat closed her eyes again, only opening them when Bran let out another roar. He half sat up before he fell back unconscious. Kat was on her feet and beside him before she could think. Her fingers went to the runes on his upper arm, as she murmured the words that came to her. Mior's chants, her own chants, and Myrddin's incantations formed a pulsing helix that enclosed the god in white light.

"It's working," Myrddin muttered sometime later.

"Only a few more. But these are deeply imbedded. It's good that he's unconscious because this will hurt like hell."

Bran was as pale as paper and his lips were blue. "Is he alive?" she whispered.

"Barely. He's hanging on for you."

"For me?"

Myrddin's gaze caught hers. "He's newly formed. You are all he has."

Tears welled and spilled over. "I can't be all he has, Myrddin. He can't be that dependent."

"It's not dependency. It's deep connection. His soul remembers you."

Kat sucked in breath and let it out. "Don't die," she whispered.

It took another hour before all the shards were out and had turned to ash. Bran lay utterly still, his heartbeat nearly undetectable. Myrddin straightened and rubbed his lower back. "Now we wait. If he wakes, good, if not, then…"

"Val's curse killed him."

The wizard nodded, reaching to pull Mior up from where he sat cross-legged. "Thank you, young wizard. If you wish it, I will teach you all that I know. And maybe you can teach me a thing or two."

Mior frowned down at the still figure. "He isn't opening his eyes."

"Give him time." Myrddin headed off, but when Kat didn't follow, he turned back. "You cannot help him now. He's in another world."

"I can't leave him alone." Kat curled up next to him and held his limp hand. She glanced at Mior standing next to her hesitantly. "Go with Myrddin. I'll watch over him."

Mior ran after the disappearing wizard, his bright voice echoing down the tunnel. "I want you to teach me!" Kat heard him shout before their voices faded.

Kat was asleep with her head on Bran's shoulder when she felt him stir.

"Kat?"

"I'm here. How do you feel?"

"Glad to be alive."

Kat began to cry.

It took some time for Bran to sit up. "I'm so fucking weak," he muttered.

"Not surprising. The last time this happened you were weak too, but then we…"

"We, what?"

Kat chuckled. "We made love in the spring. Airmid's healing spring. To celebrate."

"Wish I could say I felt up to something like that," he muttered, leaning against her. "But I can kiss you, if that's ok."

Kat felt for his face, pressing her mouth to his.

It took a long time to reach the end of the tunnel, Kat's arms exhausted from supporting him. "Are you sure you feel better? Because you don't sound it."

"The poison's gone, but it did some damage."

"That bastard," Kat muttered.

"I hit him with that spear, but it didn't seem to faze him at all."

Mior saw them first, his brooding look replaced with a

smile. "You're okay!" he yelled, rushing to hug Bran around the legs.

Myrddin smiled and nodded when he saw them. "Well done, Kat."

"It was not I who did this, Myrddin. I thank you and Mior from the bottom of my heart."

"And from the bottom of mine, for what that's worth," Bran said, attempting to smile.

Siobhan came close, shyly reaching to hug him. "I am so pleased," she murmured.

Bran's normal austere warrior expression was replaced with an uneasy grin. "Thank you," he muttered.

"How about we find our way to safety, like we planned four hours ago? I'm sure my mother is plotting against us as we stand here exchanging pleasantries."

The world outside the cave was filled with strange light. There were fairy-like creatures hanging in the air, the faint sound of chimes in the distance. Trees seemed to float instead of having roots, and what looked like a golden city was shining in the far distance. Kat gazed into the shimmering light. "What a beautiful place. We must be on another planet or in another realm. But how did we get here?"

Myrddin scanned, his expression dubious. "This does not feel right."

They'd walked probably a quarter of a mile when they heard a thunder-like reverberation that made the earth shudder under their feet. "What did I tell you," Myrddin muttered, his eyes turning dark. "She reads my thoughts despite all the enchantments I put up to keep her out."

When Kat looked over her shoulder there was an enormous dark shape emerging from the cave. The creature lumbered toward them, its piggy eyes, slits of rage. It was covered in armor-like scales, a cross between a rhinoceros, and some terrible nightmare. It was the size of a house, and when it opened its mouth, enormous sharp teeth were revealed. Kat took one more look at it and rushed to Siobhan who stood like a deer in the headlights, "Give me Tus Nua and run!" she shouted.

Siobhan handed her the baby just before Myrddin grabbed her mother's hand. A second later they whirled away. Kat called out to Bran, clutching the baby close. He looked pale, his eyes dark with pain, but he didn't hesitate as he took hold of her hand.

They rushed pell-mell under the feathery trees. Behind them the creature plowed right through them, scattering leaves and limbs. Kat heard a woman's voice singing. No, it wasn't singing, it was telling them where to go.

"There is a waterfall not far—when you reach it do not be afraid to jump in. You will be safe, but the one following will not."

Kat kept going, afraid to look over her shoulder. She could hear the thing getting closer. Siobhan and Myrddin were up ahead, flying just off the ground. The strange woods ended at a cliff edge, mist rising from the cascading waterfall. The air was alive with creatures now, big eyes watching them as they ran past. The heavy sound of the water drowned out everything, sparkling rainbows effervescing from within the spray. When the earth lifted under her feet, Kat went sprawling, the baby falling with her. She screamed when she saw Mior launch himself over the edge.

Bran was beside her, reaching down. "Grab my hand!"

Kat clutched the baby and had risen to her feet when she saw her mother and Myrddin vanish from view.

"It's up to us now," Bran panted, next to her. "Don't let go."

Kat ran next to him, one arm tight around Tus Nua, her fingers twined with Bran's. They were on the ground and then they weren't. For a second it seemed like they were suspended in a bubble of light, and then they were plummeting toward a bottom she couldn't see. The falling seemed odd, as though she wasn't falling at all. She heard a cackle, felt hands tugging at her trying to pry her arm loose from around the baby. And then she heard Myrddin yell, "It's all an illusion!" A moment after that her feet hit something solid and she tumbled, letting go of Tus Nua in the process. Screams, shouts, crying. Darkness.

The goddesses looked around. "Where is everyone?" Danu asked. "Kat was here. I had a vision."

Airmid frowned. "And where is Bran? He said to meet him here."

Morrighan scanned the wasteland. "Looks like a bulldozer the size of a large city went through this place. There is nothing left to save."

"I would have to agree," Rhiannon, the horse goddess muttered, pulling impatiently at the tight bodice of her dress. "I should have worn pants," she muttered.

"Are we in the wrong place?" Airmid asked, looking at the mud caked all over her bare feet. "Perhaps we miscalculated."

Danu gazed around. "There was a recent storm here, and a fire. Kat and her family had a house just over there," she said, pointing toward a flat area devoid of even a blade of grass or a weed. "And there was a healing spring just up there within the trees." She gazed toward the hillside of stumps with a scowl. "But there are no more trees." A gray pall hung over the land, reeking of the supernatural.

"The witch has poisoned the land," Morrighan muttered. "And Jormungand is up there," she continued, squinting toward the sky. "He's Loki's son. He's part of Ragnarok."

All the goddesses gazed upward. "He isn't moving to confront us. Why not?" Rhiannon asked.

Airmid shrugged and then started when she saw a pale-haired man coming toward them. "Who is that?"

"Looks Elven to me," Rhiannon said.

"Have you seen the ones who live here?" the man called out.

"Who *are* you?" Airmid asked, looking him over.

"I'm Val. Katel and I have a child together."

"Ah. The child who is now aligned with the witch. And where do *you* stand?"

Val scowled, running his fingers though his tangled hair. "Where do you *think* I stand? I'm here searching for her."

"We are here to meet Bran," Morrighan said. "He asked for our help."

"Bran is dead. I was taken over by the witch and I killed him."

Airmid's mouth dropped open. "The witch? Why would she want to kill Bran?"

"Because Kat cares for him, is my guess."

"Bran is a god," Danu murmured. "How could you kill him?"

"The witch provided an energy ball with poisoned crystals. If he isn't dead, he will be soon."

There was a rending screech and four people burst through the ether, their eyes wide with terror. And behind them came a monster, jaws snapping. A split second later everything went dark.

33

Kat lost all sense of what was happening. She couldn't locate Bran, her mother or anyone. She heard Tus Nua crying somewhere to her left. The monster seemed to have evaporated. And it was pitch black. Carmun loomed up in front of her, her face pale as milk. "Are you ready to face your destiny?" she hissed.

Kat stepped back, a tingle of fear going up her spine. She steeled herself, trying to stay in command, but when the baby let out a howl, she lost her focus. "The baby…"

"Leave the baby," Carmun said. "This is between you and me. You were named as my nemesis, just as I was named yours. Why do you think that is?"

"I have no idea. But as long as we're trading questions— why do you want a dark world?"

"Darkness suits me. The light hurts my eyes."

The baby continued to howl but when Kat moved to find her, the witch's fingers dug into her arm. "The baby is alive, which is more than I can say for the rest of your little group."

Kat sucked in breath, her heart skipping a beat. "She's scared." Before the witch could do anything further, Kat rushed off. As soon as she lifted her, the Tus Nua stopped crying, only sucking in noisy sobbing breaths. "Why are you so concerned with this little brat?" Carmun asked, appearing next to her. "She's isn't even a goddess. What a waste humans are."

Myrddin was suddenly next to them, his eyes as dark as Carmun's. "What are you up to now, Mother?"

Carmun glanced quickly at her son before turning back to Kat. "Just having a chat with this demigoddess who is supposed to be so strong. So far I have not observed it."

"Perhaps her strength is different than yours. Possibly empathy is a part of it. Did you ever consider that it might not be fighting that is at the root of her ability to best you?"

Carmun scoffed. "To best *me*? My strength is far beyond hers or yours, Myrddin. Your mind meanderings are annoying me now. Go away and let us confer without your input."

When she raised her hand Myrddin flew backward into the darkness and disappeared.

"My son is a disappointment. He could have been powerful, but he chose to take another path. Loki has never forgiven him."

"What could he have done differently?" Kat asked, trying to stall for time. She had no idea what to say or what to do, her mind scattering into a million scenarios of how this could end. And none of them were good.

Carmun's eyebrows rose. "He could have embraced his god powers that came from his father. Instead he chose to do simple magic." She let out a huff.

"He just healed a god. I would hardly call that simple."

"Did he now? So, the duel I set up didn't pay off," she muttered, looking away for a second.

"*You* set it up?"

"Of course, dear. My darkness is infectious. Val was ripe for the picking." She let out a chortle. "Love weakens."

"I disagree. There is no greater strength than love."

"Enough of this. What is your decision regarding the two of us?"

"Are you asking me to decide how we should fight? If so, I have no idea what to say. If we are destined to battle it out, that could take several forms. Shall we name a time and place sometime in the future?"

Carmun frowned. "I do not work that way. I much prefer the element of surprise."

"Well then, why ask? I suppose fate will have to decide. I feel sorry for you, Carmun. Not being able to feel love must be very sad for you."

Carmun looked confused for a split second before she smiled. "I will continue to plague you, Katel. Up until the moment that fate intervenes. And if I kill you before that happens, then so be it." She turned in a circle, black hair swirling around her, and vanished.

"What in goddess name did you do?" Myrddin asked, arriving next to her. "I was sure you two would be battling it out right here."

"Are they okay?"

"Everyone is fine," he murmured, glancing at the sleeping baby.

Kat let her shoulders slump. "She wanted me to come up with a plan to end this. I told her that fate would have to decide."

Myrddin's eyes narrowed. "She doesn't want this to end—she's having too much fun. My mother loves to create chaos."

Kat thought back to her time of blindness at Odin's castle, the terrible things the witch had shown her. She'd taken her memories of Bran and threatened her. So much had happened since then, and yet Kat was still alive. Carmun wanted something from her. But what was it?

Kat felt a hand on her arm and turned to see Airmid. "What are you doing here?"

"Bran engaged our services. We would have intervened with Carmun just now, but I had the sense we should let it play out."

Kat squinted into the darkness. "Who's with you?"

"Morrighan, Danu, and Rhiannon. After the gods turned Bran down, we decided to help."

"They wouldn't help? Why?"

Airmid snorted. "They found out he was brought back by a druid instead of a god. In their minds he is no longer a member of their exclusive club."

Kat thought about the physical changes, his innocence and lack of memories. "He's different now. He doesn't remember me or us."

"But you still love him."

"I...I don't know if I do or don't. Sometimes he's like a child."

Airmid chuckled. "This Bran has many of the same attitudes as the old one. He's still in there somewhere."

Kat took in a deep breath and let it out. The darkness was already making her feel claustrophobic. No auras were shining this time. "Is it night, or did the witch do this?"

"Carmun has taken the light. If she is not stopped there will be perpetual darkness," Danu said, her pale face lit up from within. "But you knew that."

"I'm supposed to stop her," she muttered "But she's too strong."

"I thought I heard you say, 'there's no greater strength than love'," Myrddin's voice intoned.

Kat scoffed. "I did, but the reality is…"

"The reality is, you're right," Myrddin finished for her. "All you need decide is what that means in real terms."

Kat laughed. "Nothing difficult about that."

Dealing with the darkness proved to be a trial, all of them grumpy and out of sorts as they struggled to find a place to sleep. Val appeared and managed to pull Kat aside. "You heard the witch. She was inhabiting my body when I threw that energy ball. You must know that I would never do something like that."

Kat frowned. "Arwen is the reason this is happening. If he hadn't been born everything would be different. Bran almost died because of you."

Val gazed at her. "I gave you magic so that you could defend yourself from what was coming, so you could walk through doors to save yourself. I am not to blame for this. I would never hurt Bran because I know how you feel about him."

Kat was crying now, unable to stop. She barely heard what he said as she fought for control. He watched her for a moment before he turned and headed away. A few minutes later a glimmer of light took her attention, and when she turned, a door had opened. Val walked through, his face a mask of pain.

It was a long time before she finally rose and headed toward the voices in the distance. She heard Danu murmur, "Being in this darkness is unacceptable."

Kat was tired from straining to see, tired of searching for a suitable place to rest. Her confusion regarding Val was sapping her energy. She knew he'd been taken over by the witch, but it still hurt to think about it. Danu was right, but where could they go?

"What about that underground place?" Mior chirped.

"It was terrible, Mior," Siobhan answered. "Those people wanted us dead. And it's nearly as dark as here. What about Odin and Frigg? I'm allowed in the Norse world, or at least I was. And I like Frigg and Freya, despite Dag's dalliance with Odin's wife. I suppose she was doing me a favor, in a way, since I was too weak to..."

"Mom, please," Kat cut in, joining them. "Past history and not in front of young ears." A second later the baby who had been sleeping in her arms let out an ear-piercing shriek.

"The baby's hungry and I have no more milk." Siobhan began to cry as she took the baby from Kat and attempted to soothe her. But Tus Nua wasn't having any of it, her screams only getting louder.

"That settles it," Danu said. "Odin may be strict regarding the gods of Otherworld, but he's never refused the goddesses."

"How do we get there?" Siobhan asked. "Last time Dag carried me."

"I can transport you, Siobhan," Myrddin said. "As long as the rest of you can travel on your own steam."

Kat couldn't see the wizard but she heard his tone and

sensed his intentions. He was hitting on her mom. Should she worry? Probably not considering everything else she had to think about. Her mother would have to take care of herself. Bran touched her arm. "Birds?"

When she shifted, her bird self could see Raven rising upward into the darkness. Hummingbird followed him.

34

The heavily carved oak door swung open, revealing the one-eyed god. Gray hair hung untidily around a lined face, thick eyebrows pushed together with annoyance. "What is this?" he roared.

Danu stepped forward. "Lord Odin, it is I, Danu. And these are my sisters, and our friends."

Odin gazed at her for a moment before turning to peer at Siobhan. "*You* have been here before. With that bastard Dagda."

Siobhan stepped back, frightened. "Dagda is dead," Kat told him, taking her mother's arm. "He sacrificed himself to save my mother from the witch."

"And what witch might that be?" he asked, not moving out of the doorway.

"The witch is Carmun, my mother," Myrddin said. "She lay with Loki and ended up with me as a result."

Odin turned to stare at the wizard. "*You* are Loki's son? You look like a mortal to me."

"My mother would agree with you. She mourns the path I've chosen. But I am not completely useless."

"Odin?" a woman called from within. "Who is here?"

Odin stepped aside as Frigg peered out. "Please come in by the fire," she invited, gazing with interest at all of them. "It is too cold out there to think."

Kat smiled and followed the other goddesses inside, trailing back with her mother who had a dazed expression on her face.

Candles burned in sconces along the walls, and the tables were covered with candelabra, a feeling of festivity relieving the overcast day. Tapestries hung on the stone walls, intricate animals and birds, woven in muted colors of reds and blues and green. The high-ceilinged room where Frigg led them had a seating arrangement centered on an enormous marble fireplace. The mantel was layered in greenery, the smell of pine mixing with the scent of the blazing wood. Odin sat in a chair fit for a king, his regal stance making his role as the ruler of the Aesir very clear.

Frigg gestured to the chairs and couches. "Please make yourselves comfortable." Once they settled, she turned to Siobhan. "You are Dagda's wife. Where is the child I helped deliver?"

Siobhan reached out for Mior who was hovering around her knees. "This is Mior."

Frigg bent to examine him. "Yes, I can see the resemblance. How is the Dagda?"

Siobhan's eyes welled. "He's gone."

"Gone?"

"He died saving my life," she whispered.

Frigg seemed shocked by this, her eyes going wide. "Died…but Dagda, he…"

"I thought you must know. He lost his god powers and

was sent back to Earth as a mortal."

"Oh! I am so very sorry. He was terribly arrogant, but also he..."

"Frigg?" Odin interrupted. "Can you get our guests some refreshment?"

Frigg rose hastily and smoothed out her blue gown. Her hair was in braids wrapped around her shapely head, her eyes bright and kind. When she headed off Siobhan let out a sigh of relief. "She's so beautiful—I can see why your father..."

"Mom," Kat warned, glancing at Odin's scowl.

"Yes, my wife was unfaithful with the Dagda," he muttered. "I wanted to kill him for what he did." At that moment Frigg arrived carrying an enormous silver tray which she placed on a table. "Ale and cider for those who would like some. How about you, young man?" she asked, gazing at Mior. Mior blushed and moved close to take the glass she held out.

"Is that alcoholic?" Siobhan asked.

Frigg seemed amused by the question. "Everything we drink is alcoholic. It will not harm him. He *is* a god's son, after all."

Siobhan sat back, her cheeks flushing with embarrassment.

"Now..." Frigg said, clapping her hands, "to what do we owe the pleasure of this visit?"

Morrighan glanced around before she said, "Earth has been claimed by the witch, and the gods in Otherworld have decided to ignore what's happening and close ranks. We had nowhere left to go."

Frigg laughed. "Yes, gods can often be quite unforgiving." Her narrowed gaze went to Odin before she turned back to Siobhan. "Oh my," she murmured, peering at the covered bundle in her arms. "Another baby? Is it the Dagda's child?"

Siobhan pulled aside the scarf. "This is Tus Nua."

"New beginnings," Frigg whispered, reaching for the baby. "What an exquisite child," she said, gazing down. "She must be about a year and a half old?"

"Yes. And I have no more milk for her," Siobhan admitted.

Frigg looked up from where she cooed to the baby held in her arms. "I am the goddess of fertility and motherhood. I always have milk." She moved to a chair and sat to undo the bodice of her dress. As soon as she pressed the baby to her breast, Tus Nua began to nurse. Frigg settled back, a serene expression on her features. "Is she mortal?"

"Yes," Siobhan answered, her eyes welling.

"I thought so," Frigg murmured.

The baby was fed and resettled with Siobhan, the ale was gone, as well as flatbread and cheese, before the reason for their visit was brought up again. This time it was Airmid who provided more details, giving the floor to Kat once she explained the darkness Carmun was causing and the need to get off Earth.

"And you are the one who Carmun wants to destroy? Why?"

Kat gazed at Frigg, wondering how to answer. "I wish I knew. Remember when I was here and Freya was taken over by the witch?"

Frigg frowned. "I had been sent away, as I recall. I remember being suspicious at the time, but Freya is my friend and I thought I was being paranoid."

"When I was blind the witch showed herself to me. I knew she wasn't Freya. She meant to kill me, I'm sure. It's why I ran from here."

"Yes, I remember now. Freya was not aware of what had happened. The witch is able to inhabit anyone without their permission or knowledge."

Kat nodded. "I have never known why she's after me. She's had plenty of chances to kill me, but she hasn't done it. Cerridwen and others have told me that my destiny lies with her. She has begun Ragnarok."

"Ragnarok? No. Ragnarok begins here in the Norse realm. She has only darkened your world."

"It is not only dark, it's scoured," Bran said. "There is not a blade of grass or a bird or an insect left."

Frigg turned to stare at the raven-haired god. "And who are you?"

"I'm Bran, the blessed."

Frigg looked confused. "I have met Bran and you do not resemble him. He came here with Kat to heal from his injuries. He has sandy hair and a very different build."

"This *is* Bran," Kat said, taking his hand. "He gave up his powers and then reclaimed them, but in the reclaiming, he died and had to start over."

Frigg peered at him. "I don't see it, but I will take your word for it, Katel. I do feel his power. He is definitely a god." Her appraising gaze traveled from his face to his wide shoulders and strong arms. She cocked her head and smiled.

Bran stared back, his gaze roaming to the baby at her breast. His gaze lingered there, watching the baby suckle.

"I don't remember you. I wish I did."

"We would like to seek refuge here until this battle is settled," Kat said, trying to break the connection between them.

Frigg tore her gaze away from Bran. "And how do you propose to settle it?"

"That's the number one question on everyone's mind," Myrddin replied. "We need time to discuss our options."

Frigg glanced at the goddesses. "Well, you certainly have a formidable army here. Against one witch? You should have an easy time of it."

Frigg's attention was returning to Bran when Kat said, "It isn't only one witch—she has many followers and some terrible birds that like to rip things apart."

"Are you asking us to help you?" Odin asked suddenly.

"No," Kat said. "We only need a place to stay where we can be safe while we make a plan."

Odin and Frigg exchanged a look. "We have a cottage where we house our guests. It is free at the moment," the goddess said. "I will show you the way."

The goddesses were mumbling amongst themselves as they trooped after Frigg. Their breath was white in the early twilight, the wide dome of sky above the forest already filling with stars. A pale moon was rising from behind the trees, the comforting sound of birds settling in for the night adding to the feeling of peace.

Kat let out her held breath, her shoulders finally relaxing. She looked forward to a real bed and the possibility of Bran lying next to her. But when she glanced at him his gaze was on Frigg. The avid look in his eyes bothered her. The world shimmered, magic in the air and in the trees, the goddess luminous within it. Frigg was irresistible.

Airmid hurried toward Frigg, her voice low as she discussed the situation in more detail. "These people are all at risk," Kat heard her say. "Their homeland has been destroyed, and without a tremendous amount of magic there will be no going back. Katel is destined to end this thing, but I fear she is not up to the task. Myrddin's mother has powers far beyond any of ours, and Kat is only half-goddess. If you have any ideas, we would appreciate your guidance. You are the Queen of Asgard and your son is the god of light and joy, exactly what has been destroyed on Earth. Perhaps Balder would be willing to come to our aid?"

Frigg turned to Airmid, her gaze one of sympathy. "My son is otherwise engaged at the moment, and I hesitate to call on him. Odin has been slated to die in Ragnarok, but my son is destined to live. I would not want to meddle with the fates by pushing him into a conflict that is not his destiny."

Kat moved closer to join in the conversation. "If this isn't Ragnarok, will we survive the real one? Will you?"

"That I cannot say since my own fate is hidden from me. Since the goddesses with you are from Otherworld, that realm's future is also unknown to me. As to you, Kat, I see nothing but darkness."

Nothing but darkness. "What does that mean?"

Her almond-shaped eyes met Kat's. "You should speak with the Norns. They are the spinners of fate and can tell you the future. All I know is that in the real Ragnarok, a winter will come, colder than any other. It will last a very long time. My husband will fight the wolf, Fenrir, who will kill him, and the Valkyrie will fight by Odin's side. You have told me that the sun and moon and stars are now missing from Earth. Ragnarok will bring the same to the Norse realm. Yggdrasil will tremble and fall, our mountains will crumble. It is Loki who will cause this. Perhaps those who manage to live through it will wish they hadn't."

Kat felt a shiver. "The dragon is already in the sky over Earth. He…"

"He's my friend!" Mior shouted, rushing up to Frigg. "He put the forest fire out. He promised to help!"

Kat grabbed him, frowning down at him. "And yet Jormungand has done nothing while the witch ruins the land and takes our light. If he's your friend why hasn't he acted?"

Mior looked up at her. "Because he's waiting."

"Waiting for what?"

"For Ragnarok," Mior said, frowning at Kat like she was an idiot.

"Perhaps the boy is right," Frigg said. "The true sign of Ragnarok is when winter comes. The dragon knows this. As I explained earlier, whatever the witch has done or is doing is not Ragnarok."

Frigg moved through an opening in the middle of a tall hedge, leading the way up a pebbled path toward a cottage of stone. Glass windows faced outward, reflecting the hillside of trees in the distance. Smoke rose from the chimney. "Who lives here?" Kat asked.

Frigg turned and smiled. "You do. I asked the servants to make a fire and stock it with food and drink. You are welcome here for as long as you like."

Kat stared at the trimmed hedges, the rose bushes that climbed the stone. "It's beautiful. Thank you."

"Thank me later after you've slept on the lumpy beds."

"I'm sure it's better than any place we've slept lately," Myrddin muttered.

Kat had walked inside when she noticed Bran on the stoop talking with Frigg. His eyes were focused on her low-cut bodice, his face flushed. Frigg's fingers moved to a curl that had come loose from her braid, a flirtatious smile on her face. She put a hand on Bran's arm for a moment before she called out, "Sleep well! We shall talk further in the morn!"

Bran stood in the doorway watching her go before he turned and headed inside.

A second later Kat rushed by him, heading into the garden to be sick. Once the contents of her stomach had been violently expelled, she kneeled on the ground, wondering why she'd made assumptions about Bran. They'd made love exactly once, and although they'd kissed several times, he had not told her he loved or indicated anything more about his feelings for her. Her eyes burned, her stomach still roiling as she picked herself up and walked slowly toward the open door.

"Are you all right?" Siobhan asked when she appeared on the stoop.

She shook her head, closed the door behind her and hurried to find a bedroom where she could be alone.

A month had gone by before the weather turned. It began with a blizzard that lasted for a week and then settled into a frigid cold that covered everything with a layer of ice. Kat vomited every day now, chills racking her body even when she was sitting in front of the fire. She was sick, but it was at least partly psychological. Bran had been absent for long periods nearly every day. She'd seen him walking with Frigg in the garden, had even watched them kiss.

This was the day she decided to spy on them, leaving the house soon after he did, and hiding behind trees and bushes. He met Frigg on the other side of the hedge, smiling down at her small form dwarfed by heavy furs. Her cheeks were rosy, her eyes bright as she tucked her arm through his. Kat crouched behind a gooseberry bush when they headed off toward a greenhouse on the other side of the garden. Through the glass she could make out the shapes of tall exotic-looking plants. As soon as they were inside, she hurried to peer through the windows.

Through the partially fogged glass she could see them

standing close together gazing at each other. It wasn't long before Frigg's fur coat was on the floor and Bran was unbuttoning her gown and tugging it off her shoulders. Frigg's golden hair lay loose around her very white shoulders, her gaze on Bran as he removed his leathers.

Kat wanted to leave, but she could not pull her gaze away. Frigg was tiny in his arms, her small breasted body almost childlike. But there was nothing childlike about what they were doing. Tears flowed down her face. She turned away and fled, trying not to hear the moans as they coupled.

Kat put a hand to her mouth, stopping to be violently ill. She gasped, wretched, tears running down her face, her stomach still heaving as she pushed herself up from her knees. She reached for snow to wash out her mouth, her tears frozen on her face, the image of them still etched in her mind. *He's not the same man, he's not the same man,* she told herself over and over, but it didn't stop the burning in her chest or the hollow feeling in her stomach. She'd totally misread the signs, and now she was paying the price for it.

She stumbled back to the cottage where she was supposed to be meeting with the others about the changed weather. Ragnarok had begun. But the real Ragnarok was inside her heart.

When she opened the door, the goddesses, Myrddin, and her mother turned toward her. "Where have you been?" Siobhan asked, frowning. "It's way too cold out there for a walk."

"I…I needed the fresh air," she lied, sinking into a chair.

"You look ill, Kat. You have not looked well for over a week now. What is going on?" Danu asked her, concerned.

Kat's hands went to her belly where her insides threatened. "I have the flu."

Siobhan's eyebrows pulled together in concern. "You look gray and you haven't been eating properly." She glanced around. "Where's Bran? He should be here for this discussion."

"He's with Frigg," she muttered.

"With Frigg?" Airmid asked. "Doing what? He's supposed to help us make a plan. He promised to be here."

"He's been gone for a couple of hours every day for two weeks," Rhiannon said, annoyed. "What is he playing at?"

Kat jumped up and ran from the room, racing toward the bedroom she'd appropriated, and swiping at her tears.

She was face down on the bed when her mother came inside. "Kat?"

Kat sat up. "He's with Frigg, Mom. Bran's with Frigg. He meets her every day and they have sex."

"What?" Siobhan frowned. "But he loves you."

"No, he doesn't love me. I assumed that this new Bran was the same as the old one, but I was terribly mistaken."

Siobhan came over to sit on the bed next to Kat. She reached to push the tangled hair back from her brow. "Are you really sick, Kat?"

"I've been throwing up every day. I'm always nauseated."

Siobhan looked her over, smiling sadly. "You aren't sick. You're pregnant."

Kat's heart seemed to stop beating for a second. "I can't be. We only had sex that one time, and…"

"You're pregnant, Kat."

Kat wiped her eyes. "How do you know?"

"Your body. Haven't you noticed the changes? Despite

being terribly thin, your breasts are bigger. You should remember from the last time."

"If I am, what should I do? Bran doesn't love me. If I tell him, he won't understand since he seems like the idiot version of his former self. He hasn't looked at me since we got here!"

"Frigg is very alluring. And she obviously had designs on him from the moment we appeared. She'll tire of him soon enough."

"And what good will that do? You think he'll come crawling back to me to assuage his pain?"

"Didn't Myrddin say he's connected to you? As I remember the wizard mentioned that his soul remembers you. You do realize that my husband, your father, was also besotted with Frigg. Dag admitted he had sex with her many times but he still came back to me."

"But you had a child together and a life. Dad loved you, Mom."

"Bran loves you, whether he knows it or not. And now you're carrying his child."

Kat wiped her eyes with her sleeve. "How can I concentrate on defeating the witch when I'm not only pregnant, but obsessed with a man who can't even see me?"

Siobhan let out a low chuckle. "You're Dagda's daughter. That's how." She reached for Kat's hand. "Come and be part of the discussion. It's meaningless without you, and it will take your mind off things."

When had her mother become so wise? Kat rose from the bed and wiped her tears on her sleeve. She took in a deep breath. "I guess I've been through worse things," she muttered, thinking about the last pregnancy. "Maybe this baby will have a normal gestation period and not turn into a monster."

Siobhan laughed. "I'm certain of it."

As soon as they returned Myrddin's eyes were on her, his eyebrows pinched into a frown. "Siobhan has spoken to you, I see. Are you ready to take up your place at the head of our little group? After all, you are the key player."

Kat nodded mutely, watching her mother head over to sit by Myrddin. Their hands brushed together as she sat down, their eyes meeting. Something was going on between them and she'd been too wrapped up in her own problems to notice. She glanced at the door but there was no sign of Bran.

She took in a deep breath, letting all her tangled thoughts drift away. "We know now that Ragnarok has begun. Soon there will be chaos on all fronts, including here. We know the mythology, and because of that we can decide what to do and when to do it. We are forewarned." She glanced at the door when it burst open, letting in a blast of snow and frigid air. Bran's dark eyes met hers before he slammed the door shut and strode toward the only chair left. "Sorry," he muttered, sitting down.

"Glad you deigned to join us," Kat said coldly, turning to look around at the others. "Now, first and foremost we have to stop the witch from forcing Ragnarok upon us before its time. Her interference in what has been set in place for millennia, has changed everything. Mior has insisted over and over that we have Jormungand's protection. That theory must be tested. I suggest we go back to Earth and find out what the dragon really thinks."

Mior, who was sitting on Airmid's lap, let out a whoop.

Kat smiled at him. "Mior will be in charge of speaking with Jormungand, with all of us at his back, of course. After that is completed, we will reconvene to decide what comes next."

"I like the plan," Airmid said, ruffling Mior's dark curls.

"I do too," Myrddin added. "First things first, I always say. My mother is a devious bitch, and I'm surprised she hasn't found us yet."

"Frigg put enchantments around the property to keep us safe," Bran said.

I bet she did, Kat thought. "We will leave for home at dawn tomorrow and don't forget to bring plenty of candles, water and food." She glanced around. "Any questions?"

"Are we coming back?" Bran asked.

Kat turned. "If you would rather remain here, we don't really need you," she told him coolly.

He frowned. "You do need me. I'm the only warrior god here."

"And I am a warrior *goddess*," Kat replied. "And you still haven't properly recovered from your ordeal."

Bran rose to his feet, furious. "I am fully recovered, ask Frigg."

Kat shook her head in disbelief. "Do you really think that screwing Frigg signifies recovery, Bran? I doubt it does. In fact, if I were to comment on your recent behavior, I would say it's weakened you considerably."

There was a collective gasp before Bran's eyes narrowed dangerously. "*She* doesn't see me as weak."

"As I said before, you are welcome to stay behind." Kat was shaking as she glanced at the group staring at her wide-eyed. She clasped her hands together in front of her. "Everyone else, be ready before dawn. This meeting is adjourned." With that Kat rose and walked sedately toward her room without looking back.

As soon as she was inside with the door closed, she burst into tears. When she glanced outside later, she saw a raven floating in the air, very black against the still white world. He hovered for a moment and then disappeared into the falling snow. She turned away, her pulse pounding. It had taken every bit of will power to say what she did. She felt drained and exhausted, her heart a heavy weight in her chest.

Dawn came too soon, Kat's sleep nearly nonexistent. Would Bran come with them or choose to stay here with Frigg? Odin had been gone for at least two weeks, his absence all the incentive Frigg needed. But he would surely arrive soon, especially with the changes in the weather. And when he did return there would be hell to pay. He did not like it when Frigg screwed other men behind his back.

She took in a breath and rose from the warm bed to glance out the window, not surprised to see another foot of snow had fallen since the night before. They were leaving here in the nick of time.

The large oak wardrobe stood open, revealing the heavy wool pants Frigg had left for her. The goddess had provided them all with a change of clothes, and if it hadn't been for what she was doing with Bran, Kat would have felt very differently about her. Surely she remembered Kat's feelings for the god when they were here the last time. But this Bran didn't look the same or act the same. Fair game.

Kat tugged on the pants and pulled on her sweater that had seen better days. Thick socks and boots came next. When she glanced in the mirror it revealed a pale and tired face with dark circles under her eyes. Her hair was a dark tangle around it. She reached back to yank it into two messy braids that she secured with leather strips. She thought of Frigg with her beautiful low-cut dresses as she stared at the filthy sweater and unbecoming wool pants, wondering why she, as a half-goddess, was so affected by the cold. Obviously, Frigg and Bran could go naked and not feel a thing, as evidenced by the two of them in the greenhouse. One last look in the mirror uncovered the sadness in her eyes, before she grabbed her wool cloak and tugged open the door.

Each person carried a leather bag filled with necessities as they trooped into the deep snow. The air was so cold that it froze the flakes as they hit her face. Frigg was suddenly there, her smile focused on the tattooed god. "I will miss you," she whispered, before turning to the group. "I wish you well on your travels, and if you ever need me you know where to find me."

Kat happened to glance back a moment later, her gut wrenching when she saw Bran pull Frigg into his arms and kiss her deeply.

When Kat took off under the trees to retch, Siobhan followed. "Sweet girl," she murmured, helping her stand and wiping off her face. "Do not let this get to you. Myrddin says this Bran is very unaware—that he barely understands himself or what he's doing. He's like a newborn babe trying out new things."

Kat was shaking all over. "How can I not, Mom? He doesn't care about me at all. And this baby," she muttered, her hands going to her belly. "It shouldn't exist."

"And yet it does. And Bran decided to come with us instead of staying here with Frigg. I have a strong feeling that things will work out between you two."

Kat took in a deep shuddering breath before following her mother back to where everyone waited. She tried very hard not to look at Bran, keeping her focus on what she needed to do to get herself back to Earth.

Kat had turned into Hummingbird and was facing into the wind and snow when she heard a caw and noticed Raven flying next to her. He spread his dark wings, shielding her tiny body from the storm as they flew side by side. Hummingbird was wary, but also knew that without Raven she would not have been able to stay in the air.

Kat sat cross-legged in the dark, seven lit candles in a circle around her. Earth's energy was wrong and she was trying to fix it. If she didn't, they would all succumb to what the witch had left behind.

"Can I help?"

Kat looked up to see Bran standing in front of her. "No."

Bran seemed confused for a moment as he stared at her. "You don't like me anymore?"

Kat sighed. "I can't talk to you, Bran. You wouldn't understand."

He squatted next to her. "Why not? You could before."

"Go away. I need to concentrate."

He stared at her for a moment before he rose and disappeared into the darkness.

"Danu, if you are close, I ask for your help," Kat murmured.

"I am here," the goddess said, lowering herself to the ground next to her. "Shall I call my sisters?"

Kat nodded.

It was a long time of chanting and intricate spells and mudras before something seemed to shift around them. "It is done," the priestess inside Kat intoned, folding forward in thanks. The four goddesses pressed their hands together and closed their eyes.

"When can I talk to the dragon?" Mior pestered. He'd been at Kat all day about it, his impatience beginning to grate.

"We had a few things to do before sending you on some wild goose chase, Mior. I don't want you to get hurt. Are you even sure he's still up there? It's so dark it's impossible to see."

"He's there. I can feel him. I can call to him and he'll come. Can I?"

Kat grabbed him and hugged him close. "You are trying my patience, you little monster. Go find Myrddin and we can talk about it, okay?"

Mior pulled out of her arms and ran, his voice echoing as he called out for the wizard.

Kat pushed the tangled hair back from her face. Their re-entry into this new dark world had them all on edge. Chanting notwithstanding, there was something unnerving about not being able to see and having the sky look like an endless black hole. Murmuring voices lifted into the strangely still air as the goddesses talked amongst themselves. She heard her mother say something about the baby, who was now without Frigg's supply of milk. She was trying to get her used to real food, but Tus Nua preferred the breast. A second later she heard running feet and Mior was panting next to her. "Myrddin's coming," Mior said.

"You need me?"

Kat started with the sudden appearance of the wizard. "I can't get used to this utter darkness," she muttered.

"Luckily, I can see in the dark, just like my mother. Mior is chomping at the bit about Jormungand. Is it time?"

"That's what I wanted to ask you. Is there any reason to wait?"

"I'm remembering the last time I had to rescue Mior."

"You thought you had to rescue me!" Mior yelled. "He wasn't hurting me!"

Myrddin ignored his outburst. "If we summon him, we must know what we want."

"We want his help to defeat the witch."

"He's already helping us," Mior chimed in. "He's waiting until the time is right."

"Okay, Mior, since you seem to know what's going on, is this the right time?"

Mior frowned. "The witch isn't here, but…" He looked up. "I don't know."

Kat let out a humorless chuckle. "He isn't a creature to mess around with, Mior. I know you would like to play with him, but this is serious."

Mior's face dropped. "But you said we needed to know if he's on our side. Isn't that why we're here?"

"Yes…" Kat answered. "But we…"

"I will go along for protection."

Kat tried to see the wizard in the dark, only able to make out the gray hair. "Can you save him if something goes wrong?"

Myrddin nodded. "Go, Mior," he said.

Mior climbed what had been the hill that led to the spring and the cave. The only one who could see him was Myrddin, who recounted what was happening. "He's there now and he's waving his hands."

Kat could hear her brother shouting and then a sound like thunder rumbled across the sky. When she looked up, she could see the bright golden scales, the enormous fiery head that moved downward.

"Myrddin, why aren't you up there?" Siobhan whispered, grabbing his sleeve.

"I'm going now." A second later he vanished.

They all held their breath as the creature moved closer still, a green-gold eye the size of a Mack truck focused on Mior's shadowy form. Myrddin joined him a moment later. The creature ignored Myrddin as he seemed to cock his head, listening.

Mior's shouting was lost in the sound of the creature's breathing, smoke rising as he lowered even further. And then he was moving away, a thundering roar sending vibrations across the bare land.

A moment later the dragon was gone and Mior was shouting as he ran toward them. "He said yes!" He ran straight into Kat, nearly knocking her down.

Kat grabbed him. "But what does that mean? What did you ask?"

"It's what I told you before. He's on our side."

Myrddin reappeared and laughed, putting an arm around Siobhan to pull her close. "Your son is a miracle."

Bran brushed against Kat. "Mior isn't afraid of anything, is he?"

Kat glanced up at the god, trying not to care that he was

so close that she could feel his heat. She stepped away and crossed her arms over her chest. "Doesn't appear to be," she answered.

"But what if the dragon is needed somewhere else? Is the battle going to happen here?" Siobhan asked, her voice shaking. "I don't know how long I can live in the dark."

"I'm planning to bring back the light, Mom."

"How do you do that?"

"It came to me when I was meditating. But once the light comes back, the witch will be drawn here."

Bran had moved close again, his hand on her arm. "I can help."

Kat jerked away from him. "Maybe Raven can help, but I doubt you can," she muttered.

"Raven?"

"Raven seems to know me and what I'm about. You do not."

"Why are you so angry with me?"

"Ask the wizard."

Bran searched out the wizard, his scattered thoughts sending conflicting ideas racing through his mind. As Raven, everything had seemed normal. He and Hummingbird were close and he protected her on the way back to Earth. But once they shifted into human form Kat had turned on him, shouting at him to back off and leave her alone. He remembered how close they'd been when he was injured, how when he kissed her, his body settled. He hadn't kissed her in a long time.

Frigg appeared in his mind and he was immediately in a state of arousal. When he kissed her, it was different than when he kissed Kat. Something was missing, but he didn't know what it was. He enjoyed what they did together, her body twisting and writhing under his as he did what she wanted him to do. She ordered him, told him what she desired. Kat didn't do that. Kat waited until he made the first move. But why was Kat angry?

"I heard you were looking for me," the wizard said, appearing next to him.

"Kat told me to ask you why she's angry with me."

Myrddin peered at him, noticing the complete lack of guile in his eyes. "You really don't know, do you?"

"She used to be nice to me."

Myrddin let out a heavy sigh, pushing his hands through his hair. "Women are complicated, Bran. And they don't like it when the men they're involved with decide to bed another. Kat is angry about Frigg. She thought you cared for her."

"I do care for her. But Frigg wanted me. I couldn't say no to a goddess like that."

"The former Bran would have turned Frigg down. That's the one Kat remembers. He's the one who loved her so much that he gave up his god powers for her."

"But I don't remember that life."

Myrddin sighed again. "I realize that. Perhaps there is some way to retrieve those memories. You were once the god of prophecy. That would seem to indicate knowledge that is not readily available to others. You and Kat have a deep connection that spans time. If you can look into the past perhaps you will find it."

Bran stared into the distance, not at all sure what the wizard was talking about. "When I'm Raven, I feel a need to protect Hummingbird."

"Ah, yes. Raven is the same as he was, while the Bran you were has changed. I will think on this and see if an idea arises. But until then why don't you talk this over with Kat?"

"She won't let me near her."

Myrddin chuckled. "Try again, dear boy, and keep trying until you wear her down."

Bran puzzled over the wizard's words as he walked through the total darkness. He had the sick feeling again. He heard Kat before he could see her, her voice echoing as she spoke to the goddesses, directing them in her newest scheme.

"I know where to find the stars," she said. "And I can coax the sun from where it hides. The witch didn't get rid of these things, she only hid them from us. If the sun is back, the moon will follow."

Bran moved into the circle of light from the many candles. "The wizard said for me to talk to you," he muttered. "I feel the sickness again."

Kat gazed at him. She laughed. "That ploy will get you nowhere. I'm busy right now."

"Please. I don't understand and I..."

"I'm not falling for that crap, Bran. It worked before you spent every waking moment screwing Frigg. But not now."

"Frigg ordered me. She said she needed my body to..."

Kat glared at him. "Get the hell away from me!" She raised her hand and sent him flying.

Airmid chuckled and Morrighan laughed outright. "What a bastard," Rhiannon murmured. "I have sworn off men."

"Bran is sincere," Danu whispered. "He is honestly clueless."

Bran heard them from where he lay in the dark. His arm hurt and his cheek had landed on a sharp rock. When his fingers touched the spot, they came away bloody. He pushed himself to standing and rushed away, his lower belly rumbling with distress. A few minutes later his guts twisted and he had to stop and pull off his leathers. He squatted in the dirt moaning as the sickness took him, his belly cramping.

Kat felt badly. Danu had explained that Bran didn't understand what he'd done to hurt her. "He's like an idiot savant, Katel. He lives in the moment and does what the moment calls for. He has no hidden agenda. If Frigg wanted him then he gave her what she wanted. I'm not saying he didn't enjoy it. What man wouldn't? But he was not thinking about you or your feelings, because he is not capable of that."

"What do I do, Danu? I still love him."

"And you're carrying his child," Danu said, dark eyes meeting hers.

"Not sure how you know that, but yes, I am, which complicates things even further. I can't have a relationship with a man who follows every whim that comes into his brain. And I can't teach him how to love, either."

"It is possible that he will recall his former self. You could facilitate it by being there for him, by loving him."

Kat shook her head, tears welling. "It hurts too much when he rejects me."

Danu gazed at her. "Without Frigg to get in the way, I doubt he'll reject you."

Kat thought about that for a minute or two. "But any time another woman happens by there's the chance he'll be led astray. I can't live like that. And what about this baby? He's like a child himself."

"I cannot tell you what to do. But if this was my problem, I would put my feelings aside and try to explain the truth. If he's like a child he has the capacity to learn. And if you haven't noticed, he has not looked upon any of us the way he looks at you."

"I hadn't noticed. It sounds like what you're saying is his thing with Frigg was an anomaly brought on by her lust."

"Exactly so. Give him a chance and see where it goes. It cannot hurt."

But Kat knew it *could* hurt.

Kat was sitting cross-legged, planning a way to find the stars when she felt someone come up behind her. The candle flickered when she turned to see Bran's leather clad legs behind her. She ignored him as she sought the right path to uncover the light. She'd pulled out all the stops in her power toolbox for this one.

"Kat? I need to talk to you."

"Sit," she ordered. "I'm in the middle of something so make it quick."

He sat next to her. "I have the sickness very bad. My

stomach hurts. I need to kiss you."

Kat lips pressed together in annoyance. "Did you have this sickness around Frigg?"

"No. It isn't the same with her. Please. I'll leave you alone after that. Just one kiss. My belly is letting go all the time now. I can't eat the food I brought back from Asgard."

Kat stared at him. "How long?"

"Ever since that day you wouldn't talk to me."

That was more than a week ago. He did look gaunt and his eyes were sunken. What if he was really sick? "There could be something else going on. Have you had any other symptoms?"

"Symptoms? What does that mean?"

"Any other feelings in your body that aren't normally there."

"My eyes water sometimes. And it hurts here." He pressed his hand to his chest.

Kat gazed into his sad eyes, suddenly sorry for him. "Okay, but only one kiss."

When his lips touched hers, Kat was transported to a garden filled with light. Birds sang and she heard a child laughing.

He let out a low moan and pulled her closer. "I...I...want you."

Kat wanted him too. Badly. But she managed to pull out of his embrace. "We kissed. That's all I can give you for now. I don't trust you."

He looked completely undone. "Why?"

"You don't love me and you just spent weeks and weeks screwing another woman."

"I…I don't know what love is. And Frigg *told* me to do the things I did. If felt good to both of us, but it wasn't the same."

"The same—as with me?"

He nodded. "She didn't cure the sickness."

"You said you didn't have the sickness when you were with her."

"That's right. I didn't. Why do I have it now?"

"You just don't understand the symptoms."

"The symptoms of love?"

"Yes."

When he abruptly shifted to Raven, the candle flame wavered and nearly blew out, the feel of feathers brushing against her. The bird pressed his soft downy head into Kat's palm. She stroked his feathers, feeling Raven's confusion and sadness. When he returned to human form, he looked utterly bereft, his eyes limned with unhappiness.

"Come here, you idiot," she murmured, reaching for him. And this time she didn't stop him when his hands roamed under her clothing.

37

The viscous substance oozed as she tugged it loose. Everything glowed, the shimmer blinding. The stretch of stars was endless, galaxies disappearing into galaxies. The stars were where they'd always been, but the curse had covered them. Her fingers worked the spells as she searched for the single spot where the dark curtain was the thinnest. Jormungand watched her, his bright scales showing her the way. She heard him in her mind, his support giving her strength as she pulled and fought with the dark. It was hours before she discovered the tiny tear that let light through. It was the size of a pin but it was enough. One finger pressing through, then another. The sound of ripping. The shriek as it began to tear and come apart. She jerked and pulled, gathering the dark into her arms bit by bit, and shredding it in her mind. It fell from her fingers like bits of dark dust and drifted away. The moon was suddenly there, a bright orb that lit up the sky. And behind it the milky way was so bright that Kat had to close her eyes.

Kat woke on her back, her eyelids warm from the

sunlight that streamed down from a cloudless sky. She sat up and opened her eyes, looking around the desert that was now Earth. Her heart sank. But in the next moment she realized that if she could do this, she and the others could bring Earth back to what it had once been. She and Mior had managed it before. When she looked up Bran was walking toward her, a wide smile lighting up his eyes.

"You did it," he murmured, sitting next to her. "I knew you could."

"How long have I been here?"

"Days, Kat. It's been three days."

He watched her, seemingly waiting for her to reach for him, but Kat turned away, too enervated to consider the look in his eyes. She was tired of wanting something she couldn't have.

"All well and good," Myrddin said later when they were all gathered together. "But we all know that Mother will recognize what's happened here. We should prepare for her arrival."

"Can't we have a moment to enjoy the sun?" Siobhan whined.

Myrddin turned, his eyes going soft. "Yes, yes of course. I didn't mean to take away your moment of happiness, Siobhan."

"Myrddin is right, though," Kat said. "Carmun will attack. And we need to be ready this time."

For the next week everyone was on edge as they waited for disaster to strike. Myrddin had headed into the ether to find food, bringing back several already cooked rabbits and a bunch of cheese and bread. He also had a skin filled with wine. "Won't last forever, but it will get us through the next few days," he said, handing Siobhan a hunk of cheese.

The baby was the only one unhappy, her screams setting everyone's already frazzled nerves on edge. Danu finally grabbed her from Siobhan, disappearing up the hill with Tus Nua in her arms. When she returned sometime later the baby was sound asleep.

"What did you do?" Siobhan asked, holding out her arms.

"I fed her," Danu said.

"You…how?" Kat asked.

Danu laughed. "You do know that I'm the mother goddess. I fed her in the usual way."

Why didn't you say earlier?" Siobhan asked, gazing down at the sleeping child. "We could have avoided hours of screaming."

"I decided not to offer until there was no other option. I knew you were trying to wean her. But the noise finally stirred me into action."

Siobhan laughed. "Thank you."

The other goddesses had been restless of late, their minds turning toward their home. Kat could see it in their eyes. "As soon as she attacks you can leave," she told them one night as they were sitting around the fire.

"If we defeat her, that is," Airmid reminded her.

"Well, yes. But I think we will with Jormungand here."

But the expression in Airmid's eyes was unsure. It was later when everyone had found their places for the night that Kat went to Airmid. "You're worried. Why?"

"I have an intuition that it won't be so easy. She's gaining strength. We are strong, but we don't have the resources she does. Her magic is far more powerful."

"We have Jormungand."

"Possibly. But there is the chance that he has befriended Mior but will not fight against his father. Loki will come with her this time."

Kat gazed into the distance. "Loki starts this thing, but according to Frigg, it begins with…"

"Yes, a terrible winter, and our weather is warm at the moment. Leave Ragnarok for a moment and think about what Carmun wants."

Kat narrowed her eyes. "She wants me."

Airmid nodded. "And why does she want you, Kat?"

"Because there's a prophecy that says I will kill her."

"You know from all the great texts that these sorts of prophecies are known to bring disaster. She wishes to reverse it before it begins."

"If left to run its course, what would happen do you think?"

Airmid shrugged. "It's hard to say. Perhaps it is a false prophecy, propagated to bring a false Ragnarok."

"But who started it?"

She raised her eyebrows. "Could be Loki, or perhaps one of our gods—maybe Camulos, the god of war. There has not been a real conflict in a very long time. The gods thrive on conflict."

"Humans do too," Kat muttered. "But false or not, it will happen. And it will play out like Ragnarok."

"Not necessarily. Not if you stop it before it begins."

The next morning Kat called a meeting to discuss what she'd been up all night thinking about. The sun was out, although there was no sign of life around them, the dirt and downed trees and rock-strewn landscape still a depressing mess. They all sat in a circle as they'd been doing for the past weeks, candles lit despite the brightness. They began with a moment of silence in which they all closed their eyes, hands held in prayer position, before Kat began to speak.

"I'm going to find Carmun before she discovers us. I will need your help, Myrddin, to suss out her Achilles heel—everyone has a weak spot. I…"

"I'll go with you," Bran interrupted.

Kat glanced at him, sorry for what she'd allowed to happen. He had no real memory of her. Things would never work between them. "I must do this alone, Bran. The prophecy says the dark goddess will prevail. Apparently, *I* am the dark goddess, the one who destroys evil."

"I will give you all I can," the wizard said. "Carmun has a flair for the dramatic which could be a weakness, I suppose."

Kat scoffed. "I'll need more than that."

"How will you find her?" Siobhan asked in alarm. "Your condition, Kat—you need to…"

"I've already worked that out, Mom," Kat interrupted, widening her eyes at Siobhan. When she glanced around it didn't seem as though anyone had picked up on her mother's unthinking statement. Except Danu, who already knew. "I will use the talents I've been given by the gods. I have Hummingbird for travel, the priestess for strength and my own goddess status for the rest of it."

"Didn't Frigg say she saw darkness in your future?" Siobhan asked.

"That could mean there was nothing to see at that moment. Everything we do changes the future, Mom. Fate is a meandering line, not a fixed point. Bringing back the stars and the sun and moon has to count for something."

Siobhan shook her head and stared down at the baby sleeping in her lap, a frown on her face.

"We are prepared to fight by your side," Morrigan said, glancing at her sisters.

"Whatever you need," Rhiannon added, pushing her mane of wild red hair away from her face.

Kat nodded. "I can reach you through the ether if I need you. But my meditations have told me that I must go alone."

"I am at your beck and call," Myrddin said.

Kat glanced at the wizard before she rose from her cross-legged position. She beckoned to him and headed away.

They walked together in silence for a while before Myrddin said, "My mother is very devious. She will not want to kill you outright, she prefers the cat and mouse game she's playing. She enjoys toying with your emotions and setting your nerves on edge."

"I gathered that. She could have killed me a dozen times over. I would rather not kill her, either."

Myrddin made a choking sound. "You think you can win without killing her?"

Kat shrugged. "I haven't had a vision of how to do it, but yes, I do."

Myrddin fingers ran through his gray tangle. "She is vain. She loves looking young and beautiful. She's obsessed with sex. If you can take away the source of her youth, you will gain the upper hand."

"The source is the energy she sucks from everyone around her. How can I stop that flow?"

"You will need to remove her young male followers. She can't last a day before she'll need their attentions again."

"She'll turn back into the hideous hag I saw rise from the depths?"

Myrddin nodded. "And she does not like that particular persona."

"It seems from what you're saying that she's like the undead or a vampire that needs blood in order to live."

Myrddin's expression went from open to guarded. "Carmun is a force of nature, Katel. She's more powerful than the goddesses you've collected, or the gods that reside in Otherworld or in the Norse realm. She may be more powerful than Loki."

Kat watched his eyes darken. "You don't know, do you?"

Myrddin frowned at her before he vanished, leaving a puff of gray smoke behind.

38

As soon as Kat returned, her mother grabbed her and moved away from the others. "Have you told Bran about the baby?"

"No, Mom. He wouldn't understand. It would be disastrous."

"I saw you with him yesterday. Are you two, you know…?"

Kat laughed. "Having sex?" she whispered. "We did yesterday, but that doesn't mean we're together. He's unaware of the most basic things."

"He needs to know. And it isn't fair of you to put the baby you're carrying in jeopardy."

"This is my destiny. I haven't had any visions about the baby, good or otherwise. If I lose it, then so be it. Maybe it wasn't meant to be."

Siobhan's eyes went wide. "You can't mean that!"

"I do mean it. Stopping the witch is my highest priority right now."

"If you told Bran I bet he wouldn't let you go."

Kat laughed. "He has no control over me. And I very much doubt he would try. Raven is the wiser of the two of them. Raven has old Bran within him, Mom. There is little future for us unless Bran changes. I can't be saddled with him the way he is now."

"He's a warrior god. That has to mean something."

Kat shook her head, her eyes welling. "Fighting? That is the last thing I want from him right now."

"Kat...I worry so about you. You seem so different lately."

"I am different. What happened at the castle changed me. I realized that getting caught up in emotion does no good. Let's talk about you and Myrddin for a second—what's going on there?"

Siobhan's face turned bright red. "He...we...he seems to like me, that's all."

Kat grinned. "He's wooing you. Are you interested?"

"I still miss your father too much to get involved that way. But the attention feels nice after everything we've gone through."

Kat leaned in to give her mom a hug. "Stay safe while I'm gone. And let yourself go for once. You never know what the future holds."

"That's what Myrddin keeps saying."

As soon as Kat was away from her mother, she regretted what she'd told her. It was all lies. She did want this baby. And she did want Bran. But her duty lay elsewhere. All she could hope for was that the baby was meant to be and that Bran would eventually remember his past. Until that time, she had to concentrate on ending this thing.

She was meditating later when she had a vision of Val. He was battling Arwen, his face filled with rage.

"Tell that bitch to leave me alone!" Val shouted. "Your mother thinks I tried to kill Bran!"

"Fuck off, old man!" Arwen yelled back. "Do you think I give a good god damn about my mother? You're so fucking weak you don't stand a chance against Carmun!" Arwen laughed and slammed his fist into Val's face, sending him reeling backward. He fell with a sickening crack as his head hit stone.

Kat's eyes flew open, her hand going to her mouth where a scream lodged in her throat. Val had told her the truth, and now he could be lying dead in Alfheim. A second later she was filled with adrenaline. It was time to go.

Hummingbird flew high into the clouds, some inner force driving her on. When the storm hit, she was caught by the wind and pulled off course, irridescent wings unable to keep her aloft. She tumbled over and over as she fell, her tiny bird heart giving in to the shriek of wind and the icy rain that slanted toward her.

Kat woke in a forest, her thoughts tangling as she tried to remember who she was and why she was here. She heard a whisper and peered into the shadows to see three mocha-skinned women wearing hooded cloaks. They were surrounded with shimmering light and stood clustered together, not five feet away. All three had long gray hair trailing across their shoulders. Their skin was unlined but it was obvious by their deep-set eyes and the wisdom that shone forth, that they were ancient. She jumped to her feet.

"We are the Norns, the spinners of fate," they murmured as one, the different tones melding together.

Kat stared at the larger than life women, her gaze going to the pale, diaphanous gowns peeking out from under their cloaks. They looked like they belonged in the clouds somewhere. She opened her mouth but was unable to utter a word.

"I am Urd," the one on the left said. "I weave what once was."

"And I am Verdandi," the woman next to her continued. "I weave what is coming into being."

"And I am Skuld," the third goddess pronounced, her voice deep and resonant. "I weave what is to be."

When Skuld's forbidding gaze met hers, Kat took a step back. She was far more imposing than the others.

"What do you want with me?" Kat whispered.

Skuld's frown deepened. "You are about to interfere in our labors."

When Kat took another step back, she ran into the trunk of a tree. She cleared her throat. "Your labors? I'm on my way to rid the world of the witch. Is that what you're talking about?"

Urd nodded, her expression solemn. "I am in charge of what once was. Evil will always exist. There is no ridding the world of discord. Opposition is what keeps it all in balance."

"But the witch has to be stopped. There is a prophecy that says that I'm the one to rid the world of evil. I'm the dark goddess."

The three goddesses regarded her impassively before Verdandi leaned forward to peer at her. "I am aware of your part in this. It is written. But it is *my* job to weave what is coming into being, not yours."

Kat gazed at the goddess whose eyes were the color of a stormy sea. "But I've been called upon to do this," she managed to squeak out of a throat gone dry. "My destiny is entwined with that of the witch."

"Destiny," Skuld said scornfully. "*I* am the one who weaves what shall be. This dispute will never be resolved. What happens is for *us* to say. It is not for *you* to decide."

Kat was suddenly afraid. There was something unnerving about the three goddesses. The dispute would never be resolved? A shiver went down her spine as she felt their power. It filled the forest and twined inside her, leaving her feeling helpless. "The witch is bringing darkness to all things. She wants to take away all light. What would you have me do?"

Skuld threw her hood back, tangled gray hair spilling across her hunched shoulders, dark eyes fixing Kat with a menacing stare. "Verdandi is the one to make that decision. It is she who weaves what is coming into being, and that design is only partially completed. This is why we are here."

Kat had to look away, any power she thought she had disappearing in that instant. "I have to stop her somehow," she muttered. "I don't want to kill her. I understand that good and evil must exist side by side to keep the balance. It's the way of the world. But Carmun wants evil to prevail and to last forever. Everything will die."

Verdandi turned to Urd. "And what say you, my sister? You have been at this longer than we have."

Urd gazed toward Kat, her forehead creasing. "The pendulum swings back and forth, more good this time, more evil the next. But in the end, it always balances out. This witch you speak of does seem to threaten that balance. I see now that she is becoming too powerful. But I weave the past, not the future. It will be up to my sisters to decide your fate."

Kat turned to glance at Skuld, her gaze going from the most imposing goddess to Verdandi, whose eyes were filled with kindness. "You both hold the fate of the universe in your hands. Would you want perpetual darkness to be the result of your weavings?"

Skuld frowned and glanced at her sister. "It is up to you, Verdandi. I take my cues from what you decide."

"This is a conundrum," Verdandi answered, "but with what I have just heard, I must carefully consider what this earth creature is telling us. Darkness cannot take all the light. That is not balance. And the pendulum will never swing back if that occurs."

"That's what I'm saying!" Kat cried out. "But how do I stop her without tipping the scales?" Kat waited for an answer, hoping they would tell her exactly how to handle the situation, but instead they began to fade, until there was only the shimmer of where they'd been. Verdandi's words played over and over in her mind. If darkness took over, the pendulum would never swing back. But they hadn't said how to stop the witch. She put her head in her hands, trying to sort through her tangled thoughts. The only thing she knew for sure was that she wouldn't have wanted those three against her.

Kat wandered for hours trying to figure out where she was and what came next. Her mind drifted as she meandered through woods so full of vegetation she could barely pass through them. And once she found her way out, there were endless meadows that stretched into valleys steeped in mists. Everything shimmered with magic. She could feel it like thick honey. *Magic is magic,* she thought to herself. *It can be used for good or evil.*

When she saw the castle, she realized that this was the same woods where she'd first met newly formed Bran and where the witch lived. It was barely recognizable without the snow. Had the witch changed the weather to suit herself? Myrddin's suggestions of taking aim at her vanity flew through her mind. If she could just stop the flow of energy that kept the witch young...she pushed aside the heavy vines and worked her way toward the path that led to the imposing edifice in the distance.

Once she came out into the open Kat saw the witch and Arwen heading for the gate that led out of the bailey. Her heart stuttered for a second, dizziness washing over her. She took in a deep breath and went to meet them.

"She's here," the witch said, gazing at Arwen. "Your mother has finally come. And she's alone this time."

Arwen frowned, peering into the distance where a lone figure moved along the path. "I'd like to see that bitch go down."

Carmun smoothed his frown lines with her fingers, caressing his cheek before she took away her hand. "Anger is not the way, Arwen. In order to prevail you must quell your rage. It takes a quiet mind to work the spells necessary to eliminate your enemies."

"My father is still alive, if that's what you're referring to. I hurt him badly, but he didn't die."

"I'm glad to hear that. Patricide can cause a person to go mad. Now, come along. We want to greet our guest at the gate."

Arwen looked back at the closed castle door. He had forgotten to bring his cloak and he was already cold. "What about the others?"

"They are all in their beds recovering."

Arwen looked confused. "Recovering from what?"

"From being drained of their precious energy," the witch replied, smiling. "Just look at me!" she said, twirling in a circle. Shiny black hair flew outward, her face rosy. "Would you like to bed me, young Arwen?"

Arwen blushed to the roots of his hair. "I...I hadn't considered it."

Carmun laughed. "It will imbue you with more of my power—wouldn't you like that?"

Arwen stared at her. "I suppose so," he said hesitantly.

Carmen made a moue of disappointment. "You are too young, it seems. But until the others are restored, I will need you to step up."

Arwen's eyes went wide. "You mean I have to screw you?"

Carmun laughed and hooked a finger under his chin. "Coming to my bed is an initiation that all my male devotees must complete. If you cannot follow through, well...you will not be part of my inner circle."

Arwen's mouth dropped open. "But I know nothing..."

"About the sexual act? I will teach you." She smiled coquettishly and unlocked the gate.

The day was nearly gone, the wide dome of sky streaked with bright color as the sun dropped toward the horizon. The land was a disaster but there was still the sunlight and the clouds to enjoy now that Kat had brought back the light. "Are you sure you shouldn't follow her?" Siobhan asked Myrddin, clutching his sleeve.

Myrddin took her hand in his. "If I feel that I'm needed I will go. Let her get her bearings and make a plan. It will not do her any good to have me hovering around."

Siobhan gazed at him, her eyes welling. "She's pregnant with Bran's baby. She hasn't told him. And this is a critical time for her to be overstressed and putting herself in danger."

Myrddin smiled, patting her hand. "Kat is stronger than you think. She knows what she's up against. Try not to worry." He peered at her. "I think it's time for us to take this thing between us one step further, don't you?"

Siobhan stared at him in shock. "I…I'm not ready."

"Siobhan. Your husband has been gone for over six

months now. He isn't coming back. I am very attracted to you. And I know you feel the same. What possible harm could come from spending the night holding each other?"

Siobhan smiled. "If it was only holding, maybe. But there's no privacy here. We live in a flat desert of nothingness where everyone can spy on everyone else's business."

"I'm can conjure us a private place. I will not push anything until you feel ready."

"You have a reputation. Kat told me about Nimue. What about her?"

Myrddin stared off into space. "Nimue sealed me into a cave for thousands of years. It's a wonder I was able to escape. There are trust issues between us."

Siobhan let out a shaky laugh. "I would think there would be, after something like that!"

Myrddin put his arm around her shoulders. "Tonight then?"

Siobhan turned when she heard a subtle cough. "Oh, Airmid," she said, extricating herself from under Myrddin's arm. "What do you think about this situation with Kat? Can she manage to keep herself safe?"

"I cannot say for sure. But I do know that she's very resourceful. I have faith in her and you should too. What she needs now is all of our positive thoughts. They will penetrate through the ether and give her confidence."

"Positive thoughts? For what?" Bran asked, joining them.

Airmid turned to the god. "For Kat. She's with the witch."

"Already?"

Airmid nodded. "And now is the most critical time for

her. If Carmun is able to push her off balance, the witch will gain the upper hand."

"Yes," Morrighan agreed, appearing at Airmid's side. "I suggest we light the candles and form a circle."

Siobhan clapped her hands. "Great idea!"

"Can I come too?" Mior asked.

Kat felt a subtle shift, as though a light had been switched on all around her.

The witch watched her curiously, a frown appearing on her face. "Your friends are with you. I can see them. And you are carrying a child."

Kat ignored her, watching Arwen. "How is your father?" she asked him. "I saw what you did."

"He's fine. Just a lump on his head," he muttered.

"Glad to hear that. I was worried."

"Come, my dear. Let us have a cup of tea and discuss our options," Carmun said, taking hold of her arm. Her skin seemed to sag for a moment, lines appearing around her mouth and on her cheeks, her eyes losing their brightness. She shook herself and glanced at Arwen. "It seems I will need you to do your duty sooner than I thought," she muttered.

Arwen made a choking sound and stared at the ground.

Kat glanced at Carmun, wondering what duty Arwen was slated to perform, but before she could puzzle over it the witch said, "Your son will service me as the others have been doing since I arrived."

Kat glanced at Arwen who looked ready to puke. He

was too young for what Carmun had in mind. She could kill him. When she turned, Carmun was watching her with narrowed eyes, a smile hovering around her mouth. *I know all about you*, Kat heard in her mind. *This baby is not long for this world.* Carmun let out a cackle and led the way into the castle.

Once they were inside, Carmun grabbed Arwen and dragged him away. The last thing Kat saw was Arwen's pinched features, the terror in his eyes as they rounded a corner and disappeared.

"She knows," Myrddin muttered. They had made a circle and lit the candles, all of them focusing their energy on Kat.

"Who knows what?" Bran asked.

Myrddin glanced at the god. "My mother knows that Kat carries your baby."

Bran's eyes went wide, his brow furrowing. "What baby? I don't understand."

Airmid put a hand on his arm. "You and Kat were intimate a number of months ago, Bran. The night you first met in the woods by Carmun's castle? That's when it happened."

Bran stared at the flame for a moment before he pushed himself up to his feet and strode away. By now the sun had set, and shadows had gathered, taking him quickly into the darkness.

"You shouldn't have told him," Siobhan whispered, glaring at Myrddin. "Kat said he wouldn't understand and I think she was right. Did you see the look on his face?"

"He had to find out sometime," Airmid murmured. "Perhaps it's better for him to hear it from us."

"He's barely capable of coherent thought," Danu muttered. "I think it's time we give him back his memories."

"You can do that?" Siobhan asked.

Danu nodded. "I had planned to talk to Kat about this, but she left before I could broach the subject. What do you three say?" she asked, glancing at the other goddesses.

"It's the right thing to do," Rhiannon agreed. "He's like a lost little boy without them."

"But it's meddling," Myrddin warned. "He was reborn as this Bran, not the one before. You will be restoring memories he doesn't have."

Siobhan glanced at the wizard. "Kat said that Raven has the old Bran's memories."

"That might be true, but it doesn't mean..."

A harsh caw interrupted the wizard, echoing in the silence. They all looked up, surprised to see Raven soaring above them, the dark shape vanishing into the clouds.

The witch and Arwen were gone for at least twenty minutes, and when they returned, Carmun was bright-eyed, her skin glowing. Arwen looked sick, his arms crossed against his chest as he stared at the floor. Carmun took him by the shoulder and propelled him toward the table. "Now that wasn't so bad, was it?" she hissed, pushing him into a chair. Arwen said nothing.

Kat watched from where she was standing at the

window, her heart going out to her son. He looked diminished, both physically and emotionally. When a dark shape caught her attention, she turned to look outside, surprised to see a raven flying by. Her heart did a somersault. Now was not the time for Bran to appear.

"Kat, please come and sit down," the witch called. "I have little cakes and tea prepared. We have so many things to discuss. Don't you think it's time we get started?"

Kat headed toward the table laden with food and took the chair next to Arwen. "What is there to discuss?" she asked. "You want darkness and I want light. The Norns are not on board with your plan, Carmun. They will not tolerate the imbalance."

"The Norns?" Carmun let out a laugh. "They represent the past. What I propose is the future."

"And you think you can beat them?"

"Of course, I can beat them, Katel. They are nothing compared to me. And they know it. It is why they came to you for help."

"They were not there to ask for help—they were there to warn me not to meddle in their affairs. When I told them what you had planned, they weren't happy."

"Really? Well, too bad for them, because it will happen, with or without their approval."

"I will ask again—why, Carmun?"

Carmun smiled. "Because I want to and I can. You have always been a thorn in my side, and now with this latest news, I find that I cannot let you live. I had thought that perhaps I could render you impotent, but now…"

"What latest news are you talking about? You mean the baby? What does the baby have to do with anything?"

"You don't know?" she asked. "Let's just say that killing you has become a priority." She cocked her head, gazing at the small bump that pressed against Kat's dress. "This is a critical time for you. You should have heeded your mother's advice. You are a stubborn girl."

When she handed Kat a cake, there were maggots crawling all over it. She pushed her chair back and ran for the door, flinging it open to retch in the bushes next to the steps.

"My dear girl," Carmun said from behind her, holding out a hand to help her to her feet. "Is this what pregnancy does? Now come along inside again and listen carefully to what I have to say."

Kat was too dizzy and sick to complain as she followed the witch and sat down next to Arwen. He looked numb, his eyes glazed, but when she put her hand on his shoulder he jerked away. She managed to drink down a cup of peppermint tea as she waited for Carmun's proposal.

"I am so sorry to inform you of your untimely death, Katel. You and your baby cannot be allowed to live."

Kat frowned, refusing to rise to the bait. "You can bring the darkness but I can restore the light. I've already done it on Earth."

"I doubt you brought any light to Earth...did you?" Carmun peered at Kat, her narrowed eyes widening. She gasped, her hands waving in the air just before the room turned black as night. "You will not thwart me. I am stronger than you are."

Kat laughed, trying not to succumb to the numbing fear in the pit of her stomach. "I am the dark goddess from the prophecy. The one who destroys evil...didn't you know that?" She moved her fingers in a mudra, sending a hex spinning toward where the witch had been sitting before the light was snuffed out. But when she felt fingernails rake down her cheek, she knew it hadn't reached its mark. Blood dripped as she rose from the chair and moved away from the table. She had to get out of here.

"You are not the dark goddess!" the witch shrieked. A second later Kat flew backward and slammed into a solid stone wall. "This baby you carry will *never* be born!"

Kat saw the magic flowing toward her in angry waves. She tried to send another spell, but the pain in her belly took over. A scream rose up as she tried to protect herself from the witch who was sending curses, one after the other—twisting snakes that entered the place where the baby rested. Cramping and contractions shot through her. "No," she whispered, trying to crawl away.

Magic swirled in bright colors, revealing Carmun grinning down at her, her lips pulled back in a rictus. "You and this fated child will not stop me. You will both die tonight. Arwen!" she shouted. "Come help me!"

Arwen appeared out the darkness, his face white with fear. "Hold her!" Carmun shouted. "Hold her still so I can cut this baby from her belly!" A knife appeared in Carmun's hand, sharp silver glinting.

Arwen looked from Kat to the witch, seemingly unable to move.

"Now!" Carmun shouted. "If you do not obey me you will die with your mother!"

Kat saw the witch through a haze. She was no longer beautiful, her face contorted and hideous, her hair lank. Her back was hunched, her dress tattered and dirty. Kat turned away in agony, her body racked with spasms. She was miscarrying.

Arwen stood between her and the witch, his hands held up to keep Carmun away. "Don't hurt her!" he yelled.

Through the witch's shouting and Arwen's muttered spells Kat heard the door slam open, a booted step. "Where is Kat?" a man's voice boomed out.

A second later she was lifted into strong arms and carried out the open door. The witch came after them, her high-pitched shrieking filling the air. Lightning bolts pierced through the darkness, catching the grasses around the castle on fire. From over Bran's shoulder Kat saw the witch head for Arwen, her face dark with rage. Carmun grabbed him by the shoulders and held him against her as she pressed her mouth to his. Arwen writhed and twisted but he could not extricate himself from her grip. And when she was finished, she threw him aside where he fell face down like a rag doll.

Kat was sick, vomiting over Bran's arm. Her belly spasmed, sending sharp pains racing. She moaned, closing her eyes on what she'd witnessed. Arwen could be dead.

The witch's voice faded as Kat bounced against Bran's chest, each movement worse than the one before. Tears of pain stung her eyes, blood trickling down her face. But it was the wetness she felt between her legs that brought the panicked cry that erupted from her mouth. The pain increased ten-fold, worse than anything she'd ever felt. She screamed in agony, trying to move her hands to her belly, but she was pinned against Bran. A haze descended and then everything went dark.

Kat woke, a moan rising up as she felt the twinges in her belly. She was lying on

her side, wrapped up in a heavy cloak and held tight in Bran's arms. A fire burned next to them. "The baby," she murmured.

"The baby is safe inside you," Bran whispered.

"You checked?"

He nodded, his head moving against hers. "There was only blood.

You must sleep now."

"But…" When Kat tried to sit up, he pulled her down, his arms locking her against him.

She was exhausted, shivering in shock. The piney scent of him filled her nostrils, his heat settling inside to warm her. A feeling of safety and comfort. She closed her eyes and slept.

When Kat woke again, Bran was sitting on his heels in front of the fire. It was still pitch black, and the forest was utterly silent. "How long have I been asleep?"

Bran turned. "A night and a day."

Gingerly she pushed herself up. "Is it night again?"

"Hard to say. The witch took the light." He turned back to the fire where a rabbit roasted. "You must eat, Kat. Are you up to it?"

Kat sat up, the smell of the roasting meat wafting toward her. "Yes. I'm hungry."

Bran moved to help her over to the fire. "We should leave here as soon as we can. The witch will find us if we don't."

Kat took the hunk of meat he handed her and bit into

it, her stomach growling. "How did you find me? I saw Raven and…"

"Raven knew where you were. They told me…Myrddin and the others told me about the baby."

"That's why you came?"

Bran made a funny sound that seemed like a laugh but wasn't. "I felt sick, Kat, not like the normal sickness, but something else. When I turned into Raven I knew."

Kat paused from chewing. "You knew…what?"

"I knew how I felt about you."

Kat gazed at the frowning dark-haired man. "You remembered?"

Bran shrugged. "It's not a memory. It was right there all the time. I was hiding it from myself."

Kat licked her fingers and reached for more, trying to puzzle out what he meant. "So, Raven told you?"

He gazed at her with an expression that seemed so familiar. Like the old Bran. "Maybe it was finding out about the baby. No one thought I would understand. But when I heard, it was as though some barrier in my mind collapsed."

Kat stared at him, unable to breathe. "The runes, Bran. They were clues. That part of you knew all along."

Bran nodded. "Yes, Raven always knew." He reached to place his big hands on her belly. "I love you and I love this," he murmured.

"I'd given up hope," she whispered. And then she began to cry.

40

The suffocating darkness did not lighten. Kat and Bran talked a long while before they snuffed out the fire. "I'm not sure where to go or what to do," Kat said once he picked her up and headed off through the woods. "I'm still reeling from what's happened between us. I can barely think."

Bran smiled, cradling her close. "It's hard to concentrate on anything right now. What I want to do is make love for the next seventeen hours, but after what the witch did to you, I think we should hold off on that."

"I feel like I'm having a dream…everything seems surreal, from the utter blackness of this forest, to this baby inside me, and what you just told me. But all that has to be put aside. I've got to stop her."

Bran adjusted her position. "Before I rescued you, Raven entered the open window leading into the room where the followers were sleeping. They were out cold, Kat. It was very strange. As a god I have the power to undo enchantments. When I left, all those young men were as free as they were before the witch got hold of them."

Kat peered up at him. "Are you saying she can't use them anymore?"

He shrugged. "She can put another hex on them, I suppose, but after what I did, I doubt they will be so willing. I imbued them with the strength to hold her off."

Kat laughed. "Without them she could wither away!" But a moment later she thought of Arwen. "She might have killed my son."

"I have to hope he's all right. Maybe Val opened a door and took him before she could do further harm."

"Val," she whispered. "Did you know he was taken over by the witch when he tried to kill you?"

"I do now. Every interaction I've ever had with him came back to me. The Val I knew would never do what he did."

A twig snapped and they heard the rustle of leaves. Bran moved behind a tree and placed her gently down, his hand over her mouth to stop her scream. "Stay here," he hissed, moving away.

Kat was mortified. *It must be the baby that's making me so jumpy,* she thought to herself. *It's time to get a grip.* She peered into the darkness but she couldn't see a thing. A second later she heard a heavy thump and an outraged cry. "It's only Myrddin!" Bran yelled.

"Thought you could use my help," the wizard said, abruptly appearing next to Kat. "I know Carmun better than you do."

"Yes, you do, but Bran and I have a handle on it. We're starving her out."

Myrddin frowned. "What do you mean by that?"

Kat glanced at Bran. "Bran cut off her supply of virile men.

But that isn't why you're here," she continued, peering at Myrddin's shining eyes in the dark. "You came to check up on Bran."

Myrddin looked surprised for a moment before he caught himself. "Seems that I was wrong to worry," he said, glancing from one to the other. "Something is very different between you."

Kat smiled. "He's…"

"I'm back," Bran finished for her. "And this time it's all of me."

It was a lot later, after they'd traveled far from the castle and the witch, that Bran called a halt. "Kat needs to rest. She's not fully healed yet."

Myrddin nodded. "I could use some sleep. And I am damn sick of this fucking darkness. Can you work your magic, Kat? Not now, but when we wake up—seeing in the dark doesn't help when I don't know if it's night or day!"

"I'm not sure I'm strong enough right now. As you noticed, Bran had to carry me. I need to conserve what I have to bring your mother down."

"Hope she hasn't recruited more followers," he muttered, frowning. "She seems to have an endless supply."

"She has to use strong magic to 'recruit' as you call it. According to Bran, they're under heavy enchantments."

"True. You mentioned your son. Perhaps you can dream tonight and find out where he is and if he's okay."

"Dream? I don't control my dreams, Myrddin. They're like visions, they come unbidden when I need them."

"Perhaps it's time that you did," he said, watching her. "We could benefit from what the Fae have to offer."

When they bedded down with the blankets Myrddin magically produced, Kat thought about what the wizard had told her. 'It's simple,' he'd said. 'All you have to do is hold the image in your mind. Try to keep it there as you fall asleep.'

Kat was deep in thought, her brows furrowed when Bran put his hand on her shoulder. "Are you feeling all right?"

"I am, especially with you to hold me all night." She turned to kiss him lightly on the lips before settling against him. Her thoughts shifted to Arwen, her mind hanging on to the image of him after Carmun sucked away his essence. *Where are you?* she asked silently as her eyes closed.

A wooded hill, shadows. The call of a night bird. Blazing candles, a bonfire. Arwen and Val sitting next to it talking.

"I'm sorry," Kat heard her son say. "I didn't know." His face looked pale and his eyes were filled with tears.

Val nodded. "She is very powerful. You were under her spell. I'm glad Kat escaped. I only hope she's safe."

"What if she recruits me again? I'm unable to say no, Dad. It was disgusting what she made me do."

"We are Fae, Arwen. And you are old enough to invoke your own magic now. It's time I teach you a few things."

Kat woke slowly, a feeling of peace settling into her as she became aware of Bran's arms wrapped around her. In the distance she heard Myrddin's snores. The dream came back to her. Arwen was safe with Val. But a second later she thought of Carmun. The witch would come for them. She wanted Kat and the baby dead.

"This has to be a communal effort," she told Myrddin and Bran later when they sat around the fire in the dark. "It will take all of us to render her impotent."

Myrddin stared at ground. "Val and Arwen could be of use," he mumbled

"Do you have any idea why she was so upset about the baby I carry? If Bran hadn't come when he did, we'd both be dead."

Myrddin shrugged. "I have no clue what goes on in her head. Maybe she thinks your baby will be strong enough to stop her."

"Hope she's long gone before that," Bran muttered.

Kat glanced at Bran. "What if we shove her into a parallel world?"

Bran frowned. "It would require a door, and also I'm not sure we'd ever get that close to her."

Kat brightened and sat up straight. "She was weak when we left—or at least she looked really old. And now she doesn't have the means to replenish."

Myrddin did not seem pleased, his eyebrows pulling together. "She'll find a way out. She always does."

Kat watched his expression, unsure what she saw in his features. "Do you have a better idea?"

Myrddin gazed at her for a moment before he rose and headed under the trees.

"What's wrong with him?" Bran asked.

Kat shrugged. "I don't think he likes my plan."

"Well I think it's a good one. But you need to get Val in on it."

By the time Myrddin returned, Kat was sitting cross-legged, concentrating on Val. Calling to him like this had worked in the past, but since the rift between them she wasn't sure he'd respond. She was still at it when a blinding brightness lit up the dark forest, a door opening to reveal the Fae man. He stepped through the opening, his expression clouded with anger. "What do *you* want?"

Kat gazed at his angry face. "I…I'm sorry, Val. I know that Carmun was in charge when you did what you did."

"I was sure you knew me better than that."

"I did, I do. I was only upset because of Bran. Arwen tried to protect me from the witch…he…"

"He told me all about it. He also said that Bran came to your rescue. I was glad to hear it." He glanced around, his gaze lighting on Bran and Myrddin standing in the deeper shadows. "Seems you have what you need. Why call on me?"

"You have control of the doors. We've come up with a plan that requires them."

"Ah, so this is all about the witch. I should have known."

Kat took in a breath and let it out. "I'm truly sorry, Val. I don't know what else to say."

Val gazed into the darkness, his swirling eyes the only part of him she could see. "Arwen told me about the baby. Did the witch hurt you or the child?"

"The baby's okay—thanks for asking."

"I care about you, Kat. I always have and I always will." He let out a heavy sigh. "Tell me how I can help."

"Has anyone seen Myrddin?" Siobhan asked the goddesses. The night had been spent in his arms, but when she woke in the morning, he was gone. It was disconcerting to give herself over like that and find him missing come morning. It made her feel cheap and terrible.

"He went to find Kat. He was worried about Bran's sudden disappearance."

Siobhan gasped. "Kat's so vulnerable right now!"

Danu put her hand on Siobhan's arm. "Kat is a goddess, Siobhan. Yes, she has vulnerabilities, but not like a human might have. Trust that she knows what she's doing. After all, this is her destiny."

Siobhan took in a deep breath. "And Myrddin is able to discover where she is? I don't understand how any of this works."

Airmid laughed. "Magic is mystifying for everyone. And the wizard's abilities are even more confusing. I have no idea how he operates." She peered closely at Siobhan. "Is there something happening between you two?"

Heat rushed to her face, nervous fingers attempting to pull through her tangled hair. She'd jumped from bed and run out barefoot, dressed only in a light shift. She glanced at the other goddesses a few feet away. "Well…yes," she whispered. "He…we…"

Airmid smiled. "I thought as much. I've seen the way he looks at you."

"But now he's gone, and I…"

"I've heard he's quite the lady's man, but he seems to genuinely care for you."

Siobhan tried to smile. "I must get dressed and see to something for breakfast," she mumbled, hurrying away.

"Mama! The dragon says that war is coming!"

Siobhan turned from where she bent over the fire. Myrddin had left her eggs and a loaf of bread. Conjured, she supposed. But cooking the eggs was proving to be more difficult than she expected. "What war?"

"He says that the witch will go away and he will keep the world from going dark!"

"Jormungand talks?"

"I hear him in my mind, Mama. But there will be a bad fight first. And many will die." Mior's face fell, his eyes welling.

Siobhan felt a jolt of panic. "Who will die?"

Mior looked down. "He didn't say names."

When she opened her mouth to ask him another question, he was already racing away. Mior was a constant source of worry, his relationship with the dragon becoming more and more disturbing as the days went by. How did he know these things?

41

The witch hovered in the air over the forest, searching. She was weak but she could still feel her son. He thought he was here to help the stupid girl and her idiot boyfriend. But she knew there was still a part of him that loved her. And that was the part she had to tap into. She let out a humorless laugh, and let herself fall through the heavy air.

Myrddin put up his hand. "My mother's here," he whispered, signaling silence.

Kat strained to hear, but whatever Myrddin was aware of was far beyond her abilities. "What should we do?" she mouthed.

Myrddin was there one moment and gone the next. Val and Bran glanced at each before Val whispered. "We need to get out of here."

"But what about Myrddin?"

"The wizard can take care of himself." Val said some

words and lifted his hand just before a door appeared. He glanced at Kat and Bran. "Come on," he muttered.

Kat grabbed Bran's hand and hurried for the opening, but when she was halfway through, her fingers slipped out of his. The door slammed shut behind her a second later. "Bran!" Kat shrieked. "You have to go back for him!" she yelled at Val.

"I can't, Kat. The doors are not like that."

Kat stared at the Fae man. "You came directly to where I was."

"That's because you called to me and I could hone in on where you were. That moment in time is gone now. Bran's a god and he's with Myrddin. They'll be fine. The important thing is that you're safe."

Kat shook her head, tears welling. "I can't be away from him right now."

Val grabbed her by the shoulders. "Think about what it is you came to do. You called on me to help and I arrived. You *will* find your way back to Bran. I promise you that. But for now, you are with me in the Norse world. This is where you're supposed to be, Kat. Everything happens for a reason."

"What can I do from here?"

"For one, you can talk with Arwen. He has a lot of knowledge regarding the witch. Let's start with that, shall we?"

Kat looked around the forest, trying to place where they were. The sky seemed wider than the last time she was here, the forest darker. "Where is he?"

Val smiled. "I'll show you."

The cave was dug into the side of a hill, stairs leading down into the underground cavern that was lit with many candles. There was little to be said for it, other than the firepit with a heavy pot hanging over it, and the blankets stacked in a corner. She thought of Val's former house, sad for him and for Arwen. This had not been a good time for either of them. At least Arwen was out from under the witch's spell. But there was no going back to their former life.

Arwen met them, his eyes widening when he saw Kat's tear-streaked face. "What happened?"

"Your mother is upset because Bran got left behind. I tried to tell her that talking with you will help decide the future."

Kat sat on a stump that had been dragged inside, wiping the tears from her eyes. "I can barely think."

Val stoked the fire burning in the center of the room, preparing something in the pot. "Drink this," he ordered a few minutes later, handing her a cup.

Kat sniffed. "This is alcohol. I can't have…"

Val raised his hand, stopping her objections. "This is an elixir, Kat. You need it right now."

Kat drank it down, her eyes watering. "What does it do?" she asked, trying not to choke.

"It will bring clarity, take away your worry and give you the confidence you need to complete your destiny."

Kat laughed. "All that and nothing for this unborn child I carry?"

Val looked at her, his expression serious. "The baby is fine. It is you I worry about."

When Kat met his gaze, she saw something there that frightened her. He was seriously worried about her. What did he know? But that train of thought came to an abrupt stop when Arwen said, "Carmun isn't really alive."

"Not alive? How do you know?"

"She was brought forth by the forces for evil. The only thing that keeps her going is the constant supply of energy she takes from others. Without that she would wither away into dust."

"I guess I knew that, but I did think she was alive. Someone or something must be responsible for bringing her here. Do you know who it is?"

Arwen nodded. "Loki."

"But why? For what purpose?"

"He wants her to do his dirty work for him so that he doesn't get blamed."

"But he doesn't want the world to go dark, does he?"

"He doesn't care. He has control of where he lives. What Carmun is doing seems like Ragnarok, but it isn't. Loki wants to kill Odin and his son early. He hates them because of their power. And since he's destined to die, he wants to change the outcome."

"And what happens when the real Ragnarok comes about?"

"Loki is hoping he can cheat fate."

Kat thought of the Norns before she glanced at Val. "Did you know all this?"

"Not until a few days ago."

Kat stared into space, her mind whirling. If the witch wasn't alive, it shouldn't be that difficult to get rid of her. But would that invoke Loki's wrath? "Myrddin says he's her son. Is that true?"

Arwen nodded. "And Loki is his father. But that was a

really long time ago. I don't know how she died or when, but she hasn't been alive for hundreds of years."

Val brought over a bowl of rabbit stew and handed it to her. "You must eat for the baby's sake," he said.

Kat took the bowl and the spoon he handed her. "Do you think I'm not eating? If there is food to be had, I eat, believe me! There just hasn't been much lately."

"You're pale, you have circles under your eyes and you're far too thin. I will make sure you have food while you're my guest."

Kat nearly choked on the stew that she was swallowing. "You sound like you did when we first met, Val. Like we're having dinner at that beautiful hand carved table of yours and Isabel is carrying platters in and out. Where is our wine and our linen napkins?"

Val chuckled. "Have to maintain some standards."

"You two are ridiculous," Arwen muttered. "The world is coming to an end and you're joking about table manners?"

"Your mother needs to relax for a moment, Arwen. I'm only trying to make that happen. First food and then sleep. Tomorrow we can regroup and decide our next course of action."

Kat nodded, spooning up the rest of the stew in her bowl.

Kat had risen early and was meditating in the dark when she heard Val stir and Arwen's yawn. A moment later light pulsed against her closed eyes as all the candles were lit at once. Murmured voices and the clink of a cup, the spit of the fire. She opened her eyes.

"Good morning," Val said, smiling. "You talk in your sleep."

"You never noticed that before?"

"This is the first time I've heard it."

Kat rose and moved toward the fire. "Did I say anything interesting?"

Val's swirling eyes met hers. "Actually, you did."

Kat took the mug of tea he held out. It was steaming hot and aromatic, the scent of peppermint, lemon and another aroma she couldn't place wafting into the air. She took a sip, waiting, her eyes on Val.

"It was somewhat garbled, but I heard the words, Carmun and Myrddin, and then you gasped, as though you'd realized something."

Kat pressed her lips together. "My meditation this morning was also related to those two. I hate to say this, but I think Myrddin has known about his mother this entire time. He's been aiding and abetting her in this endeavor. And now I'm even more concerned about Bran."

Val frowned. "He may have known, but I doubt he has malicious intent. Maybe it has to do with his mother seemingly alive again. A son can love a mother despite her being evil."

Kat snorted. "You mean like a mother loving a son who might be evil?" she whispered.

"I heard that," Arwen muttered.

Kat turned. "You were a nasty little boy, Arwen. And that was before the witch put a spell on you. I was afraid for my life. But I still loved you."

Arwen grunted and sat down next to her. He rubbed the sleep from his eyes and glanced blearily at the pot of tea. "I was testing the limits. And I went too far."

Val poured Arwen tea and handed it over. "As I have mentioned many times," Val said, glancing at Kat, "Fae children must be raised by Fae parents. You were not equipped to deal with him. But to get back to the subject at hand. If you're right and Myrddin is complicit, he needs to be dealt with."

"If it's true that he wants to keep her around, that makes him dangerous. He could have met up with us simply to prevent us from stopping her."

Val nodded. "Exactly my thoughts."

"But why is she so focused on me? If this is Loki's deal why am I on her radar?"

"Because you are the one who's been named to thwart her. And if she isn't really alive perhaps there's some other sorcery involved."

"I feel like she came into being to teach us something."

Val stared at her. "Teach us what?"

"What it would be like if we lost all our light, for one. In order to have light we have to keep our thoughts turned toward the light. People can bring darkness as easily as Carmun. I saw it in the underground city. Those people have embraced desperate ideas that don't serve them." Kat felt a twinge in her belly, her hands going there. Any tiny pain or movement still worried her. "We have to let Bran know about the wizard."

"I will open a door to the spot where you were. The moment has passed, of course, but if I'm right, Bran and Myrddin are still in the vicinity."

"Not sure why you couldn't have done that last night," Kat grumbled. "But I'll take it." When Val opened his

mouth to explain, she waved her hand. "Don't bother—
I'm not capable of understanding the intricacies of Fae
magic. But I do remember you saying the Fae can cross
space and time. That sounds promising."

Val grimaced. "It is not as simple as it sounds. For now,
I suggest we concentrate on Bran and Myrddin." He
handed her some flatbread. "Eat, Kat."

Kat laughed. "You're worried about my baby, aren't
you? I've seen that look before."

Val pressed his lips together. "This baby is…special."

Kat frowned. "More special than just the offspring of a
god and a demigoddess?"

Val nodded, looking away. "It seems so. There is power
there."

"What kind of power?"

Val turned to her. "The dark goddess isn't you, it's this
child you carry. She is the dark goddess."

Kat stared at him. "Does that mean there's something
even worse coming?"

Val shrugged and looked down. "I have no way of
knowing that."

Kat felt a shiver of fear. She took the bread that was
fresh from the warming fire, munching on it as she tried to
make sense of what Val was telling her. "How do you know
all this?"

"I'm Fae and the future often reveals itself to me. It
doesn't mean it's set in stone, but I get glimpses."

"And you've seen her."

Val smiled. "Yes, Kat, I have."

"As a baby or grown up?"

"I had a glimpse of a young woman, probably around

seventeen, with green eyes and dark hair."

"What was she doing?"

Val frowned. "She was standing in the middle of a field waving her hands and a wall of water was swirling around her."

"Water…she was controlling it?"

"That's what it looked like."

The candle flame claimed Kat's attention, sending her careening into a hazy future. She saw a raven-haired little girl with eyes the color of jade staring at her, but when she reached for her, the scene dissolved. Fire raged and she could hear screaming. Shouts.

"Kat? Kat!"

Val's urgent call broke through, startling her. "What is it?"

"It's time to go."

She rose to her feet, her mind whirling. "I'm ready when you are."

42

Bran woke from a dream in which he was alone and lost in an endless dark wood. When he opened his eyes and called out to Myrddin there was no response. He couldn't see a fucking thing and the fire had long since burned out. How long he'd been asleep was anyone's guess. "Myrddin!" he yelled again. And when he got up to explore, he discovered that the food stores were gone, as well as the extra blankets. "You bastard!" he shouted.

A moment later there was a blinding light and a door appeared. Kat ran through, Val right behind her. He rose quickly and met her halfway, his arms so tight around her that she gave out a little cry of pain. "I'm sorry," he murmured, letting her go. "When you didn't come back, I began to doubt everything."

"Val couldn't pinpoint the spot. It's why we waited until this morning."

"I don't know how long you think you've been gone, but it's been a hell of a lot longer than a day. Myrddin took off this morning while I was still asleep. The bastard took all the food and the blankets, even the one I had over me. He must have cast a spell to keep me asleep."

Val frowned. "We think Myrddin may be helping his mother."

Bran nodded grimly. "I've had the same thought. I think he took off because I broached the subject last night, wondering why we were walking in circles and not confronting her. He told me Carmun wasn't at the castle right now. I didn't believe him."

Kat took hold of his hand, placing it on her lower belly. "This baby, she..."

When the baby kicked Bran let out a gasp and stared at her, unable to breathe for a long moment. "I can feel it," he murmured.

"As exciting as this is," Val muttered, "We need to focus on the witch."

Kat let Bran's hand go and turned. "I have to tell him, Val. He needs to know about..."

Val narrowed his eyes. "Now is not the time. We are literally in utter darkness without a candle to light the way."

Kat let out a heavy sigh. "You're right."

"I have no idea what you two are taking about, but I do think the witch is the priority at the moment."

Val grimaced, nodding. "We should pursue our idea about the doors. But finding a parallel realm that prevents her from either reconstituting herself or escaping, is the catch."

Bran glanced at Kat. "The only place I know that fits that description is the one where Kat and I accidentally went. It's a paradise, but it's also seductive and a trap."

"I remember," Val muttered. "It was almost the end of

you two, as I recall." He headed off, leading the way through the silent woods.

Bran remembered too—all too well. It was when he discovered that Kat had slept with Val. He shook himself and let the anger dissipate. So much had happened since then. He grabbed Kat's hand and followed.

Kat felt it—the energy shift. "The witch is close," she whispered.

Val stopped in his tracks and pointed. "The castle is just up there."

"She's not in the castle," Bran muttered. "She's looking for us."

A shriek had them all ducking as the witch materialized out of the darkness. She was diminished in so many ways, her hair thin and lank, bits of scalp showing, her skin sagging and lined. Her dress was in tatters and hung off her skinny body like a sack. She looked a hundred years old. "You will not stop me!" she croaked. "My son is here now and will provide me with what I need!"

Provide her...was she planning to have sex with Myrddin? Kat felt ill for a second as she pictured it. It was obvious she had not *fed*, for lack of a better word, for a while. Carmun was at her weakest point. When Val conjured a door, Kat rushed behind the witch, shoving her from behind, but Carmun was too quick, turning on her at the last second. She grabbed Kat, her bony hands going tight around her neck. Despite how she seemed, the witch was strong, her fingers digging into Kat's throat and cutting off her air.

Kat was nearly unconscious by the time Bran managed to drag the witch away. But instead of attacking him Carmun pulled him close attempting to kiss him. Bran grappled with her, his arm muscles bulging as he barely kept her at bay. "Let her go!" Kat shouted, rushing up behind them. "Val!!!" Another door opened wide, a shimmering world on the other side. Kat threw herself at the witch, shoving her as hard as she could. Carmun was thrown off balance, flailing as Kat rushed to shove her again. This time the witch fell through the opening, her eyes wide with horror, her shriek fading as the door shut with a snap and disappeared.

A second later Myrddin was there, his face red with fury, dark cloak swirling around him. "What have you done?"

Kat ran at him, her power rising up as she sent him reeling backward. "You tricked us! You were never on our side! We should have shoved you through too!"

Myrddin landed on his back, his face contorting into despair. "I didn't trick you! She's my mother!" he cried out. "I...I wanted to save her, to change her, but..."

"She's a shadow spirit, Myrddin! She's not even real!" Kat screamed, standing over him.

Myrddin rose slowly to his feet, rubbing at his welling eyes. "I thought...I thought I could stop her," he stuttered. "I didn't want her to hurt anyone."

Kat glared at him. "You let that thing nearly kill me and my son. You allowed her to turn Earth dark. She nearly killed all of us!"

There was a roar and a thundering bellow as the ground began to rumble. A second later a red-haired, furious giant appeared, towering above the trees. "Where is she!" he shouted, the trees bending from the wind from his mouth.

A second later the woods caught on fire, flames exploding as a hundred lightning bolts struck the trees. Myrddin spun in a circle, his hood flying off to reveal wild gray hair charged with the sudden electricity. Flames, like angry snakes, poured from his fingertips, trees and bushes and grasses catching fire as he swung his hands. Loki fanned the flames with his waving arms, his bulging eyes wild as he helped the wizard destroy the forest and everything around them.

Kat screamed when her sweater caught fire, the wool curling into black threads. But underneath it her skin was cool, the charred wool falling harmlessly to the ground. She looked up at the towering giant, anger flowing from her like liquid fire. "Carmun is gone!" she shouted. "Go home!"

The giant glared down on her. He was on fire but it didn't seem to bother him at all. "We had a plan!" he bellowed, waving his hands at the flames licking at his wild red hair. "You were not part of it!"

"You will go back where you came from!" Kat shouted. "Without her power you are nothing!"

Loki raised his brows in astonishment, leaning down to peer at her. "You! I know you!" he bellowed. "You are the one who…" But before he could continue Bran grabbed Kat and dragged her away. A second later he was Raven and she was Hummingbird beside him, both lifting into the smoke-filled air. Below them the forest burned, dark smoke billowing upward. Cool air ruffled Hummingbird's feathers as they rose up and up, Raven flying close to protect her as they soared away.

Earth came into view as they dropped through the clouds. Bran shifted and rose first and rushed to help Kat. "Are you…is the baby…?"

"Both fine," Kat answered, her hands going to her belly. She was about to tell Bran what she'd learned when she saw Siobhan running toward them

"Kat! You're safe!" Siobhan pulled Kat into her arms and held her tight, tears flowing down her cheeks. Val limped behind her, Tus Nua in his arms. Behind him trooped the goddesses and Mior.

"Val? How did you…?" Kat's question hung in the air as she gazed from her mother to Val.

"Val got here right before you did," Siobhan answered. "He told us what happened, how you threw the witch through a door. Where is Myrddin?"

Kat glanced at Val. "Did you see where he went?"

Val jerked his head no. "Last I saw he was helping Loki burn the entire forest down."

"Is the witch really gone?" Airmid asked.

Val shrugged. "She's somewhere not here. That's all I can tell you. And she was very diminished when Kat shoved her through that door. I doubt she can find her way back."

"What about Loki?" Morrighan asked. "He will certainly exact revenge."

Bran chuckled, glancing at Kat. "Kat confronted him. I've never seen power shimmer like that. She was on fire, not on the outside but on the inside. I have a sense he'll leave it alone."

Kat frowned. "I hope you're right. I think that without Carmun to blame, he won't chance it."

It was late that night before Kat and Bran finally had a moment to themselves. Bran led her away from the communal fire up the hill and just inside the cave, where he made a bed out of his cloak and hers. "No need to be afraid of being sealed in here now," he said, pulling her down next to him.

"True enough," Kat muttered, trying to get comfortable. The rock was hard despite the wool cloaks. "But if you're thinking what I'm thinking, I'm not sure we can manage it."

Bran pulled her hair back and kissed her neck. "Are you sure?" he whispered.

43

Kat woke up and rolled over, letting out a groan of pain. Every muscle and every joint ached from sleeping on the rock-hard ground. Other twinges made themselves known as she flung her arm over Bran lying next to her. "That was not the best night I've ever had."

Bran opened his eyes. "You were right to stop me. Everything hurts."

Kat kissed him lightly and rose to her feet. "I didn't get a chance to share my news. You were too focused on my body."

He reached for the hand she held out. "I was intent on making love to you. You didn't seem to mind the attention."

Kat laughed. "Until my back spasmed."

Bran grimaced, twisting his shoulders from side to side. "Yeah, not exactly satisfying. So, what's this news?"

"Our baby. Apparently, she's the dark goddess. The destroyer of evil."

Bran frowned. "I thought *you* were the dark goddess. You know this, how?"

"Val. He sometimes sees the future."

"What does this mean? You just saved us from the witch. Is there more evil coming our way?"

"There's always evil, at least that's what the Norns told me. I don't know what it means, but I thought you'd like to know that our daughter will be more powerful than either of us."

Bran pulled her close and kissed the top of her head. "I will love her no matter what."

They were all sitting around the fire when Myrddin appeared out of the ether. Kat stood immediately, glaring at him. "What are you doing here?"

He threw down three cooked rabbits and a loaf of flatbread. "Thought you could use some food." He glanced toward Siobhan. "Can I talk to you for a moment?"

"Leave my mother alone, you turncoat!"

Siobhan stood up. "It's all right, Kat. I can take care of myself." She nodded to the wizard and the two of them headed away.

"That bastard was in league with his mother. It's a wonder any of us are alive. He and Loki set the entire forest on fire." Kat narrowed her watering eyes.

"He is the witch's son," Danu said. "It's hard to turn off love, even if the person you love is a monster."

"I don't forgive him," Kat muttered.

Bran pulled her shaking body against his. "He said he tried to stop her, to change her mind about what she was doing. He told me about their early days. How much he loved her and how wonderful she was. And he's carrying a lot of guilt about who she's become. He thinks it's his fault that she turned into what she is now."

"It doesn't matter, Bran. He had a million chances to warn us and instead he pretended he was helping us."

"He did help us," Mior said. "He saved Bran and he kept us safe in the tunnel. He isn't all bad!"

"Balance, Kat, remember what the Norns told you," Danu murmured. "There is good and bad in everyone. The only thing that matters is which one we choose at any given moment."

"How do you know about the Norns?"

She laughed. "Have you forgotten who I am?"

Kat sighed. "I want to forgive him, but he…" she looked up as her mother and Myrddin came into view. He had his arm around her shoulder and her mother was crying.

"I can't be party to this shit show right now," she muttered, rising to her feet. She headed off without looking back.

Kat discovered the pool under a scattering of downed limbs. She'd cleared them away, shed her clothing and climbed in when she saw Bran striding up the hill toward her. She ignored him, lying back and absorbing the warmth.

"Your mother is devasted, Kat. She wants to talk with you."

"I'm right where I need to be at the moment. Is Myrddin still here?"

"Myrddin's gone. He apologized to your mother and took off."

Kat sat up. "Apologized for what?"

"For making love to her and disappearing, for one. And he also explained why he attempted to help Carmun."

"Mom and Myrddin had sex? When did that happen?"

Bran shrugged off his vest, took off his leathers and stepped into the pool, settling next to her. "Just after you left the last time. Before I joined you."

Kat moved her head slowly from side to side, her lips pressed together. "Poor Mom. What was his reason for helping Carmun?"

"He said he was party to her resurrection. He knew she wouldn't last without a lot of help. He wasn't aware of her plans, though."

"As I told Val I think she was a wake-up call. We all need to be on our guard for the darkness that can take over our light. We all have it, Bran. It's like what Danu said, it's all about the choices we make at any given moment."

"Are you saying that she arrived because of our evil?"

"There are always those who think that power is the most important thing. The earlier version of my father is one of them. But not many are able to wield power without being turned to darkness. And if that happens it can snuff out the light. Those boys wanted power and they were too young to see the truth. Even Arwen wanted it until he realized the price he had to pay."

"But who was responsible for Carmun?"

"Loki wanted her to start a fake Ragnarok, but she got away from him and formed her own agenda."

"To kill you. I still don't understand why."

"Because of the prophecy. Somehow this nemesis business took root in her mind and she couldn't give it up.

Ragnarok became secondary."

"And now our baby is the dark goddess. Hopefully the witch won't come back at some future time and try to kill her."

Kat smiled. "She'll be too strong. I can feel it already. And besides that, Carmun was a husk when I pushed her through that door. She was never really alive. With any luck the world she's in won't be populated with virile men she can use to prop herself up."

"And yet we don't know which world she's in."

Kat met his frowning gaze. "I'm hoping it was that world where I lost my mind."

Bran grinned. "Perfect place for her. Seemingly beautiful but no people, and will suck out the rest of her energy. And the shadow creature from the Pinnacle is there. That will assure her death. Maybe your clairvoyance prompted Val to open the right door."

They sat together quietly for a while before Bran's dark eyes met hers. "I would say the sickness is upon me, but I know that one won't fly anymore. The water is buoyant, Kat, unlike the floor of the cave. What do you think?"

Kat grinned. "I think yes."

Bran sat back on the underwater ledge that circled the pool and pulled her onto his lap Their lips met, tasting each other, before his fingers searched out her secret places. She moaned and clung to him as he readied her, her body hot with wanting him. When he pressed inside her, the water sloshed, waves slapping against the edges of the pool as they began to move as one.

Kat was lost to herself, her love for this man taking up

all the space in her body and her mind. A pale mist surrounded them as they slipped from the ledge into the water, their arms tight around each other as they connected thoroughly and completely. At the end they held each other and cried.

44

wo months had gone by since the witch was sent off. Val had gone home to be with Arwen and to try and rebuild his world, and the goddesses had headed back to Otherworld.

"Why is the dragon still here if the witch is gone?" Mior asked one morning, squinting into the sky.

"I thought you might know the answer to that one," Kat said, maneuvering the heavy pot full of tea. She poured into the cups they'd recently found buried under a pile of pebbles and dirt.

Mior shrugged. "The people want to come up top," he muttered.

"The ones who live underground?"

He nodded. "They sent a man up a couple of days ago to look around. I told him we don't have any food. A sickness killed a lot of them. I guess that's why I had the vision."

"What vision?" Kat asked.

"About the war with the witch. How a lot of people died. It was about the underground people, not us. Their water source dried up and they can't grow anything now."

Kat let out a juddering sigh, her hands moving unconsciously to the expanding bump of her belly. "Until we get a garden going and some animals return, we'll all starve together."

"Myrddin has brought food every week, Katel," her mother reminded her.

"Yes, and I thanked him for that. But we need to rebuild, Mom. This place is a wasteland now. When it gets cold, we'll freeze to death."

"You and Mior managed it once before. Can't you do it again?"

Kat gazed at her mom. "It seems that all my energy is being taken by this baby. How about you, Mior? Any luck with reforesting the hillside?"

Mior shook his head, dark curls bobbing. He was growing up, slimming down. He looked more like Dagda every day. "I don't get why it doesn't work now," he grumped.

"Maybe because of your attitude, young man," Siobhan scolded. "Look at your sweet sister sitting over there. She always has a smile on her face."

Tus Nua pushed herself to standing and toddled toward Siobhan. "Mama!" she called.

Mior made a face. "She's just a stupid human."

Siobhan grabbed him and gave him a swat. "I'm human, Mior. Am I stupid?"

Mior scowled. "No."

Kat watched the interchange, dismayed with how her brother had changed in the last few months. Instead of his former infectious optimism, he was morose and taciturn. He was ten years old now, perhaps that was the reason for his behavior.

She turned when Bran grabbed her hand, letting him lead her away and up the hill toward the spring. She knew what he wanted. With the uncertainty about the future it was a necessary interlude they both needed.

"Can *you* do something about this place?" Kat asked Bran later when they were pulling on their clothes.

"About the landscape and rebuilding? I can turn into Raven, I can send lightning bolts, I can bring mists and fog, I can conjure spears and forecast the future. I can do a little healing and I can fight off hordes. But I can't bring a forest back."

"If you can forecast the future, what do you see for us?"

He scoffed. "Right now, I'm too in love with you to see what the future holds."

Kat stared at him in surprise. "Love makes you unable to see what's coming?"

His head twitched in a nod. "Gods do not fall in love, remember? And I found out that this applies to everyone, even within their own ranks. It is a rule and I broke it."

She smiled and reached for his hand, twining her fingers through his. "So, sex but no love?"

Bran laughed. "Yeah, I guess so."

"That's why you gave up your god powers."

"The more I cared for you the more they drifted away. This time I know I can have both. Fuck the ones who say otherwise."

Kat's thoughts went to her father and how he'd loved Siobhan so much that he brought her back from the dead. He conjured a beautiful house for her and a garden full of trees and flowering bushes. It made her sad to think about it. "My father was able to do it all—why?"

Bran gazed into the distance. "The Dagda was the great god. He had immense mystical powers, more than any other god. The reason you and Mior were able to conjure the forest was because you're both related to him."

"Then why can't we do it now?"

"Mior is going through a negative phase that suppresses his abilities. And as you've said, all your energy is being taken by the baby. Maybe after she's born things will be different."

"We can't wait that long. There's nothing here—no food, barely any water, no way to build anything since the trees are all gone. What if Myrddin decides to forego his weekly visits? We have to make a plan."

Bran shrugged. "I agree. You need vegetables. Meat. But your mother wants to stay here. I think she's hoping for a miracle."

The weather had turned sharply colder, frost lying across the flat ground where meadows had once been. With nothing to stop them, winds whistled across the land, churning up pebbles and dirt that got into hair, eyes and covered their skin and clothes in silt. The remaining underground dwellers had arrived the week before, settling in without much fanfare. They tried their best to be friendly, handing out supplies they brought along. Blankets, firewood, cups and pots for cooking, clothing, and many other household goods joined the few Kat the others had recovered; their attitudes about Kat and her family had changed drastically. They were all in very bad shape, skeletal with viruses and spots and boils on their pallid skin.

"We need to keep our distance," Kat warned one morning during their dawn huddle. "They have illnesses that we do not want to catch."

"Myrddin hasn't been here this week. What if he doesn't come?" Siobhan asked worriedly. "And wait until he sees fifty more mouths to feed!"

"It doesn't bode well, I agree," Bran muttered. "I've flown for miles searching for animals, but it seems they were all wiped out during the flood."

"It's too cold now to grow anything, even if we had the seeds," Siobhan muttered. "What will we do?" When no one answered she stared off into space, her eyes going wide. "Who is that?" she asked, pointing into the distance.

Kat held a hand over her eyes to squint at the figure walking toward them. "Whoever it is, is well-built. It looks like a god."

Siobhan jumped to her feet. "It's Dag!" she shouted, taking off at a run. Mior took off after her.

Kat and Bran exchanged a look before they rose to follow. When they reached them, Siobhan was sobbing, held in Dagda's arms. Mior clung to his father, tears streaming down his face. Dagda's blue eyes welled, his head bent to his wife and son.

Kat ran to hug him, joining her mother and Mior. Tears slid down her cheeks as his arms came around her.

"I left the baby!" Siobhan suddenly remembered, gazing up at him.

"Well, then, we'd better go and get her," Dagda said. He was smiling now, his eyes crinkling with happiness as they hurried along. "You all survived," he murmured. "I am the luckiest god alive."

"What happened?" Kat asked him.

He grinned. "They decided to resurrect me."

Siobhan let out a moan of happiness, snuggling up against him. Her eyes were filled with tears but she was smiling.

Tus Nua was screaming by the time they arrived, her eyes red, her face blotchy. Dagda went straight to the baby, picked her up and lifted her into the air until she screamed with joy. He cradled her then, and kissed the top of her blonde head. "She's grown so much," he said, gazing sadly at Siobhan.

She nodded. "You've been gone a long time, Dag."

Food had been left in a pile next to the log they used to sit on. "Myrddin came while we were gone," Kat muttered, looking through the flatbread, cheese and meats. "It isn't enough," she said, glancing at Bran. "Not for the others who are starving."

"What others?" Dagda asked, glancing around.

"The ones from Underground!" Mior said, skipping around like his old self. "They're here but they're all sick."

"Kat?" Dagda said, frowning at her. "Don't you have healing powers?"

"Well, yes, I used to," she answered, her hands going to her burgeoning waistline.

Dagda's eyes widened. "You're..."

She smiled. "It's Bran's," she said, reaching for his hand.

Dagda's frowning gaze went to the man next to her. "You are not the Bran I remember."

Bran shrugged. "Died and resurrected, just like you."

"Died? Who resurrected you?"

"I guess I resurrected myself. Either that or Raven did it. I got back my god powers."

Dagda scoffed, looking him up and down. "That's obvious. But how did this come about?"

As Bran began his lengthy explanation, Kat divided up the food and handed it around. She thought of her healing powers, remembering what she'd done for Bran. But that was early on in the pregnancy. It seemed the more the baby grew the less power she had. What would happen once she was born?

A month had gone by since Dagda's arrival. Siobhan was beyond happy, singing as she worked, her skin rosy and glowing. With Dagda's skills the forest of trees was restored, the meadow filled with herbs and wildflowers. Deer roamed the woods again and birds and the other animals who belonged there were plentiful. He and Bran were working on a house where they could all live together, the foundation of rock already in place. Wings would jut out from the main living area to afford privacy. By the time it was completed it would far surpass their former fairy house in size and in magical properties.

Bran and Kat had helped the others build their dwellings, sharing tips on how to hunt and trap. There was plenty of game for everyone. Winter was coming so any meat and root vegetables they had, would have to be preserved for the colder months. There were no canning supplies, but root cellars had already been dug.

Mior had changed his tune since Dagda's arrival, turning back into his former chipper self. He followed his father around like a shadow, hanging on his every word. Dagda didn't seem to mind, his entire demeanor changed from his former god days. Instead of the power-hungry, selfish man Kat remembered, he was humble and grateful, love shining from his eyes.

Two months later winter arrived with a vengeance. It snowed for a month straight, the weather so cold that no one wanted to do the simple chores of bringing in wood for the fire or hunting for the meat they needed. Even Dagda was becoming grumpy and out of sorts, not wanting to be the one who stepped out of the warm house. Because gods were impervious to the weather, he and Bran were the designated hunters. But they'd both grown complacent, used to the warmth and lazing around with a cup of tea and watching the storm rage outside their cozy house.

It was during the worst of it that Kat went into labor, her water breaking early one morning just as she woke up. The house was finally finished, with bedrooms for everyone, including soft beds and blankets. She woke Bran lying next to her, his eyes wide as he took in her news and the grimace of pain on her face. He held her hand, trying to soothe her, but it wasn't enough, her screams scaring the children as the day wore on. When Dagda heard her, he grabbed the children, bundled them up and headed up the hill into the woods.

It was late afternoon when Bran called for Siobhan, worried that the baby hadn't come yet. "This is normal," she told him when she checked between Kat's legs. "It shouldn't be more than a couple of hours now."

Siobhan stayed, preparing things for the birth as Kat labored on, barely aware of the world around her. She heard their murmured voices but mostly she was caught like an animal inside the pain and trying to get through it.

It was deep into the night when the dark head finally emerged, Siobhan encouraging Kat to push. Kat was so tired she wasn't sure she could, but with Bran and her mother shouting that she had to, she finally made the effort. It was only a few minutes more before the baby was there, and she could fall back exhausted. Bran smoothed the sweaty hair back from her brow while Siobhan cut the umbilical cord and cleaned the baby.

A moment went by and then another as Kat wondered why she hadn't heard the baby cry. "Is she all right?" But just as she asked the question her mother appeared beside her and placed the bundle into her arms. Kat looked down and began to cry. Bran kneeled by the bed, his head against hers, his eyes welling. Her hair was as dark as Bran's, her eyes dark too. Her skin was pale and flawless. She didn't cry, looking up at Kat with a solemn expression. "She's beautiful," Bran whispered.

But Kat was too overwhelmed to answer.

Kat spent most of her time in bed, feeding the baby and resting. The weather outside had grown worse, two feet of snow piled up against the walls of the house. Luckily magic kept the house warm, that and the fire that burned all day and night. Instead of collecting wood, Dagda conjured it, complaining bitterly about the weather. Siobhan laughed at him, as happy as ever as she made tea and prepared meals, Mior and Tus Nua following her around as she worked.

It was bitterly cold the day Bran broached the subject of a name. "Have you thought about what to call her?" he asked, lying down next to her with his legs stretched out.

She glanced at him and then back at the baby at her breast. "She's a gift."

"Yes, she is. An unexpected gift." He gazed into the

distance, a frown between his brows. A second later he smiled, turning back. *"Feirin."*

"Gaelic?"

He nodded. "It means gift. We can call her Fee for short."

When a gust of wind shook the house, Kat clutched the baby close. Trees bent in the increasing storm, snowflakes freezing on the windows and nearly obscuring the view. The sky had turned dark with charcoal clouds that blew past, chased by something otherworldly. Kat heard the sound of splintering glass and Dagda's shout. There was a sudden sense of the supernatural, a chill going down her spine. She grabbed Bran's hand, glancing down at the baby who was staring up at her with wide eyes. Feirin's knowing gaze was unnerving, the expression way too wise for a newborn. "What's happening?" she asked, glancing at Bran.

Bran's gaze met hers before he turned to look at the very aware baby in her arms. "I think Feirin knows, but she can't tell us."

When Kat glanced down, she was taken into the deep and knowing eyes, reflections of other worlds swirling within them. Her mind suddenly filled with images that flashed by, one after the other. Storms, darkness, cities growing up and collapsing again, oceans receding and then flooding across the land. Forests gone, replaced with buildings that then disintegrated as time rushed by at breakneck speed. "Who *are* you?" Kat whispered. The baby let out a little coo.

Fin

If you enjoyed this book, please leave a review!

To receive news on giveaways and new books,
please sign up here:
www.nikkibroadwellauthor.com

Facebook:
www.facebook.com/NikkiBroadwellBooks/

Pinterest:
www.pinterest.com/nbroadwell/

www.ingramcontent.com/pod-product-compliance
Lightning Source LLC
Chambersburg PA
CBHW020928260626
47169CB00006B/1617